SOMEWHERE IN THE CITY

SOMEWHERE SERIES, BOOK 2

TOBY JANE

CHAPTER ONE

It's dangerous to be too beautiful.

I know. I've lived it. Right now I'm sitting on a hard metal folding chair in the recovery meeting, enduring the way guys scope out my body and girls judge me. I've dressed down for the occasion, too—I'm no threat to anybody in my ratty hoodie, the hoodie that's been a kind of security blanket for the last six months since Dad died and everything changed.

I have on baggy jeans, and my hood is up to hide my hair. I'm thinking of dying it. Some mousy color, like muddy brown. My hair draws way too much attention.

In fact, that's what I'll do, right after this stupid meeting.

The leader gets us going with the Serenity Prayer, and then we are supposed to go around and share our "experience, strength, and hope."

I don't have much of any of the above, at eighteen, just moved here, and my biggest hope is to get everybody off my back as soon as possible.

I endure the stories. Sad ones, really. Kids ripping off their parents. Guys giving other guys blowjobs in parking lots for a few bucks to get high. I was never into any of that shit or did anything radical like that. In fact, I'd have been fine, would never have had to come to this meeting, if it weren't for the Carver boys.

But who could resist the Carver boys? The only thing to do in that pothole in the road, Peterborg, on Saint Thomas. Yeah, it all started with Connor, but then there was Keenan. I shut my eyes and indulge in a little memory starring me and the Carver boys.

Someone elbows me. "Your turn."

I sit up. The leader, a chubby lady with one of those soft do-gooder faces I'm too familiar with, gives me a hairy eyeball.

"Welcome to our meeting," she says. "Is this your first time with us?"

I nod. "Hi. My name is Pearl."

I'm supposed to say, "and I'm an addict," but I don't. I can't. It would be a lie. I just barely got going with some hard stuff and everybody freaked the hell out, and now here I am enrolled in this "day treatment" daily meetings routine. It sucks. But at least I'm not in Eureka, armpit of California, with Mom's tears and Jade's compulsive cleaning.

The group leader narrows her eyes a little because I haven't said the catechism. I remember she has to sign my attendance sheet, though, as she says, encouragingly, "Would you like to share your experience, strength and hope with us?"

"Not really, no. But thanks for asking."

A titter goes around the circle, and the leader moves on.

There's a guy across from me, long thick legs extended into the circle, his jeans just the way I like them—broken in, with split knees. He's wearing black boots and a leather motorcycle jacket that looks like it's the real deal, like he got here on a Harley or something. His arms are folded on a chest I wouldn't mind getting a closer look at, and dark brows are pulled down over eyes that look black from here.

I stare back at him, and touch my tongue to my lower lip. Then, I shut my eyes very slowly, and open them again, so he can see how blue my eyes are, how long my lashes. I uncross and recross my legs, so he can appreciate that mine are almost as long as his.

His face doesn't change and he looks away with such a bored expression I feel heat rise up my chest under my hoodie.

Well, getting him to notice me will make the meeting a little more interesting. I push my hood back so my naturally curly blond hair tumbles out like Rapunzel sending down her ladder.

He doesn't so much as glance at me, and I spend the rest of the meeting trying to get him to.

When it's finally over, I get up from my chair, unzipping the hoodie so my black turtleneck showcases my curves, but he's already walking out without talking to anybody, picking up a helmet from beside the door.

Well. That gives me something to look forward to tomorrow when I come here again, same Bat-time, same Bat-channel. And maybe I'll keep my hair blond for a while longer.

Unfortunately, my antics have attracted someone else's attention, one of those lumpish hockey-player types that think they're God's gift—not that I would know a hockey player from a pole vaulter, since we have nothing but soccer on St. Thomas.

"Hi." He actually reaches out and picks up one of my curls, rubs it between his fingers like he wants to smell it or something. "Pearl."

I yank my hair out of his hand and bundle it into my hood and zip it up again. "Howdy, fellow druggie."

That puts him back a bit, rubbing his rash-roughened chin with a hand. "Need a ride somewhere?"

"No thanks."

"I'm Steve."

"And I don't recall asking." I turn and walk out. I can feel his eyes burning holes in my back, and I can feel the other girls hating on me. Everyone judging me, like they always do.

Well, if they'd walked a mile in my boots they wouldn't envy them, I can tell you that. Not that I'm complaining. I'm not in Eureka, California, after all. Instead, I'm living in Boston with my sister Ruby and her hunky husband Rafe, and they're pretending they have some idea how to deal with me.

I don't need anything but to be left alone.

That's what I tell myself as I walk home from the meeting. It feels lonelier and more pathetic than I ever like to feel, the wind cutting through my jeans and the last of the fall leaves rolling along the sidewalk. There's a sharp wind off the Charles River, only a few blocks away from my sister's sweet old Back Bay neighborhood. I go up the stairs of their brownstone with the sandstone lions that guard the door. I've nicknamed the lions Beowulf and Odin, and I pat their heads as I get my key out and go inside.

Yeah, every time I think I'm lonely or sad or get tempted to drink or hit someone up for a line or a hit, I have to think: EUREKA. I don't have to go there. And I need to be grateful.

Up in my girly-pink bedroom, I turn my radio to the rock station and flop backwards on the bed, listening to the Top 40 of 1989.

I really am grateful to be here. Rafe and Ruby didn't have to take me in, make me the third wheel to their two-person googly-eyed love fest, especially now that Ruby's pregnant.

Right on cue, Ruby knocks on the door and then opens it. "How was the meeting?"

Ruby's so pretty. She has green eyes, long dark red hair, and the kind of heart-shaped face with blushy skin that makes guys

4

want to protect and take care of her, when nothing could be further from what she's really like: stubborn as a mule and smart as hell. She just got her law degree, and the only person who can sometimes beat her at an argument is me.

"It was fine."

"Where's your paper?"

I got so distracted I forgot to have the leader sign my attendance sheet. "Dammit, I forgot to have it signed. But Ms. Betsy can sign it next time."

Ruby comes all the way into the room. She's about three months pregnant and just beginning a little pooch of belly. "Pearl, come on. You promised. Let me see your arms."

I push up the sleeves of my hoodie, biting down on all the ways I want to tell her to back off, thinking *Eureka*. She and Rafe trying to lay down rules is really kind of funny, when Mom and Dad never could get me to obey anything.

I'm the original rebel without a cause. I don't know why it's always my first instinct to do the opposite of what everyone wants.

She sits next to me. "I hate this, Pearl. I hate having to hold your feet to the fire like this. But I just don't think you get how serious things are."

"Oh, I get it." I pull my legs up under my stretched out, comfy old hoodie. "I do what you and Rafe want or you ship me back to Mom."

"I guess that's the bottom line, but that's not what I'm talking about. I just don't think you get how worried we are about you. You have a problem."

I can't take it anymore, and surge up off the bed in a waft of anger.

"You don't get how it's really not a big deal and never was."

"Mom and I talked. She said she's thought a lot about how things started going bad with you and traced it back to a

Christmas party two years ago that you went to at the Carvers' house. Did something happen there? Something bad?"

Yeah, I remember that party. What I remember is that I don't remember.

"You know what? If I'm too much trouble, send me back already. I'm sick of the inquisition, of nothing I do being right."

I slam out of the bedroom, feeling tears at the backs of my eyes.

If only Dad hadn't died because of me.

I could have still turned things around if he hadn't died when he did. How he did. I jump on the smooth walnut railing and slide down the long curving stairs to the entryway.

I'm not a total nutcase. I grab a coat. Boston in November is pretty damn chilly at night.

Out on the street it's quiet. I head for one of the walking bridges that crosses over the freeway to the park that runs along the Charles. I just want to walk, to clear my head. I'm not looking for trouble.

But trouble has always seemed to find me.

It doesn't help to have a sister like Ruby. So good at everything, so clear about her goals, the responsible super achiever.

I missed her so much when she left for school. I realized I was never going to be able to fill her shoes with Mom and Dad, and their scrutiny began to really chafe once I got into my teens.

I didn't want the same things they did. But I didn't know what I wanted, myself. I just knew it wasn't the mellow island life on Saint Thomas, where the biggest social event of the week was the Sunday church potluck.

That's how I ended up going out with Connor Carver. He was twenty when we started going out, and I was fifteen. He worked at the shipyard in Charlotte Amalie, and he drove a souped-up Charger and smoked Marlboros. He was so hot in those broken-down jeans and the T-shirt with the sleeves rolled up around his cigarette pack...

Ah, memories. *Memories I had, and didn't have.*

The wind off the river is fierce. I tighten my hood and lean down to walk into it, feeling it smack my cheeks, and I'm so focused I don't hear the running footsteps coming up behind me until it's too late, until my head explodes with stars and the ground is coming up to meet my face.

CHAPTER TWO

I wake up on my back. The sky is dark, there are a few stars above, but ambient yellow light from the park outlines the stark branches of bare-limbed trees.

Someone is digging through my pockets, patting me down. It takes a second but I realize I've just been clocked on the head and now I'm being robbed.

Not that I've got anything to steal.

I scream, and kick at whoever's muttering, his hand in the pocket of my jeans and about to get the key I'm carrying, literally the only thing on me.

"Shut up!" He slaps me, and it snaps my head to the side. He gets hold of the zipper of the jacket and hauls it down. "Where's your purse? Your wallet?"

"Screw you, asswipe!" I yell, terrified he's going to touch me, rape me. I thrash and kick at him again. I connect with something soft and he grunts. I roll to the side to get away.

"Help! Help!"

He's pissed now and kicks me, right in the stomach. It knocks the breath out of me.

I curl up in the fetal position, my hands over my head as he kicks me some more and then I hear someone yelling, "Hey! What are you doing? Get away from her!"

I'm too busy trying to drag air into my lungs to pay much attention to the scuffle that goes on, but then someone is rolling me onto my back.

"Are you all right?"

My hood's fallen off, and he sucks in a breath at the sight of my face.

That's how I know he's a man, and he's gotten a look at my hair, and face, and since my jacket is unzipped, now he can see my body, too. Yes, it makes people gasp.

My eyes pop open, too wide, but the man's haloed by one of the park's carriage lamps and I can't see his face. I open and close my mouth a couple times, still trying to get air.

"He ran away," my rescuer says. "Just get your breath. You're going to be okay." He sits down and lifts me halfway into his arms, and we just sit there on the ground for a few minutes.

Finally, I can speak past the pain. "Thank you."

"I didn't do anything. What kind of jerk beats up women in the park?"

"He was trying to rob me, but I didn't have anything." I feel a wave of tears well up, so many tears. *I never cry.* Pearl the tough girl, that's me.

But now, my body battered, lying on my cold ass in the park in the arms of a stranger, I let it all go.

All I've been holding onto. Dad's gone. The Carvers. The move here, which has been harder than I'll ever let anyone know. I really miss Mom and Jade, even though I don't want to live in Eureka. I even cry for Saint Thomas, that pretty little cliché of an island where I grew up.

"Shhhh," he says. "You're all right now." He holds me against him, but just by the shoulders, not trying to cop a feel, and he pats my back, little gentle pats like burping a baby.

But he doesn't seem to be trying to hurry me along, get me to shut up. Most guys totally can't handle a girl crying, but he seems perfectly content to sit on the freezing sidewalk in the dark with a crying girl snotting all over his clothes.

Finally, I'm done. Pain of a different kind is taking over my body, reminding me I need to get home and probably into a hot bath.

"I'm so sorry," I snuffle. "I've just—been through a lot. I'm sorry I cried all over you."

"Don't worry about it." He's still patting, but now he's touching my hair, gently, so gently. It scares me. He's a stranger after all. I pull away, and groan because my tummy hurts, and my back, and my hip and my head, too.

"I need to get home."

"Let's get to Mass Avenue and find a phone booth. Call the police."

"I just want to get home." I can feel hysteria rising.

He must hear it in my voice because he says, "Okay. We'll get you home and then we'll call the cops."

I try to get up but I wouldn't have been able to if he didn't loop an arm under my shoulder and hoist me up against his side.

I still haven't seen his face, but at this point I hope I never have to look him in the eye after my total sob-fest breakdown.

He mostly carries me to Mass Avenue, but we can't find a phone booth and the cars can't stop on the freeway-like road, so we limp and hop up over one of the bridges and into my sister's Back Bay neighborhood, and by then it's not worth it to try to find a cab, so my rescuer and I gimp our way to the brownstone, and I was never so happy to see Beowulf and Odin.

The ten steps to the shiny black door of Rafe and Ruby's

building are just too much for me, and I collapse. He sets me gently on the bottom step and bounds up to the door, pounding on it. The door opens, and it's Rafe with no shirt on, wearing a pair of flannel pajama bottoms and looking ripped and scary.

I shut my eyes so I won't be embarrassed by how he yells, "What the hell?" and shoves past the guy who brought me home and scoops me up like I weigh nothing, carrying me into the house.

Ruby is in a tizzy. I hear her invite the stranger in, and I just shut my eyes and cling to my brother's neck, because that's the way I think of him.

Rafe, the big brother I never had, who takes care of me like a dad.

The waterworks start up again. I'm so embarrassed. He's carrying me all the way up that stupid staircase, and putting me on my bed.

"Pearl. What happened? Did that guy hurt you?"

I can tell he's getting ready to go kick my rescuer's ass.

"No, he saved me," I hiccup, hating how weak I'm being. "I got mugged."

"She needs first aid," Ruby says from the doorway. "I've already called the cops. This is Brandon. He chased off her attacker and brought her all the way home."

I open my puffy eyes enough to see Brandon in the doorway. He has short blond hair and brown eyes, and is wearing one of those preppy sweater vests with the argyle pattern on it over a long-sleeved shirt, but he'd had some sort of wool coat on, I could swear. He probably had to take it off because I got so much snot and tears on it, but I remember how it felt against my cheek.

"Brandon. Thanks so much," I say. "I don't know what would have happened if. . ." I can't even complete the thought without my eyes welling up again.

"Don't worry about it," he says. "Just relax. You're safe now." He speaks to me as if we're all alone, his voice pitched to that vibration that worked so well to have me feeling utterly safe, safe enough to unlock all the grief I've been carrying for months.

I shut my eyes and their voices fade until sirens wake me up. I'm getting checked out by the emergency personnel, and the cops are here too, and they take my statement and Brandon's statement, and I even get naked with the EMT checking out all my bruises and a lady cop photographs them and asks matter-of-factly if I was raped.

"Not recently," I say, which isn't what I meant to say. Eventually they all leave and I get into the hot bath I've begged for, and Ruby comes in with me, sitting on top of the toilet seat.

I'm sunk deep in fragrant bubbles, my eyes at half mast, the pain medication they gave me beginning to work when Ruby says, "What do you mean, not recently?"

"I didn't get raped tonight," I say sleepily. "Because Brandon saved me."

"But you were raped before."

I have only half a brain cell working by then, but I remember I'm not supposed to tell and I shut my eyes, shut my mouth.

"Pearl. Please. Help me understand what's been happening with you. Tell me." Ruby's voice is so soft, and trembling with her own tears. "I know something is wrong, something more than Dad's death. You never used to be like this."

"Like what?" I feel that old defensiveness rear up to push her away from getting too close to my pain.

"Like this. Angry. Self-destructive. You aren't the Pearl I know, that I grew up with. Did something happen at that party at the Carvers'? Mom thinks it did."

"People change." I slide all the way down into the bubbles

and under the water to shut her out, and when I finally have to come up for air, she's gone.

The next day I'm hurting. Like, really hurting. I can't even get out of bed. Ruby's worried and calls a doctor that makes house calls, and I get checked out again.

"Bruising and muscle contusions," the doc says. "She'll be all right in a few days. And probably won't run off alone at night to the park, right?" He's a cherubic-looking old guy with a potbelly and pink cheeks, and I hate the way he implies this is my fault, what happened.

I get more painkillers and I'm shocked when Rafe comes to my door, his long hair in a ponytail, dressed to go out in jeans and a sweater. "Get up, Pearl. You've got half an hour to get ready for your meeting."

"What? I can hardly walk!"

"Get up off your ass and get dressed. I'm taking you, in whatever you're wearing, in twenty minutes." He leaves.

All my loving older-brother feelings go flying out the window as I curse a blue streak and haul my sore body out of bed and dress in my usual all-black. My hair is a disaster, a waist-length welter of matted curls that I went to sleep on soaking wet. The mugger didn't get my face, but that's about the only part of me that didn't get bruised.

Well, at least I'm going to have some "experience" to share at the meeting today, I think resentfully.

Rafe drives me to the door of the church hall where they hold the meetings.

"Do I need to walk you in?" His dark blue eyes are still angry, and I'm realizing he's not someone I want to piss off. "Because if you need help, I'll walk you in. And if you're thinking of leaving, I'll sit with you on my lap and make sure you stay in there."

"I don't need these stupid meetings," I say, for the hundredth time. "I am not an addict. I was just playing around."

He just stares at me, a muscle jumping in his jaw, and I decide to make the best of it. "Whatever. You're a jerk. I don't know what my sister sees in you."

I open my door and get out, slamming it hard, and limp into the building on my own steam.

The meeting's just getting started, and I sit next to the leader. "I'm sorry, I forgot to have you sign this," I say, giving her the signature paper from yesterday.

She looks at me, can tell something's wrong because my eyes are swollen to slits from crying and my snarled hair is a mess.

"Are you okay?" She signs the paper, for yesterday and for today, too.

"No. I was mugged last night," I say, and my eyes well up.

That's how I end up being the first one to share.

"Hi. I'm Pearl. And I don't want to be here today because every muscle in my body is screaming in pain right now. I was mugged last night, and if you want the truth, it happened because I ran away from the house and went to the park looking for trouble. Looking to score. I was mad at my sister when I left the house, but I didn't realize what I was really going to the park for until just this minute, as I'm telling you."

I can't believe how good it feels to tell the truth for once, to a whole group of people who have been there. I tell about the mugging, and I even unzip my jacket (because my beloved hoodie is in the wash) and show the bruises on my midsection and back.

"He kicked me and kicked me. He was mad I fought back

and that I didn't have anything to steal. He was probably looking to score, too."

And I sob and cry on the leader's shoulder right in front of Hot Motorcycle Guy who's across the circle from me again. He's listened to my whole story, stone-faced.

But I don't care if he looks at me or listens to me or even notices me. For once, I don't care what anyone thinks. Screw him, anyway, and all the guys in the world who only want one thing from me.

I get tons of hugs, and the whole meeting turns to stories of getting assaulted for drugs or assaulting others for drugs, and by the time we end and all hold hands and say the Lord's Prayer, I actually feel peace coming to me through the familiar words. I know I'm a part of this group, for better or worse. *I'm in the right place.*

CHAPTER THREE

"How was the meeting?" Rafe asks. He's pulled up at the curb and pushed open the door of his Mercedes for me. I get in.

"Fine." I'm not ready to admit he was right about making me go to the meeting.

We drive back to the house in silence, but finally, when he's pulling into the garage, I ask, "Are you mad at me? Because you seem mad."

I don't like how my voice comes out small, like a little kid's, but I realize I don't want him mad at me. I need him and Ruby.

A lot.

He sighs, turns off the car. We sit in the dim garage and he clenches and unclenches his hands on the wheel.

"I'm mad that you ran out of the house and put yourself in danger," Rafe finally says. "And I'm mad someone assaulted you. I need to tell you straight, Pearl. If you can't take your program seriously, going to school seriously—if you're going to freak Ruby out all the time and be out of control—we're going to have to send you back to your mom."

The tears well up from that deep place that, once it got started, I can't seem to shut off. "I'm sorry, Rafe. I get it. I'll be good. I want to stay."

He looks at me with those dark blue eyes that I can see melt my sister but only make me nervous. He sees too much. "I mean it," I say. "I'll take it seriously."

"Good. Then you won't mind that we have a counseling appointment for you this afternoon. A woman who specializes in trauma."

I swallow my curses and anger. This shrink can have a crack at me, no problem. She won't get anywhere. "Sure."

He grins. "Was that a "sure" I heard? Now I think I'm the one that's high."

I sock him in the arm as he laughs, and we're back to normal.

It's Sunday, thank God, so I have another day to get ready for school. After another Percocet and a nap, I face my closet and think about school Monday. I haven't been applying myself at school or trying to get friends, and that needs to change.

All the usual reasons. The girls don't like me because I'm too pretty, the guys like me to hit on, but they're all just pimply babies in my opinion. The truth is, I've just been skulking in and out and doing the minimum. But after my talk with Rafe today, I know I have to turn that around.

Like it's easy, transferring to a big Boston high school halfway through senior year from a place like St. Thomas. But I haven't really given it a chance, I know, and there's got to be some halfway measure between my all-black stealth clothes and wearing shiny boat shoes with pennies in them like some prep-school dork.

I pick out a different outfit than usual for Monday. Jeans, the soft caramel-colored half-boots Ruby gave me, and a blue sweater with a snowflake pattern around the neck that I've never worn. I'll probably look ridiculous in it, like a Barbie milkmaid, but if I wear this to the therapy appointment it will help me fend off the shrink.

I put on the outfit and spend another half-hour brushing my hair and finally get all the tangles out. I put on a little mascara and lip gloss, and look in the mirror. I look like the Swiss Miss chocolate girl, sweet as sugar and twice as pure.

I want to vomit. If they only knew.

Someone knocks on my door and I yank it open before I remember I was going to be good and nice.

"What?"

It's Mrs. Knightly the housekeeper, and her sweet face crumples at my tone. "Miss Pearl. There's a gentleman to see you downstairs."

I frown. "Who?"

"He says you met last night. His name is Brandon Forbes."

Brandon. My rescuer. I dread seeing him by the cold hard light of day, but I owe him thanks at least, and I'm curious about him. I have a sense that he's older than me, but not that much. "I'm sorry I was snappy, Mrs. Knightly. I appreciate you coming all the way up here to tell me."

She perks up. We've had a bond since the first day I arrived. She's lovely to me, brings me little things she finds at the flea market she thinks I'd like, and I do the same for her.

"It's okay, honey. I can't believe what happened to you."

"Yeah, it sucks. But I'm feeling better. Now I guess I better get down there and thank the guy who rescued me."

"Oh, then I want to thank him, too."

Mrs. Knightly follows me down the long curving stairs to the yellow parlor, where Brandon's sitting on the silk couch talking to Rafe. Brandon stands up. He's better-looking than I realized last night. His eyes widen at the sight of me, and I surprise both of us by running across the room to hug him.

"Thank you so much," I say into the soft wool of his preppy-looking sweater.

"Thank you, Mr. Forbes," Mrs. Knightly says behind me. "You did a good thing, helping our Pearl."

His arms come around me and he pats me with that little baby-burping pat. "You're welcome. I'm glad I could help." His voice is a low comforting rumble that makes me feel good, just like it did last night, and I can feel him stroke my hair, which is a floating tumble all around us, sticking to his sweater by static electricity as if magnetized.

Rafe clears his throat. I pull away and pat Brandon's shoulder and smile up at him. "Really. Thank you."

"So nice of you to come by and check on Pearl, but she needs to get ready for an appointment with a trauma counselor," Rafe says, as we gaze at each other.

I thought Brandon had brown eyes, but it turns out they're hazel with specks of green and gold, and he has a very nice mouth that I wouldn't mind getting a taste of. I can see he's similarly taking inventory and he says, ignoring Rafe, "I'd like to take you for a walk in the park sometime. Not at night. Revisit the scene of the crime. I think it would be good for both of us."

"I'd like that," I say. My hair is still stuck to his sweater, the long blond strands reaching out like quivering antennae to attach to him.

"How about tomorrow?"

"After school. Two-thirty?" I ask.

"I'll pick you up."

And I hug him again, because I just have to, and he pats

me, and I can feel Rafe glaring at Brandon and he growls about the time, and finally Brandon lets me go and we say goodbye. Suddenly life is looking a whole lot better to me than it did before, in spite of having to go to therapy.

CHAPTER FOUR

Dr. Rosenfeld is a sparrow-like woman with salt-and-pepper hair and no makeup. She wears one of those awful natural-fiber dresses over a turtleneck and socks under her Birkenstocks. I keep my face neutral and shake her hand as briefly as I can get away with, looking around.

Dr. Rosenfeld's office is decorated all earthy-crunchy, with avocado-green walls, a big bison skull on the wall dangling a dreamcatcher, and some really messed-up art on the walls featuring more skulls, flowers, and dripping blood. A client probably gave it to her. Her office is in a fancy building downtown on the 20th floor; Rafe brought me since Ruby's working on some business contract for McCallum Enterprises.

I wish I had some idea what to do with my life when high school ends, which isn't that far away. Maybe I can use this time with the counselor to talk about that, which is something I really need help with.

I sit in the middle of the tweedy couch so I have a lot of room around me. Dr. Rosenfeld goes and sits in an office-type chair across from me. There's a coffee table with a big tablet of paper and a set of pens.

"So. Your brother-in-law says you were attacked in the park last night."

"I was mugged. Yeah."

"But someone rescued you."

"Brandon Forbes. Thank God."

"So, tell me what happened."

I really look at her for the first time. She has a plain face, unapologetically lined, and deep brown eyes. Silver-and-black hair hangs in a neat helmet shape, like she put it on this morning.

"How is that going to help me?"

"Trauma can grow and magnify when it's locked up inside. Every time you tell your story, it's like letting light and air over a wound. It helps it heal."

This makes sense to me because I already feel so much better after talking about the attack at the twelve-step meeting. I relax a little bit against the couch. I might as well get my brother-in-law's money's worth, at least about the mugging.

"I was mad at my sister and decided to go for a walk, get some air." I tell how the mugging happened, and finish with, "and then, when Brandon held me in his arms and I knew I was safe, I just cried so hard. And I haven't cried hardly at all, since Dad died."

"Why do you think that is?"

"I..." I choke on all the secrets I'm carrying. "I don't know. I think I was just letting it all out."

"Letting all what out?" Her eyes are sharp, but kind. Still, I'm not ready. I don't trust her. In general, but specifically not to run and tell Rafe and Ruby even though I signed confidentiality paperwork.

"I don't want to talk about it. I want to talk about what to do after high school. I'm graduating this year."

"Ah." She sits back, as if she knows exactly what's going through my mind. "We can certainly do that, but I want you to know that everything you say in these sessions is protected, totally confidential. Except if you are planning to hurt yourself or someone else, which I'd have to break your confidentiality to prevent. My job is to help you heal, and to do that you need to know your secrets are safe with me."

"Maybe another day I'll talk about that," I say, refusing to take the bait but liking how straightforward she is. "Can we discuss my future?"

"Sure. It should begin with what you like to do."

"Yeah. That's the thing. I'm not sure. I thought I'd end up working in the hospitality industry since I grew up on Saint Thomas, but then we had to move." We talk about that for a while, and how I came to live here in Boston. It's a colorful story and takes the rest of the time, and I only get to tell her that I like fashion and design before our time is over.

"I'm seeing you again in three days," Dr. Rosenfeld says. "I'm looking forward to seeing you again, Pearl." She says it like she means it. She walks me out, and she and Rafe exchange pleasantries, and then we're on the way home.

"How was it?"

"Fine," I say. And I won't tell him he was right to bring me here, too.

CHAPTER FIVE

The next day I'm still sore but I'm moving better. I wear the blue sweater and jeans I picked out to school, and it seems to help things go a little better. A couple of girls give me a smile or say hi. I even get waved over to a table at lunch with several girls that I know aren't cool but aren't the bottom of the barrel either, and that's good. I can't eat much, because my stomach still feels upset and I walk stiffly from the bruises, but I don't tell anyone what happened. We're still at the "so how's the weather" and "what movies do you like" stage. I'm just happy not to get a cold shoulder for once.

After school I walk the five blocks quickly home because I'm looking forward to meeting Brandon.

He's already at the house, and Ruby's talking with him in the yellow parlor when I unlock the front door.

"So you're at MIT," Ruby is saying. "What year?"

"I'm a junior," Brandon says. "Majoring in engineering."

I push the door in, eavesdropping. Engineering? At MIT? I can't help contrasting Brandon with my first boyfriend, Connor Carver, whose talent was running drugs and fixing cars. But Connor was so hot it didn't matter what he did. Brandon's nerdy. He wears argyle sweaters, for Heaven's sake.

But Brandon makes me feel good, and safe, and so what if he turns out to be boring? Boring is what I need right now.

I try not to think of Hot Motorcycle Guy with his long legs and burning-coal eyes.

"Hi, Brandon," I say, coming into the yellow parlor. I've taken a minute to put on some cherry lip gloss and mascara earlier and my hair looks good, so I'm not surprised when he looks a little dazed when I give him the patented full-wattage Pearl smile.

"You should be a model," he blurts out. "You're every bit as gorgeous as the girls my mom works with."

"What?" Ruby says. "Your mom works with models?"

"Yes. She owns the Melissa Agency. They have offices here in Boston and in New York."

"Do you really think so?" Ruby gives me a critical once-over. "She's tall enough, but don't you think she's a little—full bodied?"

"Hey!" I put my hands on my hips. "I'm standing right here."

"She has a nice shape. She'd have to lose a few pounds but I wasn't thinking runway. She'd be better for magazine work," Brandon says to Ruby, looking me over with the same assessing air. He picks up a handful of my drifting, creamy-silver curls, lets them drop through his fingers. "This hair will photograph amazingly well."

"Why don't you introduce her to your mom?" Ruby's being really persistent, and I'm getting a little angry and embarrassed.

"Hey!" I say again. "I'm not interested in modeling."

"I think she'd be mad at me if I didn't," Brandon says, and finally addresses me directly. "Don't worry about it. Modeling is the most competitive field ever. It would be a miracle if she looks twice at you, no matter what I say."

This immediately gets my competitive streak going, and I want to impress this unknown Melissa of the Melissa Agency. *His mother.* Probably a battle-ax.

"I thought we were going for a walk."

"And so we shall." He extends his elbow for me to take. "How are you feeling?"

"Bruised. But lots better."

"Here's your coat," Ruby says, and hands me the black wool coat with a hood on it that I picked out at a thrift store. It's like my friendly hoodie, only bigger. I get into it and immediately feel like myself again.

"See you in awhile, Ruby."

She waves us out the door like a den mother. We walk out of the brownstone and I pat the lions' heads. "Bye, Odin. Beowulf."

Brandon has a nice warm laugh. "Those your pets?"

"Low maintenance. That's how I like them," I say. We walk along the sidewalk and over to the bridge across Massachusetts Avenue, retracing our steps from before.

"I can't believe you half carried me all the way home," I say, snuggling into Brandon's arm, rubbing against his coat. "What were you doing out at the park alone? I never asked you."

"I had a tough equation I was working on. Sometimes I walk at night, and it helps me unsnarl the problem."

"Did you figure it out?"

"Weirdly enough, I did," he says, as we get to the park and walk along the wide cement walk that borders the Charles. In the afternoon sunlight, crew teams glide along the river's smooth green surface like water striders, and the last of the fall leaves blow along in a light breeze. "I left your place, walking back to my frat house, and I suddenly knew the answer. So I had to run all the way back and write down the next step before I forgot it. So you helped me too."

"I'm glad I'm good for something." I don't mean for it to come out so sad sounding, like a little girl with a case of hopelessness. He looks down at me, and I like that he's at least three inches taller. I'm five-nine so I don't get to look up at people that often.

"Pearl. You're at the beginning of what's going to be an extraordinary life."

"Really? You think so?" So far, my life on Saint Thomas was sheltered and boring. Then, things happened and it all changed. Now I'm wishing I could get back to boring, but extraordinary? I never thought of myself that way. Ruby, yes. So smart and pretty, she was always going to do big things. Me? I just wanted... I don't know yet. But I never had a sense it would be anything extraordinary.

I like that he thinks so, and I hug his arm. "Thanks for saying that."

"I am going to set you up an appointment with my mom."

"I don't know. Modeling." I kick some leaves. "I'm not sure I want all these people looking at me."

"It's not really you they're looking at. It's the idea of you. Kind of like this old coat you wear, and that ratty old hoodie. The model persona is a disguise."

"I never thought of it that way, but I can see what you're saying," I say, glancing at a billboard I can see across the park of Cindy Crawford. Her hair blows like a wheat field, her skin is burnished metal, her lips a sculpture.

I wonder what the real Cindy is thinking and doing, if she even kind of looks like that poster. Brandon might be right.

"I know I'm right," he says, and squeezes my arm. I must have said it out loud. "We're almost here."

I feel my heart speed up as my mind goes back to the other

night walking along here, my head down, preoccupied—and the whack like stars exploding that knocked me down.

Brandon steers me off the main cement path to a spot between two thick bushes. The ground is trampled grass and looks unremarkable.

"This was where I saw him assaulting you."

"It was so dark. And I was wearing black. I can't believe you saw me," I say, and shudder.

"You screamed, remember? I wouldn't have spotted you if you hadn't, I was so preoccupied with my math problem."

"You came and fought him off," I say, trying to imagine being Brandon, going to a stranger's aid in the dark against a possibly-armed man. "I can't believe you did that for me." My eyes fill up and I sniffle.

He hugs me. "I would have done it for anybody. We can't just let evil happen in the world and turn a blind eye."

But some people did. A lot of people did. Including some I thought were friends.

I flash to that Christmas party, the Christmas party I can hardly remember, and that back bedroom in the Carvers' house where I woke up, to what was done to me.

I discovered what happened from the blood and mess I was lying in, from marks on my body from teeth and lips, from drying stains of nameless fluids I'd known nothing about until that night.

I never should have had that drink in the big red plastic cup.

I feel an overwhelming nausea and turn away, retching, beside one of the bushes.

Brandon pats my back, awkward but tender. I stay bent over awhile, gasping, thankful I hadn't eaten much at lunch. Finally, I straighten up. He hands me a Kleenex in one of those little plastic packets. So tidy, so organized. I pat my mouth. I can't look at him.

"I think I should go home now."

He doesn't ask if this was a good thing for me. Therapeutic. I can't tell if it was. I only know I remembered more today than I'd ever let myself before, and I desperately want to forget again.

To feel better.

I think of the oblivion of the drug Connor introduced me to, the dreamy half-light, a floating and magical feeling like I was insulated, like nothing could touch or hurt me.

I want it, fiercely. I should go to a meeting, but that's not what I plan to do.

I am walking so fast toward home, Brandon's jogging a little to keep up. I've almost forgotten he's there because I'm thinking of where Ruby keeps her household money and that I know where I can make a buy. As soon as I ditch Brandon.

"Hey. Are you okay?" He takes my arm and I resent the intrusiveness of him touching me. I shrug him off.

"Fine, thanks. But listen, I just want to get home. I think I need to talk to my shrink about what happened." This is guaranteed to make him leave me alone, and it does.

"Okay, I understand. I'll call you with a meeting time for the modeling thing."

"Sure." I stop myself from saying, "Whatever" because Brandon doesn't deserve that. He's been a total gentleman, gone above and beyond in every way.

He walks me all the way to the sandstone lions. "So I'll see you tomorrow. If I get a meeting for you."

"Okay," I still won't look at him.

"Listen." He puts a hand on my arm, turns me. I won't look at him so he tips my chin up and I finally have to meet his warm brown eyes. "I'm sorry this happened to you, Pearl. But you're going to be okay."

Once I'm high, I'll really be okay.

"Sure. I know," I say with fake cheer. "Absolutely. Thanks again." I turn away and skip up the steps as if cheerful, and give a little wave at the top.

He's frowning, hands in his coat pockets, as I shut the door on him and go looking for my sister's stash of grocery money.

Rafe is down at the docks, according to a note on the counter, and Ruby's at work at McCallum Enterprises. They are both such busy, responsible, good people it kind of makes me want to hurl again.

The place to score is by the public bathrooms on the Common, and after I've found the hundred-dollar bill Ruby leaves for Mrs. Knightly in a cookie jar, I dress in my usual all-black, braid my hair and stuff it inside my hoodie, and leave the house again.

I trip down the stairs without patting Odin or Beowulf and walk briskly to Boston Common in the low light of evening.

It's getting colder, and the wind cuts through both my hoodie and my coat, but pretty soon I'm going to be feeling warm and very, very good. I give some thought, as I walk, to where I'm going to get high.

It has to be my bedroom. I can just leave a note that I'm so emotionally wrecked from revisiting the site of my assault that I took a sleeping pill and went to bed. That should work to keep Ruby and Rafe from checking too close.

I get to the bathroom, and sure enough the skinny black woman with dreads who sits on the bench with her bag of yarn and knitting needles is still there. A customer is just getting up from sitting next to her, a preppy-looking dude in a bomber jacket with his hand in his pocket from something she handed him.

I head for her like a heat-seeking missile. I'm so intent that I jump as I feel a hand on my arm. "Hey."

I whirl around, and my hood falls off. I'm looking into Hot Motorcycle Guy's face—a face more rugged than handsome. One angled black brow is split by a scar. His mouth has full, curling lips that look hard—brutal, even, as is the grip he has on my arm.

I try to yank away. "Hey yourself. Let go of me."

"No." He clamps down harder and turns, physically dragging me away from the woman with the bag of knitting. I panic and start flailing, fighting to get away, opening my mouth to scream, but by then he's hauled me into the lee of the bathroom and has both hands on my shoulders, pushing me back against the wall.

I realize he's released me, and shut my mouth slowly. His hands still bracket me in, and his big body cuts the wind in front of me.

"Calm down. I'm not going to hurt you. I'm trying to help you." His voice is deep and low. His eyes aren't black like they looked from across the circle of the meeting. They're a brown so dark it's like Kalamata olives. I stare back, a rabbit hypnotized by a snake. I find my breathing slowing. Falling into sync with his.

His sculptured lips look delicious. I like the stubble on his cheeks, the row of steel earrings in one ear, the black, chain-covered motorcycle jacket he wears, and the broken-in black jeans and belt covered with gunmetal studs, and the black sweater that's tight against his amazing body.

"I'm trying to help you." He's close, so close I can see the long, thick lashes around those dark-olive eyes. That gorgeous mouth comes closer, and I tip my head and my eyes half-close. The chemistry between us is magnetic. I can feel him trying to resist it, but still getting closer. *Kiss me, please*, I think, and then, unbelievably, he does.

His mouth *is* brutal, but in a good way—hot and consuming, confident and taking. No warmup needed, our tongues tangle deliciously. I grab his jacket with one hand and the massive slope of his back with the other and haul him in closer, giving back promises to fulfill some of the simmering attraction we've felt from across the circle of the meeting.

He smells spicy and tastes like cinnamon, and I love the way he kisses me, like a starving man getting to a feast. I feel exactly the same, hungry and out of control, but wanting to savor the moment, too.

He finally breaks away and lifts his head, looking down at me. My vision is fogged, my breath hitches, and I'm panting like I ran a mile. My breasts tingle, I can feel how hard my nipples are, begging for him to touch them. There's a warm pulse between my legs.

"You're trouble, Pearl," he breathes into my mouth. "A whole lot of trouble." And he sets his mouth on mine again, and I feel my nerve endings sizzle like I'm struck by lightning, every hair on my body upright and quivering, and all I want is *more, more, more.*

Finally, he wrenches his mouth from mine. His hands are still pressed against the wall on either side of me. So far he hasn't laid a hand on me, though mine are all over him, and everything I feel just makes me want more. "I should take you home."

"To your place?" I whisper. I realize I don't know his name, because the whole time he's been coming to the meetings he hasn't said anything but "Pass," when it's his turn to share.

He chuckles, a bass rumble. "No." And he takes me firmly by the arm again, and pulls my hood up over my hair. "To your place."

He takes my hand. He's wearing soft leather gloves with the fingers cut off, and his hand is strong and warm and feels so good in mine. He walks me down the path to a nearby parking lot where I spot the big, black motorcycle I'd already checked out at the twelve-step meeting.

I'm still dazed, my body flushed and ready to follow him anywhere. Even behind the dumpster would be fine, I'm not picky. He could haul my jeans off and be in me in two minutes flat.

I'm so turned on by this idea I stumble, and he hauls me up against his side. He's big and hard as a boulder I want to climb, but alas, we're at his motorcycle already.

There's a spare helmet in one of the locked saddlebags, and he hands it to me. "What's your address?"

I tell him, and he sets the helmet on my head, and puts the strap under my chin and tightens it. I look at him, longing, straining toward him, and he smiles and kisses me hard and quick.

"Bad girl. Tempting me like this." And he kisses me again. "Ever ridden a motorcycle before?"

"Yes." Connor had one. We rode all over Saint Thomas on that old beater off-road bike.

"Then you know you need to hang on." He swings a leg over the cushy, black leather seat and backs up the big shiny bike, and kicks the starter. It roars into life like lions growling around a wildebeest.

I get on behind him, my thighs tight behind his legs, my arms clamped around the studs of the belt around his muscular midsection, and the feeling I have as we roar out of the parking lot is *exhilaration*.

"Don't take me home, yet," I yell into the wind cutting our faces. "Take me for a ride."

I feel the rumble of his chuckle and see him nod, and then

we're whizzing down Mass Avenue and through the tunnel, and I howl like a wolf into the echoes and spiraling lights and rushing cars, yelling with excitement and something a lot like joy.

We go across the bridge, and the Charles is turning black as the sun has set, and we circle through the dark and spinning lights and high-pitched wail of the wind, and finally back around to the city. I lean into his leather-clad wind-shadow and watch the sights go by, and decide, for the first time, that I really love Boston.

I don't remember I was going to the Common to get high until he's pulling the bike up at the steps of Rafe and Ruby's brownstone and I'm getting off, feeling warm and deliciously hungry and excited and even a little bit happy.

"Can you come in?" I ask, taking off the helmet and shaking out my braid.

"Not today. See you at the meeting." He takes the helmet and stows it in the bag and revs the motorcycle.

I can't believe he's just leaving me like this. I can't just let him go. I lean over and kiss that hard, tender, tasty mouth, and I bite his lower lip a little at the end.

"Okay. See you at the meeting."

He roars off. I'm still vibrating all over with the feeling of all that power between my legs.

Turning to face Beowulf and Odin and a flight of ten stairs with light spilling through the glass window in the shiny door at the top, I realize I still don't know his name.

CHAPTER SIX

It's too much to hope that Ruby and Rafe didn't start worrying and looking for me when I came home; Ruby yanks the door open before I can stick the key in.

"Where were you?" Ruby's cheeks are red, her green eyes flashing. I've always thought Ruby looks great in a snit, and I'm feeling so good I just smile, what Connor used to call my 'shit-eating grin."

"Didn't know I had a curfew," I say, strolling in past her, wondering how I can get the hundred-dollar bill back into the cookie jar without her noticing.

"Who was that guy on the motorcycle?"

Oh damn.

"What, spying on me?" I head for the stairs. The best defense is always a good offense. "Keeping an eye on me like an old lady peeping at the window?"

This pisses Ruby off to no end, as I knew it would.

She actually growls and stomps her foot, and chases me up the stairs. "Pearl, for God's sake. We're responsible for you.

Didn't Rafe talk to you about... about if you can't follow the rules?"

"What rule did I break?" I reach the landing, fold my arms over my chest. I can feel how taut my nipples are from the cold and from being so close to Hot Motorcycle Guy. "I left you a note that I was going for a walk on the Common."

"I know you did, but that guy dropping you off—that wasn't walking home from the park!"

I relent, because I'm kind of happy right now and there's no sense pissing Ruby off when Motorcycle Guy really did help me. He distracted me so totally I forgot all about getting high.

"I ran into him at the park. He's a guy from my twelve-step meeting, okay? He gave me a ride home. He was totally sweet, too."

Well, maybe not sweet. Sweet tasting, though. My body lights up, remembering his kisses.

"Oh." Ruby's still got her hands on her hips. "How did the outing to the park with Brandon go?"

I shake my head, feeling the happiness I had for a few minutes draining away. "It was super upsetting."

"Well, you can talk to Dr. Rosenfeld about it tomorrow because you have a really busy day. Brandon called here and left a message that he has an appointment for you to meet his mother about the modeling thing. He'll pick you up right after school. And you have your lunchtime twelve-step meeting; Rafe and I are busy tomorrow so you can take one of the cars to school and go to it at lunch yourself. Then, you have Dr. Rosenfeld at six."

"Okay." I feel smothered by all of this. I just want to get to my room and lie on my bed and fantasize about Hot Motorcycle Guy. I wonder how old he is. Rafe and Ruby will probably think he's too old for me. They even think Brandon is too old for me, I can tell.

But I'm eighteen now, and I was never a young eighteen.

Ruby hugs me, and I hug her back, now that the fight is over. "I just worry about you, that's all," she says in my ear.

I pull away. "I'm fine. The bruises are a lot better today, and even though going with Brandon to the park was upsetting, it was a good thing to do. I just need to keep moving forward."

"Well, come down to dinner in half an hour or so." Ruby smiles. "That guy was awfully hot."

"I know," I grin. "He's *so* hot."

"What's his name?"

"Oh." Now I can feel my own face heating up, and I fib. "I can't remember. He said it in the meeting, but I didn't want to tell him when we met up that I didn't remember it. I'll find out tomorrow at the meeting."

And I'd find out a lot more, if I possibly can.

CHAPTER SEVEN

I dress the next morning with the meeting in mind. Narrow black jeans and cuffed heeled boots that make my already-long legs look like forever, a sweater tunic I've never worn before that Ruby gave me for Christmas, supposedly matching my eyes; and my hooded old coat to cover it all up whenever I want to hide. But I don't want to hide, this time. Not today. Because I'm seeing Hot Motorcycle Guy at lunch, and then I'm going to meet a famous modeling agency owner after school.

I'm not worried about what I look like for Dr. Rosenfeld. The woman wears Birkenstocks with socks underneath, for God's sake.

The morning flies by. School's actually not so bad when I'm paying attention, and at recess the girls from yesterday's lunch wave me over again to their middle-position table under a tree with all the leaves already gone, but some little round hard-looking nuts still stuck on it. I point up into the bare branches. "What kind of tree is this?"

"Horse chestnut. You gotta watch out, the wind sometimes knocks those off and they can hurt," one of the girls, Kayla, says.

"Are those from the song, "chestnuts roasting on an open fire?"" I ask.

She looks at me curiously. "Where did you say you're from?"

"Saint Thomas. Virgin Islands. We don't have horse chestnuts there. Lots of coconuts, though."

"Oh, that's so cool," she squeals. "Do you have pictures? Is it as beautiful as they say?"

"Probably more beautiful," I say, thinking of the water of Magen's Bay, so close to my childhood home, a turquoise so clear it shimmered, lit as if from within by the sun's reflection off the white sand bottom. "It's pretty boring to live there though."

"How could it be boring?" Another girl, Megan, asks, leaning into my personal space with bubble-gum breath.

I end up telling stories about life on the island until the bell rings. "I can't sit with you at lunch today," I say, feeling some actual regret. It's been nice having people to sit with, talk to, who weren't treating me like slime. "I have an appointment. See you tomorrow, though?"

And we end up exchanging phone numbers.

Things are definitely looking up. Maybe I'm not as socially doomed as I'd thought.

Lunch rolls around and I just about jog to the vintage BMW that's one of Rafe's collection. This one's not restored yet. It's not like the guy doesn't have enough to do, but he likes to buy old cars and tinker with them and fix them up. Ruby's driving a convertible Jag he fixed up and gave her for her birthday that about made my jaw drop.

Still this one runs, and it's a Beamer, which isn't a bad thing to be seen driving, so I'm feeling pretty swank as I pull up at the church parking lot where they hold the meeting. Mostly I'm dying to see Hot Motorcycle Guy again.

I sit in my usual spot, saying "hi" to a few people, and try not to keep looking around for him. The meeting gets started with the usual ritual protocols of Serenity Prayer and reading some quotes, then we get underway with sharing.

And Hot Motorcycle Guy never appears.

I cycle rapidly through the stages of grief I have the misfortune of knowing from Dad's all-too-recent death. First, denial: "He's in the bathroom. He's coming any minute. There's no way he's not coming after that kiss. No one blows me off like this." Halfway through the meeting I find myself bargaining: "I'll be good if he just shows up. I won't just jump his bones. I'll be hard to get, a real lady if he doesn't dump me before we even get going." Anger comes next, and I mentally swear a blue streak and pick at my jeans, tearing a hole in the knee as the endless meeting progresses. Finally, after I've briefly reported to the group that my bruises are better and I'm going to therapy for the attack, I realize I've accepted that he isn't there, and the meeting was okay anyway.

I feel exhausted, though, as I get my paper signed, and I have a couple more hours of class and then the modeling meeting.

I can't stand the thought of going back to school so I cut for the first time, going straight home after the meeting. After all, I need to look good for Brandon's battleax of a mother.

No one's home, as I knew they wouldn't be. Even Mrs. Knightly comes in later in the afternoon, so I revel in a bath and scrub myself all over with a loofah sponge. The bruises from the attack are still lurid, and I go gentle on those areas, but there's no denying I feel 100% better after I get out, buffed and clean, and rub myself all over with baby oil.

I've read up on modeling a bit since this opportunity appeared, and I know we have to start with the blank canvas of my un-made-up face. She'll need to see me without enhancement.

But that doesn't mean I can't make sure my skin and hair is as good as it can be.

I've already washed my hair and put on a super conditioner. I blow-dry it into a welter of luscious curls with a diffuser and slather on a clay mask. I lie down in my thin cotton robe with a couple of slices of cucumber over my eyes to tighten any puffiness.

I must have dropped off to sleep because next thing I know, a deep chiming wakes me up. I sit up and the cucumber slices fall off.

The chime comes again. It's more like a peal of bells, I decide.

It's the front door. Someone's there.

I try to remember when the last time was that I was home alone and had to answer the door, and realize it's never happened before.

I can't go answer the door looking like this.

I run across my room and glance out my window, which overlooks the street and the door. I don't know what I was expecting to see, but it's not a black Harley parked on the sidewalk in front and the top of Hot Motorcycle Guy's head as he rings the bell again.

I run out of my bedroom, hop on the curving banister, and slide down to the entry, smooth as snot. I run across the black-and-white marble of the entry and yank open one side of the huge door.

He's walking back down the steps.

"Hey!" I yell.

He turns, and busts into a huge grin at the sight of me. I realize I've never seen him smile. "Nice get-up."

I wrap my arms around myself, aware that my robe is

printed with cats in various poses, I'm barefoot and naked under the robe, and I have a mud mask on my face that's beginning to flake off like something out of Night of the Living Dead.

"Hey. I don't know what to call you," I say. He comes back up the steps.

"Magnus."

"Magnus? What kind of name is that?"

"Roman. I think."

"Do you have a last name?"

He's reached the top step and is smiling down at me. "I think you lost something," he says, and lifts a cucumber slice off my robe and holds it out to me on his finger. "Here."

I feel a world-class blush roar up my body and I'm grateful the damn mask hides it. I snatch the cucumber off his finger and throw it in the bushes. "What are you doing here?"

"I couldn't make it to the meeting. Wanted to make sure you knew I didn't blow you off."

"Okay. Come in. I can't stand out here in my robe." I withdraw into the house. He follows me. Looks around.

"Nice place."

"Yeah. My brother-in-law's. I'm Pearl. Pearl Michaels." I stick a hand out.

His dark eyes are sparkling with mirth as he takes my hand. "Magnus Thorne."

"That's a great name."

"My parents thought so."

"Well, thanks for coming by. It was a good meeting." As if I didn't spend the whole meeting wondering where he was and torturing myself.

"Yeah. I had a work thing. Wanted to get your number."

"Oh."

We look at each other. In spite of my mask and goofy outfit,

I can feel the air crackling with the energy we seem to spontaneously generate. "Um, it's right here."

I turn to the old-fashioned rotary phone Rafe keeps on a little marble stand with a pad for messages. I copy the number, hand it to him. "Here."

"And here's mine. In case you're ever tempted to slip again." He hands me a card. I glance down at it. MAGNUS THORNE and a number are printed on it. Nothing else. Who has a card like this? And I don't like that he's trying to set himself up as my program buddy. I don't want him for that.

"What do you do, Magnus Thorne?"

"A little of this, a little of that," he says evasively. "Well, I just stopped in to say hi and get your number. You look like you're getting ready for a big evening."

"A modeling interview," I find myself saying. "I don't usually primp like this."

"I know." He winks. "But then, you don't need to."

"Nice of you to say so, but this is different."

"I imagine. Well, I better go."

"I wish you didn't have to." I gaze at him and pout, thinking about kissing him. His nostrils flare. He can tell what I'm thinking about.

"You're adorable. But no." He flicks a crumbled bit of mask off my shoulder. "Knock 'em dead. I'll see you at the next meeting, and call me if you feel tempted."

"Tempted. Interesting choice of words," I say, and he laughs as he goes out the door and shuts it firmly.

I glance at the clock. "Shit!" It's one-thirty and Brandon is picking me up at two-fifteen. I race up the stairs and into the bathroom.

CHAPTER EIGHT

It takes every one of the remaining forty-five minutes to get the mask out of all my pores, smooth everything, finish my hair, and get into my black outfit. I also pack a sundress and grab an evening gown out of Ruby's closet in case Melissa wants to see me in different clothes. I'm waiting in the foyer when Brandon drives up in an older Mercedes that I'm guessing belongs to his mom. I hurry down the stairs and pat Odin and Beowulf's heads for luck.

Brandon inhales deeply as I slide into the car and put the clothing bag between my feet. "You smell like baby oil. And you look amazing."

"Oh, yeah." I'm blushing again, dammit. "I buffed my skin really nice in case your mom wants to take some photos. I know I can't wear makeup but I thought I'd try to look my best."

"Melissa. She goes by Melissa. I'm not allowed to call her Mom." He puts the car in gear and we glide away from the sidewalk. "I'm glad you wore what you did, and no makeup. An initial shoot and interview are interfered with by makeup and distracting clothes."

"I know. I did a little reading."

"So did you change your mind about wanting to do this?"

"I like the idea of it being challenging," I say with total honesty. "This is going to sound bad, but I'm always the prettiest girl. I want to see how I measure up against the best."

Brandon slants me a glance from those intriguing hazel eyes, and it's both hot and speculative. "Competitive, are you?"

"I guess."

"Well, you've come to the right place. Keep the confidence going. All the successful models I know have attitude."

The Melissa Agency is located on the twentieth floor of a silver building. That's what I call it, because the arc of it looks as seamless as poured mercury. Whizzing up in the elevator, I take Brandon's arm and press close, feeling nervous. He smiles down at me. "I've never brought a girl to meet my mother before."

"Oh, God. Really? But it's not like we're a couple or something."

He shrugs, and I realize, looking into those warm hazel eyes, that he's interested in me. I wonder why it took so long to sink in. And I like him, a lot. He's nice and he rescued me, and he's probably a whole lot better idea for a girl like me than a bad boy in black leather named Magnus Thorne.

The elevator opens into an atrium-like entry filled with pots and pots of hothouse orchids. Paper birds hang on invisible filaments and flutter on the unseen breeze. It should be a little cheesy; instead it's enchanting. The receptionist behind a modern arc of desk inscribed with **The Melissa Agency** looks up at us. She's totally gorgeous and should be a model herself. I feel a quiver of doubt, looking at her wide brown eyes, high cheekbones and shiny smile. I'm a long way from Kansas, also known as Saint Thomas.

"Brandon! This the new girl we've got booked in?"

"Sure is. This is Pearl Michaels."

The receptionist leads us into another area surrounded by closed doors marked with titles: Hair, Makeup, Clothing, Runway, Studio mark just a few. At the far end of the hall, I spot the sanctum sanctorum, marked by brass script spelling out *Melissa*.

"Brandon. Geez. What's it like to have someone like this for a mom?" I whisper, clutching his arm.

"You're not the only one to go to therapy," he says, with a wink. He drops a kiss on the top of my head. "You'll be fine. Knock 'em dead." He hands me over to the receptionist, whose smile congeals when she sees his gesture to me.

"We have you booked with a photographer for an initial shoot," she says. "Good you don't have makeup on and your clothes are okay. So I'll just send you to Hair." She knocks on that marked door.

"Come in!"

I enter, and a towering black woman, working on a stunning brunette in one of her two chairs, smiles at me. "Come have a seat."

I sit in the remaining chair, and in a moment she's sifting her hands through my hair. "My name's Francine."

"I'm Pearl."

"Good healthy hair, Pearl. This looks like natural color."

"It is."

"Well, I see you have some natural curl. I'll just throw it in some hot rollers and give it a little more body."

The brunette, her head in a hood, leans out to wave at me. "Cynthia Twining." She has a British accent.

"Pearl Michaels."

"You come here a lot?"

"First time. I'm... auditioning, I guess you call it?" I scrunch my nose, unsure.

"Oh, a modeling virgin," Francine tosses my hair, using her fingers as if they were salad tongs. "I'll give you my two cents. Don't freeze up in front of the camera. Think of that clicking shutter as your boyfriend's eye on you, and show him all the best parts. Seduce that camera. Make it want you."

"Oh," I say faintly. Cynthia smiles from her chair.

"Francine knows what she's talking about. She's been here at Melissa for ages, making us look beautiful."

"It's a tough job," Francine quips, and we both laugh.

The makeup woman comes in when my hair is done and checks me over. She daubs some seemingly-invisible makeup on my face with a sponge.

"You have good skin," she says. "But I can tell you've been in the sun."

"I grew up on Saint Thomas." Until this moment, I thought having a tan was a good thing.

"Well, you should be okay until your twenties," she comments. "Take off the clothes, get into this robe."

"Oh, I thought I'd have clothes on for the pictures." I immediately think of the bruises blooming all over my torso and thighs.

"We start out in bathing suit, so we can get a full picture of your body. Here you go." She hands me a tiny black bikini. I don't have a choice and I don't want to explain the situation to her. I figure the bruises will tell their own tale and the photographer can choose to take the pictures or not. I go behind a screen and get into the suit.

From the other side of the screen I hear a light tenor voice. "Pearl? I'm Chad Wicke."

I get into the robe they provided and belt it hastily, coming out.

"Hi." I shake his hand. Chad looks like a cliché fashion

photographer to me: slight build, shag haircut, purple shirt, Converse tennis shoes paired with striped trousers.

"Come with me. We're doing the basic audition shoot, so that will include a full body series, some with clothes, and a series of head shots. We just use a black background and light you, see what happens. Bring your clothes bag. For the sake of time, we'll have you change in the photo booth."

I bring the bag and follow him into a door marked Studio 1. Chad points to a corner filled with light glaring from huge bulbs on stands. The background is a black drape and a single metal stool awaits. I feel my heart rate pick up, my palms prickle. I'm intimidated.

"Over there on the stool," Chad says, already absorbed in doing something with a bank of cameras. He punches the On button on a boom box, and the room fills with Madonna singing something naughty.

I think about what Francine said about seducing the camera, but I'm not ready to be exposed yet. I drop the robe, walk into brilliance that hits me like a wall of heat, and sit on the stool.

Only I don't just sit. I balance myself right in the middle of the small metal seat, drawing my legs up under my chin. I wrap my arms around them, resting my chin on my knees. I can feel my hair tumble down around me, a curtain of creamy curls.

I'm delaying the moment Chad sees my bruises as long as possible.

He turns and lifts his camera, grinning. "Shy girl. I like it. Open those eyes wide, Pearl. You look amazing, like a bird on a branch."

Between his reassuring, enthusiastic commentary and Madonna's crooning, I find myself relaxing. I even think of Magnus Thorne kissing me, and I lick my lip and give the camera some sexy.

"Okay, good. Now it's time to show me everything, Pearl."

The moment of truth.

I uncoil from my pose on the stool and step in front of it, splaying my legs wide, thrusting my hips forward as I arch my back, resting my elbows on the stool.

"Holy crap! What happened to you?" Chad exclaims, but his camera never stops clicking. I glare at him defiantly, my head thrown back as I look down my black and blue body into that clicking eye.

"I got mugged two nights ago," I say. "Boston is a great town."

"I love the attitude, Pearl. You've got nothing to hide, you did nothing wrong, and that's what your body is telling me. You're a survivor."

"I'm a survivor," I repeat. I feel my eyes fill. I move back behind the stool and change my pose to demure. My eyes are shiny with tears as I let the camera see all the feelings that I've been hiding, fleeing, sedating. Shame, fear, grief.

"Okay. Now give me some more of that sexy attitude. I liked how you started in that pose on the stool with nothing but your face speaking, and that was before I saw how amazing your body is, how you already know how to use it to express yourself."

Chad may be a mousy little fashionista, but he knows his business. I feel myself morph into the seductress I know I can be, turned sideways with my butt raised and legs straight out, leaning on the stool and looking at the camera, imagining Magnus. He's walking toward me, about to kiss me. I can almost feel it, and the chemistry crackles in the air like static electricity.

"Okay," Chad finally says. "Great. Now get some clothes on, your black outfit is fine. We'll see how clothes hang on you."

"Not that well. I tend to fill out clothes rather than have

them hang," I say ruefully, but go through some more changes and shots with the outfits thrown on over the bikini.

Finally, it's head shots, and this is where Chad's genius shows up again.

"I am going to tell you a feeling. And I want you to shut your eyes, and feel the feeling. Then open your eyes, and show it to me."

He's moved in closer, has some of the lights dimmed, uses a shiny umbrella on the side to do something soft with the light.

"Anger," he says. I don't have to dig very deep for this one. I open my eyes and feel the feeling suffuse me, tightening my face and shooting fiercely out of my eyes.

"Sorrow," he says.

I don't have far to go for this one either. Tears actually leak out of my eyes and I feel them catch on my lips.

"Joy. Lust. Anticipation. Nervousness. Excitement. Contentment. Pride. Jealousy. Gratitude."

I'm exhausted when he finally lets me off the stool. "Go get a bottle of water, use the bathroom, and you can crash for a few on that couch." He points, all the while looking at his camera as if he can't take his eyes off it. "I think we have a few useful images for Melissa to look at. I'm going to process."

He disappears.

I glug down the water bottle, take a pee in the small closet-like bathroom, and collapse on the couch. No one told me modeling was such hard work.

CHAPTER NINE

I've somehow fallen asleep when Chad comes and wakes me up with a shake on the shoulder.

"Time to come meet Melissa. I put together some quick contact sheets for her; she has them already. Can I get you anything?"

My stomach grumbles and I realize I haven't eaten since breakfast, but during the clothing section of the shoot, Chad has already told me I have to lose fifteen pounds, minimum, for any kind of work in this field.

"No thanks."

He hears the rumble of my tummy and grins. "Just cut back and you'll peel this baby fat right off."

I'm back in my basic black and I follow him down the dimly-lit hall with its spotlights on magazine covers—probably all Melissa models. I drag my feet, but seconds later Chad is opening the door with the glamorous name on it.

The first thing I see is Brandon sitting in a chair in front of the desk, and my face breaks into a big smile of relief as I see him. Then my gaze goes to the imposing figure behind the desk.

She doesn't look like a battleax, but she doesn't look like a pushover either. Her hair is a soft gold pageboy and she's wearing a plum-colored suit with a spray of lily of the valley in the lapel pocket. Her eyes are huge, heavily made-up, and the same shade as Brandon's, a changeable light hazel. She smiles. "Welcome to the Melissa Agency, Pearl. My son has been telling me about you."

I notice the swath of contact sheets spread across the desk's pristine surface but keep myself from glancing at them with an effort as I cross the room and extend my hand to her. "Thanks so much for giving me this chance, Ms. Forbes."

"Melissa, please. Sit." She points to the chair next to Brandon. There's no room for Chad to sit, but he's come to stand at Melissa's shoulder. He hasn't taken his eyes off the proof sheets.

"Look at the range, Melissa. I was pulling stuff out of her she didn't know was there."

"I see, Chad. And yes, we all know you're the best portrait photographer ever, and that's why you work for me." She rolls her eyes a little at the enthusiastic young man.

"Can I see?" I ask hesitantly. Brandon reaches over and squeezes my hand reassuringly as I lean forward.

Melissa pushes the sheet with my body shots on it toward me. I wince at the sight. The bruises are vicious-looking in black and white, a patchwork of violence stippled across my ribs, hips, thighs and stomach. The photo of my defiant pose is strangely beautiful and disturbing.

Melissa taps it. "This is genius, Chad."

"It was all Pearl." He smiles at me. "I just told her to show me everything, and she did."

I hang my head and feel my neck heating up. "I didn't know whether to tell you first or not. I decided just showing was better."

"Just showing is always better," Melissa says. "That's what

I like about these test photos. You're common enough looking, quite frankly. We have busty blondes up the wazoo around here. But you know how to act, too, and that's what we need for magazine work. Quite frankly, you're too heavy for runway or even catalog, but I can see you doing specialty magazine work. I'd like you to come back and we'll develop a full portfolio."

She turned to Brandon. "Good eye, son. There's hope for you yet."

"I aim to please, Melissa," he said coolly. "But give it up. I'm not taking over the business."

She flaps a hand. "Give it time. Now take this young lady home." Melissa shook an admonishing finger at me. "You need to lose fifteen to twenty pounds by the time we do the portfolio shoot. You have two weeks."

"What? Two weeks?" I'm appalled. I know how hard it is to get weight off. The time frame seems ridiculous.

"Talk to the other girls. They're full of tips." Melissa flicks her fingers. We're dismissed.

Brandon squeezes my hand again and Chad leads the way out of the office, his face lit with excitement.

"You're the first no-background model we've discovered in ages," he says. "I can't wait to do your portfolio shoot."

Out in the hall he admonishes me the same way Melissa did. "You have to take that weight off. It's rounding out your cheeks and filling in where there should be shadows. You have a chance at this if you can work hard and follow directions. No partying—it wrecks your skin."

"Yes, master," I quip, and Chad laughs. Brandon is strangely quiet. As we get on the elevator, I feel a surge of excitement.

"This could be what I'm meant to be doing after high school!" I exclaim as the elevator doors shut. "Thanks so much for setting this up for me." And because I'm happy, and grateful, I kiss him, leaning up to plant my lips square on his.

I don't expect the kiss to get hot so fast, but Brandon's arms come around me and draw me up close, one arm wrapped around my waist. The other hand comes up to cup my jaw, and he angles my face to get better access to my mouth.

He tastes like mint, and smells of something expensive, and I love how deliciously solid and strong he feels. I sense a wonder in our exploration that feels good but not edgy and almost scary, like when I kissed Magnus. I feel glowy and good as the elevator doors open and he lets me go reluctantly.

"What time is it?" I ask, a little lightheaded from the kiss and no food.

"Five o'clock."

"Crap! I have a therapy appointment at six. Can we grab a drive-through bite and you drop me off? I'll see if Rafe or Ruby can pick me up."

"Sure." He walks me to the garage and when we get into the Mercedes, he takes my hand again. "I'm wondering if I should have brought you here. It's going to complicate things."

"How so?"

"Because I want to date you. And I never date models." He reaches over and hooks me to him by the back of the neck for another long kiss.

"Think of me as the girl from the park that you rescued," I say, when I'm back in my seat and buckled up. "Besides I'm not a model yet."

"But you will be," he says, brow knit darkly. "I haven't seen such good proofs in a long time."

I ignore that. "What was that your mother was saying about getting into the business?"

He navigates the garage and back onto the busy avenue, heading for a nearby Burger King drive-through. I decide this is my last fast food for the next two weeks, but I'm already drooling at the thought of the burger.

"Melissa wants me to take over when she retires. I want to be an engineer."

"You have to do what feels right to you," I said. "But maybe there's some way you can do both. After all, you rescued me. And solved your math problem."

He grins at me. "I have to remember you're only eighteen and in high school. You're pretty mature for your age."

"Age is just a number. I haven't been young for a long time," I say, and feel the truth of that weighing down my bones.

CHAPTER TEN

Dr. Rosenfeld smells faintly of patchouli as she welcomes me into the office. "Good to see you again, Pearl."

"Likewise." I feel myself still glowing from the photo shoot and Brandon's kiss. "I've had a lot going on. I think the question that I need answered about what to do next might be answered."

I filled her in on the meeting at the modeling agency. She smiled. "So you felt energized by this?"

"Not at the time. Believe it or not, I fell asleep as soon as Chad was done taking the photos. I had no idea it was so exhausting. But later, after the meeting with Melissa..." I trailed off, not wanting to tell her I'd kissed Brandon. I didn't want to get into any of my stuff with guys with her.

"Tell me more about this young man who rescued you and brought you to the agency." It's like she's psychic, and I narrow my eyes.

"He's nice. He's gone above and beyond."

She leans forward. Her sharp brown eyes could be

described as "twinkling." Today the socks she's wearing under her Birkenstocks are purple, and I fix my gaze on them.

"Come on, Pearl. I wasn't born yesterday. This guy likes you. Do you like him?"

I look up at her. "I do, yeah. He took me to the park where the attack happened yesterday." I grind to a halt, remembering what happened at the park. What it sparked.

"And?"

"It was his idea. He thought it would be good for us both to go back there in the cold hard light of day." I stop again, feeling myself struggle. I don't want to tell her what happened. But to get my brother-in-law's money's worth, I need to. "I got really sick when I saw the place. Actually retched in the bushes. It was so embarrassing."

"What did Brandon do?"

"He patted my back. Walked me home. It made me realize what a big risk he took, trying to rescue me in the dark. Who knows if the mugger was armed? And yet he drove him off."

"So you were feeling grateful."

I thought about that blur of a walk home, how all I wanted to do was get high. "No, actually. I felt sick, and terrible. And I wanted to get high. I couldn't get away from Brandon fast enough."

A long silence as she waited for me to tell her more. I opened the drawing tablet on the coffee table in front of me and began drawing a picture.

"Tell me what happened next," she prompted softly.

I continued with my picture. It was a green hill, with a rainbow coming out of a cloud, and a house with a wide veranda nestled against the hill. The turquoise water of a bay sparkled in front of the house.

Home.

Saint Thomas.

"I said goodbye to Brandon, and found my sister's house-keeping money and went to the park to get high. But someone stopped me. A guy from the twelve-step meeting. He distracted me, took me for a ride on his motorcycle; brought me home. It worked. I didn't use for one more day." I told her how I'd shared about the attack in the meeting, how much better it made me feel.

She nodded. "This is all good, but I think there are things you aren't telling me. If you're going to get the most out of therapy, you have to be totally honest."

"What if you tell Rafe and Ruby?"

"You have total confidentiality, unless you threaten to hurt yourself or others. Drugs, sex, criminal activity—it's all protected. I could lose my license if I told anyone."

I let this sink in. "Okay. Maybe you can help me with the memories that are making me want to use. I can't tell them at a meeting." I feel my eyes prickle. "I had sex with my boyfriend for the first time at a Christmas party two years ago. I don't remember it." I tell her the memory I had with Brandon at the bushes in the park. "I think I had a rufie or something. It was Connor who had sex with me, but I don't even know because from then on, Keenan, his brother, acted like I'd slept with him, too. They told me what a great lay I was the next day. I didn't remember anything but Connor handing me a drink in a red cup."

"But you stayed with him after that?"

I nod. "Him, and Keenan, too. They—I don't know how to explain it. I felt like it was my fault. I'd let them sleep with me. Once it had happened it was too late, I wasn't a virgin anymore. And I grew up religious, so I figured. . ." I couldn't put into words the feelings of shame and dirtiness, the sense that I'd brought it on myself.

"You were date raped. By brothers. That's not right, Pearl."

It sounds bad when said like that.

"Well. It got worse," I say. "Connor is a mechanic, but he also sold drugs. He... got me into it."

"How do you feel about him?"

I shut my eyes. I remember Connor's lithely-muscled café-latte body. Remember his dark eyes boring into mine. Keenan, two years younger, is just as gorgeous. The memory of the two of them with their hands on me still lights me up, and I shiver.

"I don't know."

"I think you do."

"Okay. I felt about him how I felt about the drugs he gave me. I craved them. Both of them." I put my face down in my hands, feeling shame sweep through me in a wave. I just want to forget, to feel better. To be anywhere but here, facing what I've been fleeing.

And that isn't even the worst of it.

"Pearl. Listen to me." Dr. Rosenfeld says. I raise my eyes. They're open too wide and feel dry. I keep thinking of the woman at the park with the knitting bag.

"You were what? Sixteen? And how old were these boys?"

"Connor is twenty-two and Keenan is twenty."

"So first you are raped..."

"I don't know if I was. They say I was drinking and partying and loving every minute of it." Some part of me, having accepted their version, wants to believe it. The alternative is too terrible. I'm not even sure I'd have ever left them if Rafe and Ruby hadn't taken me away.

"It sounds like you were drugged. Raped. And then sold a bill of goods, and deliberately hooked on heroin." Red flags of anger brighten Dr. Rosenfeld's cheeks. "Your sister and brother-in-law are very worried about you. They suspect something happened to you that changed you. And I concur. This was not your fault."

"No. I know what was in me. What's still in me. I love sex, I love heroin. I am who I am." I stand up, casting off the awful idea of having been a victim. It's not a role I can play, any more than hide the bruises of my attack. "Connor and Keenan showed me who I am. And I'm grateful for it." I walk to the door, and out through it. I feel ten feet tall, filled with a righteous sense of something—not anger, but something like victory.

I wonder if my face shows it. If I were photographed now, if that feeling, so defiantly triumphant, would show on my face. Because I know how great it is to be pleasured by two men who adored my body, the experience enhanced by drugs. I wouldn't want to have missed it.

I get outside Dr. Rosenfeld's building to discover night has fallen. That burger I ate, without the bun, feels like a lead ball in my belly as I stride along the sidewalk of midtown. I'm not entirely sure how to get home but I know the general direction, and keep heading there, just angling across streets.

Walking is clearing my head.

I come down from the weird high of that dark place and feel shame again. See the situation as Dr. Rosenfeld sees it. Wonder how I live with myself. And realize I'm approaching Boston Common and the woman with the bag of knitting.

I reach into the pocket of my jeans, take out the card I slid into the pocket. MAGNUS THORNE. He specifically told me to call if I was tempted. I lean against a brick wall, shutting my eyes. Debating.

I remember the pinwheeling colors of lights spinning by, Magnus's solid presence blocking the wind that cut my face, the studs of his belt under my hands, the thunder of the engine between my legs.

I need to be distracted like that again.

I look around and realize I'm only a few blocks from the

Common. I find a phone, dig a few coins out of the bottom of my purse.

"Hello?" His voice is a sharp bark. Not friendly at all. I remember I'm calling from a pay phone and he won't recognize the number.

"Magnus? It's Pearl."

"Pearl. Hey." His voice changes, warms. It encourages me.

"I'm tempted."

"Are you?" His voice is playful now. I can almost see the crinkles around his dark eyes, the curl of his lips.

"I'm a few blocks from the Common. I had a really upsetting therapy appointment, and... I realized I was heading back there. To the park."

A long pause.

"I'll come get you. Where are you?" Back to an unfriendly bark.

"Corner of Beacon and School Street."

"Wait for me." He hangs up brusquely.

I hug myself in my coat, leaning against the building. My eyes move up and down the street, because it's dark here, and I don't feel safe anymore.

Anywhere, if the truth be known. I was drugged, raped, and whored out by my boyfriend to his brother. *And I went along with it.* I feel sick again and want to retch. Want to forget. Wish I could. Wish I could experience that weird victorious feeling I had in Dr. Rosenfeld's office, but it seems fleeting as a mirage, some trick of belief and emotion I can't get to again.

Thankfully, no one approaches me and twenty minutes later, the Harley pulls up. Magnus looks dangerous in that sleek black helmet, his leathers gleaming, the buckle on the ankle of his boot catching a stray beam from the streetlight. He does not look like someone who's keeping me from falling off the wagon —more like he's planning to take me to hell.

And if Magnus asked me to, I'd go there. I deserve it.

I pull away from the wall and approach. He takes the helmet off, shakes out his thick, coarse black hair. "Tempted, huh?"

"I can't joke about it," I say. "Please. Just make me feel better. Like you did before."

He looks at me for a long moment, and nods. "Motorcycle therapy. Got it." He points to the saddlebag on the back. "Helmet."

I put it on, and swing a leg up behind him, my purse sandwiched between us, my arms tight around his waist. The motorcycle roars into life between my thighs, and I immediately feel better.

CHAPTER ELEVEN

Magnus takes us in the opposite direction this time. A new set of roads, highways, and byways, and finally we're arching along a bridge at full speed. I hold on tight, and his big body is a rock in the sea I'm clinging to, battered by the wind and waves of emotion, thrilled by the speed. We just go and go and go, and finally he circles back and heads to Ruby's neighborhood.

At the bottom of the stairs, in front of Odin and Beowulf, I get off the bike. "You have to come in and meet my sister and her husband. Otherwise I'll catch hell. They've got me on a short leash and they'll never believe you're my program sponsor."

"I'm not your sponsor," he snorts. "But I'll admit to being a sucker for a pretty face." He doesn't get off the motorcycle. The multi-paned door at the top of the stairs opens and it's Rafe, striding down the stairs, looking every bit as intimidating as Magnus. Magnus takes off his helmet and hangs it on the handlebars.

"Who's this, Pearl?" Rafe says, with no effort at politeness.

Magnus puts down the kickstand, swings off, shakes Rafe's hand.

"Magnus Thorne." Just the way he says his name liquidates my core.

But Rafe's hard blue eyes are still on me, and my brother-in-law points to the door. "Get in the house."

I think of objecting and decide not to make a scene. I hurry up the stairs and inside. Ruby's standing under the chandelier in a silk robe, red hair all adrift, and she's frowning.

"Dr. Rosenfeld called us. Said she was worried about you, that you ran out of the session and she didn't know where you went."

"I'm okay. Did she tell you what it was about?" I ask, testing Dr. Rosenfeld's stated confidentiality policy.

"Of course not. But I'd like you to tell me." Ruby comes over, puts her hands on her hips. "And that hot guy with the motorcycle brought you home. What the heck is going on?"

I've got the door cocked because I can hear the low rumble of male voices down at the bottom of the stairs, and I'm also hearing my sister work up to a tantrum.

"Magnus is a friend. From the program. Yeah, I got upset in the therapy session and left early. I got kind of—tempted on the way home, and scared, too because it was dark. So I called Magnus, and he came and gave me a ride home."

"It's well over an hour since you left the therapy session," Ruby says tightly. "I don't see how it took that long to bring you home."

"He helped me!" I exclaim. I hear the motorcycle thrumming into life outside, and I feel desperate, afraid that Magnus will be scared off by my family, by my neediness. And that I won't get to say goodbye. I wrench the front door open and fly back down the stairs past Rafe, but the motorcycle is already disappearing around the corner by the time I reach the curb.

I stare down the road for a long moment, feeling abandoned, knowing it makes no sense.

I turn reluctantly and head back inside the house. Rafe is talking to Ruby, holding her close. I feel a stab of envy at their bond—of the way Rafe curls long fingers around the back of Ruby's neck and draws her under his chin, as if she were precious.

I want to be loved like that.

"What did you say to Magnus?" I growl at Rafe, my hands on my hips. "I hope you didn't give him any shit. He helped me!"

"Maybe he did." Rafe turns to me, calm and cool. "He says he's looking out for you from the program. So your story checks out. But you should have called us, not him. We were planning to pick you up after the therapy appointment."

"Geez, you guys are stricter than Mom and Dad ever were," I say. "Besides, I couldn't call you because you don't have motorcycle therapy." I feel a grin break over my face. "I highly recommend it for whatever ails you."

Neither of them crack a smile, but I see a dimple hovering in Ruby's cheek. She gets it, oh yeah. After all, she married Rafe at a ridiculously young age.

I run upstairs and throw myself onto my bed, shutting my eyes to relive the entire ride, feeling the roar of noise, the wind, the lights, the solid feel of Magnus in my arms. Motorcycle therapy after real therapy after my harrowing first experience modeling.

Maybe I'm going to have an extraordinary life, after all.

CHAPTER TWELVE

I manage to peel off fifteen pounds by the time I go back to the Melissa Agency for my portfolio shoot. It's not easy. I'm grumpy most of the first week, my stomach shrinking and growling, but it must be endured and I set my mind to it. I take to jogging after school, too, and enjoy going along the Charles. Winter's first snowflakes kissing my face and the ruffled water on the river is a new experience. Brandon joins me often and I know he does it at least partly because he doesn't want me going alone.

I am not worried about jogging alone. Rafe bought me some pepper spray, and I'm defiant that way. I won't hide from anything or anybody.

Magnus is driving me crazy. He seems to have decided he's like a big brother or something, and while he'll give me rides home from the meeting and has appointed himself my "non-sponsor" program guardian angel, he keeps his hands to himself and keeps his distance, except when he lets me cling to him on the motorcycle.

Brandon, on the other hand, has no such problem. He tries

to kiss me every time he sees me, and I have to be tactful fending him off. But I'm too busy for dating, and I don't want to sleep with Brandon and mess things up at the Melissa Agency.

When I think about it, the three-and-a-half months since I left Saint Thomas are by far the longest I've gone without sex in two years, and I miss it. I'd take Magnus any way he wants me in a heartbeat, but he won't have me. Between sexual frustration and starvation, sleep has been hard to come by in the last few weeks.

But now the moment of truth has come. I meet with Melissa, after weighing in with Gazelle the receptionist.

"Congratulations on losing your first fifteen." Melissa meets me by the door this time and runs an eyeball over me. I'm sucking in my stomach. I haven't been anything but hungry for two weeks and I haven't been this slim since seventh grade, but taking a few looks at magazines has already told me this is not going to be enough to get me on those pages. "Part of what we're looking for is the ability to work hard, endure discomfort, and follow directions. You're still too heavy, but Chad can work some magic and, if all goes well, get enough good images for a working portfolio."

She gestures and I follow her to her mammoth desk. "Here's our standard model agreement. I understand your sister's an attorney. You should have her look it over, but it's the usual for the industry. Twenty percent of your fees. We are a management service, not an employment agency."

"Thank you for this chance." I pick up the contract and tuck it in my purse. "Modeling seems so glamorous but I can already tell it's a tough job."

She leans back against the desk and folds her arms looking at me speculatively. "It's not often we get someone as old as you in here who has never thought of modeling as a career, and yet

is charismatic enough and has the necessary physical charac-
teristics."

"I would never have thought of it if Brandon hadn't
suggested it."

She smiles conspiratorially. "And I appreciate that. I have
plans for that boy."

I smile back. "So I've heard."

Now she frowns. "What did he say?" And I realize that this
dazzling, powerful woman is starved for bits of news about her
son, for insights into what's really going on with him.

"He really loves engineering and solving problems," I say
cautiously, careful of the line of confidence I'm treading. "If
he's given problems to solve, and it's presented to him that way,
I bet he'd get more involved."

Melissa's still frowning, but now it's because her busy brain
is ticking over what I've said. Her face clears and she pushes
away from the desk. "Well. Something to consider." She pushes
an intercom button on her desk. I can see each of the rooms has
a labeled button. "Chad, I'm sending her down."

"Roger that, Chief," Chad says tinnily, and Melissa smiles.

She's very beautiful when she smiles.

I turn and go, the modeling contract in my purse and an
afternoon in front of the hot lights ahead of me.

Melissa tells me the feedback on my portfolio is great. She's
filling up bookings for me, and most of them are for lingerie
where my fuller form is appreciated. My first ad shoot takes
place at the Institute of Contemporary Art, and it's for underwear. Outdoors, in what is rapidly becoming winter.

Standing in the concrete courtyard of modern sculptures,
wearing a long black fake fur coat over a tiny black lace demi-

bra and panties, striking a pose as if gazing into the eyes of a lover while thirty-degree wind whistles across my nipples is no one's idea of fun, but I soldier through it, heated between wardrobe changes in a portable plastic closet with a space heater on an extension cord.

Ruby comes home a few days later, her green eyes wide. "Oh my God! Pearl! You're on a billboard above Massachusetts Avenue in panties. Dad would roll in his grave!"

"Let's go see your moment of fame," Rafe says. We pile into the four-door antique Jag, and moments later we're getting honked at as we drive as slowly as possible on the busy thoroughfare beneath a mammoth billboard.

I'm a twenty-foot lingerie-clad giant, standing with one arm around a sleek silver sculpture, the other on my hip, long blond curls blowing in very real freezing wind. The dark furry coat and tiny black lace panties set off my creamy skin and my hair looks like an iridescent silver curtain. The only spot of color in the photo, making a whole lot of naughty promises, is my pouty, shiny, bright red mouth. It's the size of a Volkswagen Beetle.

I can't believe that's me. Both hands come up to cover my mouth. "You're right about Dad rolling in his grave," I say, and my eyes fill.

"Oh, Pearl, I didn't say that to make you feel bad," Ruby reaches back to touch my shoulder. "I said it because you're so damn sexy that it must be God's gift."

"Some gift. I'm never going to live this down at school," I say miserably.

I didn't expect to be an underwear billboard after my first photo shoot! I think back to what Brandon said about Cindy Crawford—*it's not really her. It's the idea of her.* And now I know that idea's a little overwhelming to live with, let alone become.

We circle back home, and there's a black Harley pulled up illegally on the sidewalk in front of the house.

"Oh, thank God. I need motorcycle therapy after what I've just seen," I exclaim, hopping out of the car and bouncing over to Magnus.

He's leaning on the Harley. His arms are folded over his vast chest, and taking one look at his smoldering dark eyes, I know he's seen the billboard.

"Get on. We're going for a ride," he says. And I hope like hell he means it in more ways than one.

CHAPTER THIRTEEN

I swing onto the Harley and give a little hop to sink into the padded seat, my thighs tight against the back of Magnus Thorne's muscular legs. I tuck my face into his jacket, inhaling the smell of leather and the trace of intoxication that's just him, feeling something deeper than arousal but not sure what it is. My arms slide under the jacket to circle his waist. I feel the cool metal studs on his belt, the way his big body flexes as he cranks down the starter, the way my touch makes his belly tighten.

I smile, inside my helmet.

If all it took to get his attention was a twenty-foot billboard of me in black lace lingerie hanging over the traffic on Massachusetts Avenue, then it's worth it.

My sister Ruby and her husband Rafe, my guardians, haven't said a word as they watch us leave. After all, I'm over eighteen and Magnus has been a gentleman up until now, taking me out when I need "motorcycle therapy" and acting a whole lot like my twelve-step sponsor while refusing to be called by that title.

But something has shifted, and I can't wait to see where he's taking me.

There's a hypnotic quality to riding a motorcycle in the dark. So many sounds, sensations and sights whirling past and through me make it almost impossible to process. I lean my head on Magnus's back, out of the wind, and watch and listen and feel. I just *am*, in this moment, and wish it could go on forever.

It's a relatively short ride this time. He takes me outside of town, through gently-wooded suburbs, and then we're turning down a narrow lane bordered by pines. The road is rutted, with deep ice-filled puddles. I cling even tighter as he slows the bike way down and we make our way through and around some serious potholes.

I lean my head out to peer around him as we slow and he turns the bike into a towering dark barn; I have just enough time to spot a log cabin with smoke coming from the chimney before we're folded in darkness that smells like horse manure and musty hay.

He rolls the bike to a stop, drops the kickstand. I lean over and hop off.

I lose my balance, though, and luckily still have a handful of his leather jacket to grab. His arms come around me as he stabilizes me. "Careful."

His voice is a little hoarse. I feel how reluctant he is to let go of me and we stand there in the dark pierced by the bike's headlight, helmets still on, but it doesn't feel awkward. It feels like *anticipation.*

I finally let go of his jacket and take off my helmet, shaking out my waist-length tumble of blond curls. "Where are we?"

He hangs his helmet on the handlebar of the bike and puts mine on the seat. "Home."

"You have horses?"

SOMEWHERE IN THE CITY

"My mom does."

He snaps off the bike's headlight. Total darkness falls, warm and velvety compared to the chill outside. I hear a soft thump of hooves in the straw and a snort. I love horses. I used to ride on Saint Thomas when I was younger.

"Got any lights in here?"

Magnus must have already been going to turn them on because almost immediately, warm spots of brightness glow into life, bulbs dangling down over a couple of stalls.

"Hello, baby." I approach and speak to the sleek black horse with a white star on his face, leaning his head over the stall door into the wide aisle. "Aren't you a handsome beast." I find a handful of dropped hay and hold it out to the horse, who nibbles it off my palm with velvety lips.

"Oh, what a honey you are," I say, leaning close to stroke the horse's neck, breathing in that horsy smell that has always made me happy.

"I like the way you say that." Magnus's deep voice stirs the hair beside my ear, sending a shiver sizzling down my nerves. "This is Onyx."

I am still stroking the horse but now I turn, lean into Magnus, and for once he doesn't move away. I tip my face up to look at him. The light bulb behind his head lights his shoulder-length hair in a dark halo that makes me think of fallen angels. But then, he's always reminded me of a fallen angel, with his black-olive eyes and brooding mysterious presence that is somehow reassuring and always, always makes me feel good.

"I saw your billboard," he says.

"I did too." I bite my lip now, and glance up, but he's backlit and I can't tell what he's thinking. "I never expected that. Kind of a shock to have that be my first modeling job."

"Good God, woman. You're a twenty-foot billboard in black panties!"

"And a bra," I add. "I did have a bra on, too."

"Not much of one." He seems to be clenching his teeth. "I've been trying to be good, but that..." Words apparently fail. He grabs me, hauling me against him. Onyx jerks away with a little neigh. Magnus folds me close and kisses me hard.

Oh, so hard.

Our teeth click as our mouths collide, clumsy with too much wanting. I dive into the kiss and it suffuses my body with delicious feeling that uncoils from the center of me and shimmers out to my extremities and back again, rippling waves of sensation.

I don't remember ever being this hungry, this desperate, for either Connor or Keenan, previous boyfriends who took me down a dark road.

But Magnus has been on my mind since I first caught sight of his long muscled legs protruding into the circle of the twelve-step meeting where we met. I've been trying to get him to this moment ever since.

The kiss has the quality of a motorcycle ride—all consuming, too much to process. Thinking isn't possible, only feeling. Mouths hungry on each other, tongues tangling, I run my hands all over his big, hard body, feeling through his clothes what I've only imagined. His heavy shoulders. The broad solid chest, whose nipples tighten as I slide a hand under his shirt. A long ripple of washboard abs that shiver and clench under my hands. His back, a vast wall of muscle—and that's when I feel something that stops me cold.

Tucked into a leather holster under his arm is a gun. I feel its chill, boxy shape lightly to make sure, scared I'll accidentally set it off.

I tear my mouth from his, arching back. "You're carrying a gun!"

He hasn't let go of me. My hips are pressed to his. One big

hand is spread over my breast, kneading and circling, the other is on my ass, doing the same. It feels glorious. The only thing that would be better than what he's doing right now is if he had four hands, and was touching both breasts and both ass cheeks at the same time.

And we were naked.

"Yep. Gun. I'll get rid of it in a minute." He leans in for my mouth again.

"Magnus?"

There's a voice calling his name. A woman's voice.

CHAPTER FOURTEEN

Now I push back and get some distance, and Magnus finally responds, but he doesn't turn. I realize it's because his erection was pressed against my belly.

"Hi Mom," he says, perfectly calm and collected. "I brought home a friend." He shrugs out of his jacket, and I think I see him wink at me as he folds it over his waist and turns to face his mother. "This is Pearl. Pearl, this is my mother, Raven."

"Hi." My voice comes out squeaky. "I was just meeting Onyx. What a beauty he is!"

She's approaching and one of the dangling bulbs catches her in its spotlight. She looks amazing and way too young to be his mother. She's dressed in a full denim prairie skirt, cowboy boots and a plaid lumberjack shirt hung with a heavy silver-and-turquoise squash blossom necklace. Black hair as long as mine streams over her shoulders and past her waist, but a dramatic streak of silver frames her face. Her eyes are deep-set, fringed by thick lashes, and the same color as Magnus's.

"Hello." She takes my hand, sandwiches it between both of hers. Those penetrating eyes look into mine and I have the distinct feeling I'm being probed somehow. "Where did you meet my son?"

I open my mouth. We're supposed to have anonymity and not talk about the program, so I don't know what to say.

"Met her at a park in Boston, Mom," Magnus says easily. "We've been spending time together and I wanted her to see where I live. What are you doing out here?"

"I saw the lights. Wanted to make sure it was you." She hasn't let go of my hand and I don't know what to do as her gaze seems to chisel into my brain.

"Well, now you've seen it was me and you've met Pearl. She's cold from the ride on the bike." Magnus slings an arm over my shoulders and pulls me to him. "We're going in, Mom. See you in the morning."

He hauls me beside him through the barn.

"Nice to meet you," I call over my shoulder. She's not looking at us any more, all her attention on Onyx as she strokes and pats the horse, her voice a low, hypnotic crooning.

She makes me shiver. Not in a good way.

Magnus feels that and squeezes me tighter as he opens the door of the barn. We trudge down a cleared path, patchy with the thin blowing of snow that's begun.

"I can't stay long without calling Rafe and Ruby," I say reluctantly, wondering if his mother is coming in behind us. But then I spot another cabin, and that one has light coming from the windows and smoke from the chimney. His is lit dimly by an overhead porch light and there's no fire going inside.

"Brace yourself," he says, but too late as a big golden retriever hurtles out of a back room and heaves itself against me in enthusiastic greeting, emitting a loud bark.

"Oh, hello," I say, dropping to my knees. The dog swipes my face with his tongue, and I'm fending him off, laughing, as

Magnus turns on the overhead light and kneels beside a black potbellied wood stove.

"Meet Whiskey," he says. "Whiskey, this is Pearl. Pearl, would you mind letting him out while I get the fire going? He should do his business."

"Sure." I open the door, and the dog bounds out onto the porch, barking joyfully. I see the dark shape of Magnus's mother leaving the darkened barn. The retriever bounds across the patchy snow to greet her and she puts a hand on his head. I can feel her eyes on me even from this distance, and I lift a hand in a halfhearted wave.

Raven doesn't wave back, and Whiskey bounds away to tinkle against a tree as she disappears into her cabin. I get the feeling Magnus doesn't bring friends, female or male, out here very often.

"Hey." He's come up behind me, crossing his arms over me from behind in a cozy gesture that makes me lean back against the wall of his warmth. "Come inside. The fire's going."

"You have to tell me how you're a guy in recovery with a golden retriever named Whiskey."

He squeezes my shoulder briefly, steps away from me into the kitchen. "One of the last things that I did before I got sober was almost hitting this stray pup wandering in the road. Swerving to avoid him, I wrecked my truck and hit a tree. I was shitfaced, but I got out and found the pup to see if he was okay. He'd been abandoned—skinny, matted, no collar—so I took him home. Named him Whiskey, to remind me that for me, drink is deadly."

"Wow. Good story. Do you have anything to eat? Anything —low calorie?"

He laughs as Whiskey pushes past me into the cabin. "I can feed you, yes. We need to talk. I'd offer you a drink, but... we don't do that, even if you were legal."

He takes the gun out of the shoulder holster, sets it on a shelf above the stove. It's the kind of gesture that appears habitual. Apparently he's often carrying the weapon. I frown at it, at the matte blackness of it that seems to soak up light.

"Why do you carry a gun?"

"For protection."

"Why do you need protection?"

He shrugs, going into the kitchen and opening cupboards. "How about hot chocolate?"

"Yes, please." I've been so deprived lately, my mouth immediately waters thinking of the taste of chocolate. I can tell he's not going to say anything more about the weapon on the shelf.

"I have some bean soup and cornbread I can heat up." He begins preparing the food as I sit at the counter that doubles as a table, looking around. The cabin is very small, consisting of a front room, a back bedroom, a bathroom, and the kitchen off to the side. I like the feel of the place. It's decorated with rustic wooden hand-hewn furniture and bright Native American blankets.

I suddenly know Magnus and his mother are Native American. At least, partly. I'm filled with curiosity.

"Tell me about yourself, Magnus."

"Why don't you start, and tell me about the billboard," Magnus says. He's trying to divert me, but I let it go.

"I was as surprised as you were. I did an awful photo shoot in the Museum of Modern Art sculpture garden a week or two ago. It was like, thirty degrees, and they had me in that bra and panties set. Didn't need a fan to blow my hair. That breeze was pure freezing-ass nature." I shiver in memory. "Here's my career in modeling so far. I go to the shoot or location site. I let them fix me how they want. I wear what they tell me and pose how they tell me, act and express the feeling they tell me they want. I get paid eventually, though I haven't seen any money yet. I'm shooting most days of the week since they did my portfolio."

Magnus hands me a plate of celery sticks. "Appetizer."

"You are too kind." I grimace but take the snack and crunch away. "So that's it. They like me in underwear, mostly."

"God is testing me." Magnus's gaze is hot as he looks up at me from the stove where he's stirring a pan that emits delicious smells.

"Why not give in?" I say, and bat my eyes. "I'm far from a virgin and I'm over eighteen. I'm a consenting adult. And I'm telling you, I hereby give consent."

"No." He shakes his head, taps the spoon on the edge of the pan. "I'm six years too old for you, and you're new in the program. One of the cardinal rules: don't sleep with hot young chicks trying to get clean."

I am trying to get clean, but it's a little scary how I keep trying to score every time the going gets rough.

"So why don't you ever share in the meeting, Magnus? I feel like you know everything about me, and other than giving me motorcycle therapy and kissing me a few times—not enough, by the way—I don't know anything about you."

"What do you need to know? I'm in recovery too, even if I choose not to share, I go and I remember I'm an addict and I work my program, part of which is helping others in recovery. I can't help it if you glommed onto me like gum on my shoe."

"Gum on your shoe!" I sit up indignantly. "I resent that! If I remember correctly, the first time we talked it was because you manhandled me up against a bathroom wall and kissed me."

He serves the heated soup into bowls, puts a pile of cornbread on a plate, and puts all of it on a tray and carries it over to the stove, now crackling warmly. He sets it on the hearth.

"I was distracting you from making a buy, and well you know it. We might as well eat over next to the heat source."

I pick up the mugs of hot chocolate and follow him, breathing in the sweet steam. "Mmm. Smells heavenly." I sip, roll my eyes in delight. "Tastes heavenly. But we aren't done talking about how I'm gum on your shoe."

"I shouldn't be doing this," Magnus says, handing me one of the bowls. Our fingers touch and it's hotter than the ceramic. "I know it. And yet, I can't seem to help myself. So you may be gum but I'm letting you stick, and that's my fault. No more talking. Eat." His mood seems to have darkened, and now I know the score.

He's my program big brother, at least in his mind, and it's not appropriate to have a relationship with me.

I mull this over, spooning up the bean soup rapidly but foregoing the corn bread with difficulty. I pick up my mug and wrap my fingers around it, sitting cross-legged and gazing into the flickering fire behind the closed grate.

"I like you," I finally say. "A lot. I haven't had good relationships with men so far. I wish I could have one with you, because I trust you." I gaze at him over my mug. I know the feelings I'm projecting. That trust I told him I felt. Attraction. Desire.

I can feel those feelings vibrating through me, and I know my face, so reflective, is showing them to him. I know, because the camera is teaching me that this is my special superpower.

He looks away, his eyes hooded. He opens the door of the stove, stirs the coals with a poker unnecessarily. He hasn't eaten much of the soup, nor any of the cornbread. His chocolate is untouched.

"I need to take you home. I never should have brought you here."

And just like that, he piles the bowls, stands up with the tray, plucks my empty mug from my hand, and heads for the kitchen. "Get your coat on. It's getting late."

I almost hate his mother for interrupting us in the barn, or I'm pretty sure this evening would have a whole different ending. Even as I reluctantly get my coat on, I realize I don't know much more about Magnus than I did when he picked me up.

But I've seen his cabin, and met his mother and his dog. That has to mean something.

CHAPTER FIFTEEN

Mercifully, no one from school recognizes me as the giant porn queen over Mass Avenue. It must be hard to imagine it could be me, which reminds me of the Cindy Crawford thing. *It's not me. It's the idea of me.* I stay really covered up at school, even keep my hair on lockdown in a braid inside my hoodie most of the time. I'm thrilled when Ruby, who commutes Mass Avenue every day under the billboard, tells me I've been replaced by a Stolichnaya vodka ad.

Melissa calls me at home after school a few days later. "I have a big job for you, but it's in Europe."

"Europe?" I squeak. "What?"

"Magazine work. I told you that's how we're marketing you. There's an Italian lingerie company, La Dolce Vita, who wants to use you for a whole campaign. It's on-site work. In Venice."

She pauses to let this sink in, and I squeal again. "Venice! I'm all over it, even if I have to let it all hang out in the Grand Canal in thirty degrees!"

"That's probably exactly what it will be," she says. "Do you have a passport?"

"Yes. But what about school?"

"I anticipate you're going to be doing more traveling from here on in," Melissa says briskly. "You should plan to drop out or get a GED."

Her words are so bald, so matter-of-fact. While I've never been passionate about school like Ruby was, being a drop-out doesn't sound good either.

"That will never fly with my sister," I say.

"Put her on the phone," Melissa says.

I go get Ruby, who's resting before dinner listlessly, having lost her appetite with the morning sickness that seems to ambush her at random times.

"Melissa has big news and needs to speak to you."

I hover in the background as Ruby gets all hard-nosed on the phone, throwing around legal terms like "coercion" and "null and void" as she haggles with Melissa. Finally, she hangs up the phone, bright red spots of battle on her cheeks.

"The agency is going to pay for a home schooling program for you if you want it," she says. "So you can do your work on the trip. Melissa says the Europeans really like your look, so you're going to have a lot of shoots over there and she thinks you should take this chance. Do you want to go?"

"Yes," I say without hesitation. "Yes, I do."

Who wouldn't want to travel everywhere, baring it all and freezing her titties in front of the world?

CHAPTER SIXTEEN

Venice in winter is mysterious. Fog creeps along the narrow stone alleys, drifting like smoke up from the pea-green water of the canals. Sound has a muffled quality. The only things I hear clearly are the peals of the church bells, the rumble of boat engines on the waterways, and the rush of the pigeons' wings as they scatter before me on the cobblestone streets.

I love the city with an instant passion. Around every corner is some new vista or tiny vignette. Even the doorways and windowsills are ancient and picturesque, the stone colorful and pitted with age, flowers growing in the cracks and every building filled with secret frescoes.

I love how stylish the women are, how friendly the men. They say "Belissima!" when I pass and blow kisses—not raunchy, like catcalls in America. The people are warm, happy in a way I haven't seen outside of Saint Thomas.

Initial days of shooting are so long that I fall into bed at night too exhausted to sightsee even a little bit. Three days in, they hold the campaign kickoff party with the Italian ad agency handling the Dolce Vita account, and I'm the main event. The creative team is a tight-knit group of young, hip professionals who chatter in Italian around me as I stand, smiling bravely, in a slim silver gown. The hairstylist has done my hair up on my head in an elaborate pile of curls that are studded with tiny, battery-operated Christmas lights.

I look like a flashlight.

My job is to stand on a dais during the PR party and periodically unzip the dress, which fastens down the front, and stroll in my La Dolce Vita panties through the party, smiling and handing out elastic garters inscribed with the company's logo.

Everyone ogles and comments in Italian. To each other, not to me. They pet and touch me, which would never fly in the United States. I can't even be offended because I know I'm honored to be chosen as the new Face and Body of La Dolce Vita, and from what I can tell, they mean well by it.

On my dais, the dress temporarily zipped back up, holding the tray piled with garters, I spot a familiar face across the room.

Brandon Forbes.

I see him scanning the room, looking for me, but he hasn't recognized me in my get-up.

"Brandon!" I call, waving, and hop down from the dais to hurry through the crowd, turning heads along the way. "What are you doing here?" My face is wreathed in a huge smile.

"Came to see how the gig is going," he says, smiling back.

I put one arm around his neck and kiss him. "Thanks for coming," I whisper in his ear.

"Attenzione," says my shoot director, a skinny brunette named Odile. "No kissing the guests."

"Oh, pardon," I say, backing off. "I'm sorry."

"Do another turn around the room with the garters," she barks.

I stiffen, humiliated that Brandon is going to see this part of my job duties, but there's no help for it. I head back to the dais, where I unzip the dress, hang it on the silver mannequin they set up, and pick up my garter tray.

Brandon is white-faced with anger as he watches me forge into the crowd, smiling stiffly in my lingerie, looking for anyone not already sporting one of the lacy garters.

Odile is trying to talk to him, and I can tell she's one of the 'Forbes-ifiers.' That's what I call the models, agency employees and connections who seem to kiss up to Brandon or his mother.

I make another loop around the room and then climb back on the dais and into the flashlight dress. At least I get to cover up sometimes.

Brandon brings me a glass of champagne. "It's Italy. You're legal drinking age here," he says.

I think of the program and that I'm not supposed to drink. But I don't go to the program for drinking, I go for drugs, and surely this situation counts as one for which I should be anesthetized.

"Bottoms up." I clink glasses with him. "Thanks for coming." I swig the champagne as fast as I can and look for more.

"Melissa wanted me to check on you."

"I doubt it," I say, twinkling at him over the rim of my refilled glass.

"Okay." He frowns. "I wanted to check on you. I had no idea this party was such a meat market, with you as the main course."

"I'm the new Face and Body." I shrug. I'm actually getting used to not really being me. It's gotten easier to become the idea of me. "I get to cover up part of the time. Last year the girl was done up as an ice sculpture and she wore nothing but body paint all night. Odile made sure to tell me that right away so I wouldn't get an attitude. Apparently the Italians think Americans are prudes."

"Yeah. I wanted to warn you that the Europeans have different standards but I didn't get to talk to you before you left."

"It was a whirlwind. I said yes to the campaign, there was some contract dickering, and the next thing I knew I was on a plane for Italy. I'm supposed to be here for two weeks, at least. They're working me hard." I describe the shoots so far. "It's a fantasy theme, so they're dressing and making me up as all these amazing creatures. Yesterday I was a mermaid."

"Sounds fun."

"Not really. I work all day and fall into bed too tired to see the sights even a little bit. Can you pull some strings and get me out tomorrow? I haven't seen hardly anything yet."

"Done." He looks down at me with that warm browny-gold gaze. "You look a little like a flashlight in this outfit."

"I know." We laugh.

Brandon gets me off work the next day early, at a mere four p.m., but the light is already going. I sponge off the fantastical makeup I wore for today's shoot riding the public carousel. I was dressed as a fairy in wisps of green lace, my hair stiffened with wires and wound with flowers and tiny lighted stars. The team really is creative, and I'm figuring out how to communicate, even if it is mostly with gestures and pointing.

Still, it's a relief to get into my basic black, my face clean, and skip down the steps of the studio where we do our costuming to hook my arm into Brandon's. As usual, he makes me feel safe, and the glow of attraction warms me too.

It really has been a long time since I've been with anybody.

I can't help the way his arms around me heat up everything inside.

"What do you want to see first?" he asks, dropping a kiss onto my hair, still stiff with glitter. "Phew. What is this stuff?" he wipes his mouth, but the glitter is still on his lips. I smile as I brush them off, and they feel firm and supple under my fingertips.

"Fairy dust," I say. "I want to ride a gondola, and get something to eat. I haven't had anything but espressos all day."

Brandon tells the boatman something in Italian and he nods and replies, choosing our route. I settle close beside Brandon and he pulls up a fur-lined blanket over us. The gondola is as magical as they look, poling down the watery avenues between the buildings at a stately pace.

Moon and lanterns gleam on the still water. The boatman, astonishingly, begins to sing and though I can't understand the words, my eyes prickle with tears at the heartfelt sound of his voice.

"I'm a long way from home," I say, and tuck my head against Brandon's shoulder.

"Where is home?"

"Saint Thomas will always feel the most like home." I hadn't realized it until this moment as the words come out of my mouth. "But I don't think I'll go back there any time soon."

"It's only a plane ride away, and the Melissa Agency books bikini shoots there more often than you'd believe."

"Really?" I look up, and he kisses me.

It feels good. Warm, and thorough, and sweet too.

I think of Magnus with a pang. I didn't tell him goodbye either, though I left a message on his machine.

And here I am, kissing Brandon.

But Magnus doesn't want me.

I try to get back into the feel of Brandon's arms around me.

I'm in a gondola, floating down a canal, being kissed by a lovely man, and the boatman is singing. It's the stuff of dreams. My life has changed so much since that day Ruby came and dragged me out of the Carvers' house.

We eat *osso bucco* at a restaurant where there are no menus, only the family dinner special, which is delicious. Afterward I'm yawning, exhausted.

"I have to get back to my *pensione*. They're getting me up at five a.m. tomorrow."

"Slave drivers." Brandon snuggles with me in the boat all the way back to my *pensione*, a picturesque building close to the major landmark, Saint Mark's Square or Piazza San Marco, as the locals call it.

At the door of the stone building, Brandon tips my chin up and kisses me deeply. Insistently. Telling me something, asking for more in the way he holds me. I'd be lying if I said it didn't move and quicken me. I feel deeply conflicted as I finally detach myself, getting a little distance but clasping his hands in mine.

"Watch out or you'll get invited up, and I'm pretty sure that's against my contract rules," I murmur against his mouth.

"It's not. I did my homework and checked before I came," he murmurs back, his hand sliding up my waist to circle my hardening nipple. It feels fabulous and my knees weaken.

I put my hand on his, detach it from my breast. "Then I have to tell you, I'm just not ready. We have to talk about this, and I'm too tired to tackle that tonight." I kiss him again, feeling bad about the disappointment I see in his changeable eyes. Right now they're amber in the streetlamp's glow. "Thanks for coming to Venice. Really."

I go inside. As I climb the narrow wooden steps, my hand sliding up a thick wooden rail that looks like it's been there a hundred years, I wonder what my problem is. I can't explain it to Brandon until I know, and all I know right now is that I don't feel right about having sex with him. That I'm worried about what will happen with Melissa if something goes wrong between us. It's a handy excuse, but there's more to it than that. I almost want to call Ruby and tell her, talk it over, but I'm afraid to get her worried so far away—and there are the long distance charges.

I fall on top of the narrow bed with its feather-filled mattress and silky cotton sheets. The shutters that look out over a small side canal are battened down for the night. I feel alone, and not in a good way. My body is still tingling from how Brandon woke it up. I feel a hungry longing for something...for someone to be with.

And the truth is, it's Magnus.

As soon as I think of him, I feel a pulse of heat between my legs. I take off all my clothing and slide between the silky sheets, naked. I've never had to touch myself before. I'd always had someone do it for me, but I know I won't sleep without some sort of release.

What is it about Magnus? Brandon's just as handsome, and better boyfriend material than my dark, brooding, mysterious, gun-toting, Harley-riding friend.

But it doesn't matter. Magnus has called to me ever since I spotted his long muscled legs wearing those split-kneed jeans and battered boots.

My breath quickens as I imagine Magnus's big, calloused hands on me, sliding up and down the curves of my hips to my breasts, circling around my ass cheeks like he knew just how to do, a sensation that heats my core instantly. His mouth was a point of heat in the cold, radiating warmth all through me. His kiss felt like it was bringing me to life. The sensation of the heavy, hard shape of his erection pressed against me, promising pleasure, is unforgettable.

I want Magnus. That's the problem.

And apparently I'm not as much of a slut as I thought I was, because I know I will break Brandon's sweet, kind, protective heart if I sleep with him just because he wants me to. And I can't do that. I won't do that, even if I'm lonely and tempted.

I cry and feel sorry for myself. I eventually find release in my lonely bed, but it's unsatisfying and I fall asleep with tears drying on my cheeks.

CHAPTER SEVENTEEN

Pounding on the door wakes me the next morning.

"*Bon giorno!*" Odious Odile sticks her immaculately-coiffed head into my room and shrieks at the sight of me. "*Dio non voglia!* What have you done?"

"Crying." I pull the covers up over my head.

"I don't believe it. You've been screwing the Forbes boy!" she exclaims, and unbelievably, she yanks the covers back and exposes my nakedness as if expecting me to be hiding him underneath me.

"Hey!" I'm done with her bullying. I bound out of bed, breasts bouncing. "I sent Brandon back to his hotel last night, not that it's any of your damn business. I'm here to do a job and you have nothing to say to me beyond that. Now get the hell out of my room!"

Odile flinches as I tower over her, close to six feet of pissed-off Amazonian woman.

"Screwing isn't in the contract!" she dares to yell at me once the door is closed.

"It is, too; he checked. But there was no screwing!" My voice rises to a howl of frustration.

"You have five minutes, then we start docking your pay," Odile yells back.

I kick the door and hear her scuttling down the stairs.

The nerve of these people! I'm being treated like an indentured servant, maybe even a slave! Who knew modeling was such a shit detail?

Getting mad was the best possible thing to get my blood going. I jump into the closet-like shower and wash my hair. It's given me energy; energy I badly need.

They're going to have to blow dry my hair out now, and that will give my swollen eyes more time to go down. Hopefully we're doing more distance shots today and the puffiness won't matter too much.

I need to talk to Brandon. And come to some sort of decision. Maybe what I need to do, I think, rubbing my scalp under the thin stream of warm water, is take a break from men entirely and work my 12 step program and my therapy when I get back to the States. Ruby told me she got into a real situation with several guys she was dating before she and Rafe got engaged, and the only way out was to swear off men altogether.

That might be a good solution. I could buy time. Time I obviously need, to work on my new, crazy career, to really get into my clean lifestyle, which still feels far from solid, and time to figure out how to seduce Magnus.

I smile, under the flow of water. Because that's my real agenda, no doubt about it. What Pearl Michaels wants, she always eventually gets. And Pearl Michaels wants Magnus.

After the difficult start to the morning, the cameraman takes one look at my puffy eyes and, after a voluble stream of Italian with Odile, they decide to do the distance shots. So today I ride in the prow of a gondola, hang my hair out of a stone window in the dank and grim Bridge of Sighs, and feed the pigeons in Piazza San Marco.

It's a productive day and by the end I've still got energy to meet Brandon, who suggests we start our evening's activities with hot chocolate at a coffee bar.

"Hot chocolate? Why not coffee?"

"You've never had anything like Italian hot chocolate," Brandon says.

I can't help remembering the hot chocolate Magnus made me with a pang. But this hot chocolate is entirely different. It's so thick and dark, it looks like a mug of tar. I stir and it's almost the consistency of pudding. I use a spoon to sip it.

"Oh my God." The chocolate is like pure melted candy bars, so thick and rich it makes me shiver. I shut my eyes in bliss, savoring every drop. I know I can't have this whole cup. Two more spoonfuls, I tell myself. That's all I get. I'm supposed to be losing another ten pounds, but who can do that in Italy? Still, I have to try.

I open my eyes, and Brandon's watching my face, grinning.

"Oh, God," I breathe. And I see the exact moment that the way I say that turns him on. His hazel eyes darken. He leans in and kisses me.

He tastes like chocolate. The kiss is so sweet, so good, it makes me moan a little and lean toward him on the bar stool. All around us we hear laughing and teasing comments in Italian, but everyone's used to public displays of affection in Venice. You can't turn a corner without encountering some couple plastered against each other in a doorway or kissing in a gondola.

107

I eventually remember I was going to take a time out from men. I realize, uncomfortably, that it's not going to be easy.

I tear myself away and pick up my spoon again, looking around the bar. It's open to the street on one side, with a few little tables, but mostly the bar is a bar, a gleaming wood-and-brass expanse filled with customers leaning on elbows and sipping espressos, tapping cigarettes on the edges of ashtrays, and generally blowing off steam in the way of an American bar —but without the alcohol.

I love it.

I let myself have two more mouthfuls of the chocolate and push the mug back to Brandon. "I can't afford the calories," I say regretfully. "I get why girls in this business stick their fingers down their throats, though."

He frowns. "You aren't doing that, are you?"

"No. But I've been tempted." I shake my head. My hair, straightened today and still filled with silver glitter, catches the light and shimmers like tinfoil. "We have to talk."

"Not now." He sets the mug down, pushes it away, throws a handful of *lire* on the bar. "Let's go to Murano. We can still catch the sunset."

"Murano?" I slide down and let him tug me by the hand out the door of the bar.

"The glassblowing island. This whole country is organized around community specialties. Murano is a ferry boat ride away. It's a whole island where everyone has something to do with the glassblowing trade that put Venice on the map a few hundred years ago."

Brandon leads me unerringly to a dock where it's only a few minutes until a motor launch with a cowling roof arrives. Inside is lined with plastic-covered, padded benches. A few lire for the boatman, and we are motoring down the canal to the great expanse of the Grand Canal, a huge waterway lined with high-end palaces and elegant waterfront hotels.

We pass by a replica of the great Lion of Venice, and as I admire the landmark, Brandon fills me in on the story. "The original bronze statue is in Saint Mark's Square, and has been a part of the city since the twelve hundreds. Over time it became the symbol of the city."

"Seems like you're really familiar with Venice. How many times have you been here?" I ask, tucking my trailing tin-foil locks into my hood. We are still getting a lot of looks, but no sense attracting too much attention.

"Maybe a dozen times," Brandon says with a shrug. "Melissa does a lot of business over here, and this is one of her favorite cities."

"So...you never mention your dad." The boat hits a wave, and a wind-tossed wavelet blows spray over us. Brandon uses his sleeve to wipe my face, and the gesture is so tender I feel bad all over again.

Dammit. I don't want to hurt this man, all for a guy who's already told me how it is for him.

The certainty I felt last night wavers.

"My dad died when I was ten."

"Oh no. I'm so sorry. My dad died... recently."

It's been seven months. I know to the day and time when my father died. I see his face going white then red, his mouth opening and closing, the way his eyes rolled back.

I hear the sound of his head hitting the floor.

I shut my eyes and cover my face.

"I know, Pearl. Ruby told me your father passed. I'm the one who's sorry, reminding you of it." He puts an arm around me, draws me close.

I don't deserve to be treated so nice, and I shrug him off.

"It's okay." I swipe tears and salt water from my cheeks. "Looks like we're almost there."

Murano is so small I can see from one end of the island to the other as we approach, and every inch of it is covered with buildings. We hop off the launch and Brandon takes me to his favorite glassblowing house, a barnlike structure warm with the heat of the furnaces. I'm fascinated with the way the glowing molten glass, the texture of thick honey, is manipulated and fired and blown by the muscular men working it in their aprons, pulling and twisting and blowing with pipes.

Brandon buys me a tiny, clear Pegasus sculpture as we leave. "Food now," he says, towing me out of the factory and down a narrow alley toward some unknown destination.

Even with the enchantment of the glassblowing, I can't seem to shake off the terrible memory I've had of Dad's last moments. I tuck the box with the tiny Pegasus in it into my capacious purse and resolve to put it behind me.

The cafe he takes me to has no sign outside. It's just a wooden half-door and a room with tables inside set with beautifully woven red cloths and candles on them.

It's very romantic. I feel dread curdle my ravenous appetite. I know this situation can't go on. I have to jump one way or the other.

Brandon orders for us in Italian, exchanging pleasantries with a proprietor who evidently compliments him on his choice of dinner companion if his fulsome commentary is any indication.

"So tell me about your dad," I say, unable to leave the subject that's nagging at me like a sore tooth.

Brandon shrugs, looks at his hands in the candlelight. They're graceful, clean-lined. "I idolized my dad," he says softly. "He was a businessman, had his own company. He was a lot of fun. Enjoyed being a dad, because he coached my soccer team and liked to take me to work at his office. He had a heart attack." Brandon looks up at me and his golden-brown eyes are filled with candlelight. "It was very sudden."

"My dad went suddenly, too," I whisper.

Brandon takes my hand. His thumb slides across my knuckles. It sends a warm tingly feeling up my arm and south from there.

I take my hand away. "Brandon. I really like you, but..."

"Oh, here we go," he growls. "I don't want to have the 'I really like you, but' talk. Not tonight. Can we save it until I leave? I promise I won't try to kiss you or pressure you."

I open and close my mouth. He must have been reading my signals. It's another point in his favor that he's picked up on them.

"I'm actually going through a lot. Personally." I duck my head and feel my hair slide down over my face in a protective curtain.

"I know. And I can take a hint. So can we rain check this conversation and just enjoy Italy?"

"And agree not to talk about our fathers any more, either," I say. He pours a glass of chianti for each of us from the ever-present carafe on the table.

"Agreed. With pleasure." I pick up my glass and with that, we toast.

I feel like I've got a reprieve, and I'm grateful to Brandon for giving it to me. We ride back to Venice and I sleep much better that night in the *pensione*. The shoot goes better too, because I'm able to focus. Brandon must have said something to Odile, too, because she's more respectful, bringing me water and other basics to keep me going.

Each evening Brandon and I do some activity in and around Venice: Visiting art museums. Taking in the glorious, gold-frescoed churches. Wandering street markets. I feel my relationship with Brandon deepen. He makes no romantic gestures to me other than hugs and holding my hand, and I find I'm both grateful and a little disappointed.

I can't sort my feelings out, and suddenly it's time for him to leave. I still have a few days of shooting left.

"I'll see you in Boston," Brandon says. He's dressed in a camelhair wool overcoat over tailored trousers, and looks every inch the successful young businessman. I go up on tiptoes and kiss him on the mouth. He tastes good.

"You've had chocolate without me," I scold.

"Didn't want you to get tempted," he says. "I'm looking out for you." He touches my lips with a finger. "See you back in the States." And he hops on the motor launch that goes to the airport, and I'm on my own again.

I'm tormented with thoughts of getting high that night. I tell myself to just hang in there and the mood will pass, but in my explorations with Brandon I've spotted a dance club with some shady characters. I'm pretty sure I could make a buy there. My body, sexually frustrated, exhausted and starved, twitches and tortures me. The craving crawls along my nerves like a spider, and I stare at the ceiling, my eyes too dry.

Barely able to make myself stay in my lonely bed, I decide to call Magnus. Long distance bills be damned. I'm supposedly making money, not that I've seen any.

I take out the dog-eared card he gave me from the side zip where I've stowed it. I have no idea what time it is in the States.

MAGNUS THORNE. Just his name, and his number.

What does he do? Something that involves needing a gun for protection. It can't be good. But he's been good to me, and he'll understand what I'm going through.

I dial the phone. It takes a while to get through as I have to access an international operator, and agree to charges that will come to my room, and other rigmarole that almost makes me lose my resolve. Eventually I hear ringing.

"Hello?" his voice is thick with sleep. I picture his black hair mussed, his dark eyes half-open, his big body naked in the bed I glimpsed from the kitchen of his cabin. The thought makes me flush all over, and all he said was hello.

"Magnus? It's Pearl."

A pause. "Pearl. What's wrong?" I can almost see him sitting up in bed, the bedclothes falling around his naked waist.

"I'm so sorry if I woke you. What time is it there?" I bite my lip, looking at my clock.

"It's really early. Or very late. Are you all right?" There's alarm in his voice.

"Oh, no, I'm okay. I'm sorry." My voice wobbles on my second apology. "There's no emergency but—I just need someone to talk to."

"So you thought you'd call big brother Magnus to chat." I hear amusement and annoyance in his tone. It feels like his voice plucks at my nerves, making me tingle and light up.

"Not big brother. Never that," I say. We both just breathe for a moment.

"This must be costing a fortune. Aren't you in Italy?"

"Yes. And... I'm tempted. You're the only person I could think of calling."

"Yep. I'm your non-sponsor. Tell me what's going on." His voice is intent, serious, and the dark we're both in across all the miles feels like a confessional.

"The shoot has been going okay, and I should be done soon.

Brandon came to visit me here." I hear Magnus suck in a breath. *Good.* Maybe he's a tiny bit jealous. That'll serve him right for withholding on me. "Anyway, we've been going out every evening. Doing stuff. Seeing sights. It's really great here," I gush.

"Get to the point," he growls.

"Well, Brandon left today. And it did something to me, triggered me."

"So you have feelings for him?" I'm pretty sure Magnus is grinding his teeth.

"I don't know. I just know I remembered something really terrible while he was here, something I haven't been letting myself think about, and when he left—it's been hard. I just want to get high. I found a place where I could buy."

"First of all, commit to me you won't go out again tonight. You don't have to think about anything past right now. Can you do that? You won't go out again tonight?"

"Yes," I sigh the answer. I've promised Magnus I won't go out tonight. I'll keep that promise. It's all I have to decide right now. The relief is tremendous, if probably short-lived.

"What is this terrible thing you remembered?" His voice softens.

I snuggle deeper into the sheets, hugging my pillow, the receiver pressed to my ear. "How my dad died. How it was all my fault. I killed him." I feel the words catch in my throat. My eyes fill and tears well up. "Oh shit. I'm crying. I'm going to look terrible again tomorrow. Odile will have a fit."

"Tell me," he whispers.

I wrap my arms tighter around the pillow for comfort, the phone digging into my ear. "Dad came to the Carvers' house to get me. He hadn't called first. The family tried to stop him from going to the back bedroom where we were. That was the only warning I had, the sound of the dogs at their house barking, my dad's voice shouting, and the sound of his boots on the floor. All of that woke me up, but I'd been partying late. Partying hard. And I was still in bed with them..." My voice trails off. I'm crying harder, trying to muffle my sobs in the pillow.

"Them?"

"Connor and Keenan. My boyfriends. We'd gotten high the night before, and spent the night in bed. Using. Having sex."

A deep silence. I can hear the miles hissing between us. It feels like eternity, like a bad dream, like the distance between galaxies. He now knows the worst about me, what a slut and a whore I am. He's going to despise me now, like I despise myself.

I take a breath and go on. "Dad yanked the door open. I sat up in bed but I didn't have any clothes on, and Connor and Keenan were there too. He just. . ." I see it again, in horrible technicolor slow motion. The way his eyes bulged, his mouth opened and closed, the terrible color in his face that came and went. The sound of his head hitting the floor as he went over backward. "He had a stroke. He died."

"Oh, Jesus. Pearl." Magnus sounds so sad. I'm crying hysterically now, too hard to talk. He listens for a time and finally when I'm winding down I hear him say, "Your dad wouldn't want you to lose your sobriety thinking about his death, would he?"

"No, he wouldn't," I eventually say. Dad and I always had more conflict than he had with my sisters, but I knew he loved me. Knew it bone deep, knew he'd have hated to be a source of pain to me. But no one gets to choose the moment of his death, how it happens. And I'd been the one to bring on his, and way too soon.

"That's not the only bad thing, though," I continue. "The Carvers didn't want Dad dead in their house, didn't want anyone to know they'd allowed the boys and me to shack up in the back bedroom. So my boyfriends and their dad Len grabbed

Dad's arms and legs and hauled him outside, all the way to his car. Stuffed him in the front seat. And we pretended he died there."

I'm sobbing again. The shame is overwhelming.

"I'm sorry that happened. My God. It must have been a wake-up call."

"You'd think. But all I wanted to do was feel better, and I knew how to. So I just did more of the same, deeper and deeper, until Rafe and Ruby dragged me to Boston. I hate myself!"

The surges of pain and shame are so bad that only physical pain in my body will do. I dig my nails into my thigh, gasping at the blinding fire erupting in my skin as blood wells from the scratches.

"Pearl. What are you doing?" Magnus's voice is a whip crack cutting through the blur of tears, the overwhelming chaos of emotion.

"Nothing."

"You're doing something to yourself. Stop it. Now." I feel the fit of madness receding, some sort of calm taking its place, a dissipation of the extremity. I can't mark or hurt myself. Magnus told me not to. And the swelling from crying will be bad enough to deal with tomorrow. Maybe I can pretend I'm sick, but then I'll have to stay in the room all day. With no TV, no drugs, no alcohol, nothing to read and no boyfriend.

I'll be jumping out the window by noon.

"I know you're hurting right now and you've never let yourself feel your pain before without medicating it. Well, there's another way." Magnus's voice is low, hypnotic. "Turn on your back."

I let go of the pillow and roll on my back, the phone still plastered against one ear.

"Take off whatever you're wearing." His voice is so sure, so commanding. I do what he says. *This is Magnus. I trust him.* He's going to make me feel better, and as I shuck off my sleep tee, I begin to have an idea how.

"Are you naked and on your back?"

"Yes." My voice comes out a whisper. The wavering light of yellow street lamps reflects off the waters of the canal outside my window and dances in liquid patterns on the plain white ceiling above me. I'm here in Venice, magical Italian city, and he's somewhere on the outskirts of Boston, but I can almost feel him in the room. My skin feels sensitized, blowing hot and cold, tingling with excitement. My nipples harden. "Tell me what to do."

"Touch your breast. Tell me what you feel."

I shut my eyes, reaching up to fondle the firm, soft tissue of breasts that Ruby thought were too big for modeling but turned out to be just right for lingerie ads. "It's round, and soft. It feels good. Silky."

I hear his breath catch, and heat flushes my body, setting up a liquid warmth between my legs. I imagine it's his big hands stroking my breasts.

"Circle your breast. Around and around. Trace the shape."

It's my own hand doing it but my imagination turns it to Magnus's hand. Here, in the dark, it feels possible and real.

"Take hold of your nipple. Roll it between your finger and thumb. Pull it upward at the same time."

I gasp at the sensation, at the heat radiating out from that hardening peak to light up nerve endings all the way to my melting core.

"Pinch it. Hard."

I cry out involuntarily, my back arching, as the sharp pain somehow translates to pleasure. "Isn't this better than hurting yourself?" Magnus still sounds harsh, arrogant. "You won't do that anymore."

"Yes," I say. "I mean, no. No I won't." I'm panting. My voice sounds scratchy. He chuckles and it sounds a little strained.

"Now, the other side. Begin with circles." He talks me to the peak of the other breast and then has me flick my nipple, and once again I cry out.

"Prop the phone against your ear. Use the pillow to hold it in place. Did you do that?"

"Yes."

"Now slide both your hands down your body from your breasts to your hips. Back up."

I obey, my hands traveling and sliding. It feels amazing. My skin feels like velvet, my shape firm, all dips and smooth hollows.

"Do it again."

I've begun to writhe on the bed, my eyes closed, my whole body alight with delicious sensation and anticipation.

"Open your legs. Slide a finger in. What do you feel?"

"It's hot. And—slippery." I feel my cheeks heat at my bold words, but I'm just describing what I feel. I realize in that moment that all the sex I had with Connor and Keenan wasn't even the beginning of what there was to discover in the hands of someone who really knew what he was doing.

"Oh, hell," he mutters. And I know he's enduring his own kind of suffering. The thought warms me even more.

"I wish you were here," I breathe.

He doesn't answer that. "Tell me what you're feeling."

"I'm swollen. I'm so—tender. It feels fat like a cherry, just waiting to be sucked on."

Now it's his turn to gasp, then he says, "Sit up a bit. Slide two fingers inside, and rub with your thumb."

I rearrange myself so I can reach that far, touching myself in a way which I've never tried in my limited self-explorations.

Moments later I'm exploding in an inarticulate, melting, shivering orgasm.

Slowly reassembling myself a few moments later, all I want is for him to feel this ecstasy too. "What are you wearing?" I ask.

"Boxers. Tee shirt." His deep voice is strained.

"Take them off."

I hear rustling. The sound of his breathing.

"Did you like telling me what to do?" I ask.

"Yes."

"Did you imagine your mouth on me, your hands on me?"

"Yesssss," he hisses through clenched teeth.

"Well, now my hands are on you. First, at the top of your head. Sliding through your hair. Oh, it feels so good. And I'm kissing you. My tongue is making love to yours. Do you feel it?"

"Yes. Oh, God, Pearl."

"Put your hand on yourself. Slide it up and down. Hard, fast. It's my hand on you, so tight, so hot, so good."

I have a different style than he does, with his brusque commands, but I can tell by his hitching breath that it's working.

"One hand is working below, the other is on your nipple. Circling it, rolling it. Now I'm licking it. Pinch it. I'm biting you."

He moans.

"Don't stop. Don't stop what you're doing. Keep going, because now I'm sliding my tongue down your ribs, kissing you over your abs. I'm at your groin and I'm taking you in my mouth. Deeper and deeper, all the way. My tongue can't get enough of you, my hands are all over you, you fill me in every way there is. Now ride me hard."

Seconds later I know, by a guttural cry, that he's found his release.

Another extended moment in the darkness. Thousands of miles of separation and yet so intimately together. Our breaths have fallen into sync.

"What is this, Magnus? What is this between us?"

"I don't know," he says. "But you'll sleep well tonight. And you won't use or hurt yourself for another day. And you've told me your worst secret, and you survived."

"How do you know that's my worst secret?" I ask.

He laughs, an abrupt snort, and hangs up. I snuggle, still naked, down into my silky sheets and fall immediately asleep.

CHAPTER EIGHTEEN

Odile is furious, as I knew she would be, the minute she sees my swollen, puffy face the next morning.

"You models! All the same. Your boyfriend leaves and you fall apart!" She actually grabs my arm and gives a yank. I yank back, stepping up to loom over her. She may be mean as a snake, but I'm big enough to stomp her.

"I need at least half a day off. If you can arrange some sort of spa treatment to bring down the puffiness around my eyes, I'll agree to it," I say with deadly cool. "And if you ever lay a hand on me again, you won't be able to use it."

Odile gives me a look and decides I mean it. "I'll book you in for a facial and de-tox treatment. But now I have to call the team and reschedule today's shoot, and we're out time and money. I'm taking that out of your pay."

"You can take that situation up with Melissa, but I'm pretty sure that's illegal. I'm going for a walk."

I brush past her and go down the steep steps of the *pensione*. One of my last days in Venice, and it's gorgeous today. Chilly, but the sun is out and there's no fog. I've grabbed my old wool coat, and a few days ago I bought a soft blue scarf at one of the street markets that Brandon told me brought out my eyes. I wrap that over the stream of my hair and around my neck, and walk to Saint Mark's square. I buy a hot chocolate at one of the cafe bars and a small packet of biscotti.

The crackers are for the pigeons and doves.

I find a spot to sit in one of the wire chairs in the grand expanse of the Square. The gold on the cupolas of the church gleams in the rich low winter sunlight, and sipping my chocolate, birds pecking around my feet, I feel good being alone.

I remember Dad for the first time without the agonizing shame. His sunburnt face, thinning blond hair, the same blue eyes I have. His broad shoulders and work-worn hands. His big heart to help others, his generosity. I cried at his funeral on Saint Thomas, true, but I never really grieved for him. I couldn't afford the emotional price tag then. But now I think of how he tried to rescue me from the Carvers, from what was done to me and compounded by my own choices—and I begin to cry again, but it feels clean and good.

"*Bella.* You okay?" An accented Italian male voice, a soft touch on my shoulder. The waiter's come to check on me, worried.

"*Si, si. grazie,*" I say, snuffling into a napkin. I really am okay. It's kind of a miracle, and I have to give Magnus credit for that. I need to check if Odile got me any reservations at the spa. "*Telefono?*"

The waiter lets me use the cafe's phone to call her. "Got you in for treatments. Come back to the *pensione.*"

The next few days pass in a blur. I'm able to resist temptation to use by being totally exhausted at the end of each day, and while I fell in love with Venice, I'm ready to be home in my pink bedroom at Rafe and Ruby's by the time I get on a plane for Boston.

Soon I'll be seeing Magnus again. I decide I have to force things to come to a head between us. I can't go on wishing and wanting and hoping, confusing Brandon with mixed signals, when it's so obvious to me that Magnus and I are meant to be together.

Ruby and Rafe pick me up at the airport. "How was Italy?" Ruby's grinning as she hugs me. "Your ads are showing up everywhere. You're a star!"

"It was amazing. The only bummer was that I couldn't eat everything in sight. Have you ever had Italian hot chocolate?" I'm so excited to tell them about all my new experiences, and I feel lighter.

Telling Magnus about Dad really did start to lift that stone off my chest.

We catch up in the car, and Ruby says, "Melissa called the house yesterday. You have an 8:00 a.m. meeting with her. She sounded pretty serious. I hope it's not any trouble."

"It could be," I say, thinking of Odile's frequently-pinched expression.

Melissa doesn't get up from behind her sleek desk when I'm shown into the inner sanctum the next morning. "Good morning," I say. "I brought you something." I set my gift on her desk.

Surprise flickers in the lift of her elegant brows as Melissa opens the simply-wrapped brown paper package I've set in front of her. She uncovers a silky scarf in a leopard print. She holds it up against her gold blouse. It looks perfect.

"How thoughtful. Thank you, Pearl." She looks up and her hazel eyes are serious. "Close the door please."

I get up from my chair and close the door of her office, feeling apprehensive.

"Let's review your performance on this last assignment," she says, sliding the scarf aside and opening a file. "First of all, everyone on the team felt that you did well, considering it was your first time in a foreign country on a shoot."

"Even Odile?"

"Even Odile." Melissa finally smiles. "But that brings me to something important and personal I need to discuss." She makes a pyramid of her fingertips, with her perfect scarlet nails touching. "I don't want you to see Brandon anymore."

My mouth falls open a little, feeling a pang. Or a twinge. Something painful. "Why not? We didn't do anything inappropriate."

"Because I need both of you to focus. You have jobs to do. You lost most of a day's work after your emotional breakdown after Brandon left, and he isn't doing well either. He had a semester break at MIT but took two more days off to go to Italy. His concentration and his studies are suffering."

"I would never want to do anything to hurt him." I can feel my face flushing. "It was all his idea. Visiting me. Taking me out every day."

"I know." Melissa taps her nails together, looks at me over them. "But you're both distracted, and I need it to stop. I want you to break up with him."

I feel my mouth tighten into a line. Paradoxically, I want him now that I'm being told no. That's how I work. "Do you get to tell me what relationships I can and can't have?"

"As a matter of fact, yes." Melissa takes out my contract and shows me a highlighted section. *"Model will abstain from substances, activities, and relationships that have a deleterious effect on her appearance and health."*

She tapped the sentence. "Your appearance was definitely affected the day after Brandon left. And his grades are dropping. Enough already."

I sit back in my chair. It really is a good thing I didn't sleep with Brandon or let things get any more serious. "Wow. I can't believe you get to dictate to me like this."

"Believe it. And break it off. Now. Or you'll be let go from this agency." Melissa's eyes are opaque and hard as bronze. "And if you ever want to work in this industry again, you'll make a good excuse to him that he believes."

"Yeah, you wouldn't want your son to find out that his mother is dictating who he can and can't see. He wouldn't take that well." I stand up. "Is there anything else?"

Her face softens a little. "I like you, Pearl. You have a future in this business. But you have to stay focused. No boyfriends. They'll only drag you down."

I had no idea modeling was not only hard work, but often uncomfortable. It's constant dieting, working out, no partying and no men.

"Talk about false advertising," I say. "Everything I promise in those ads. All a lie."

Melissa smiles. "Now you're catching on."

CHAPTER NINETEEN

I've withdrawn from school due to my new schedule, but I still need to make it to the lunchtime meeting, where I'm hoping to see Magnus. I'm surprised to get a message at home from Megan and Kayla wondering where I went, and that makes me feel good. I have to get in touch with them when I have time, water the tiny buds of our friendship with some attention.

I hurry to change into jeans, boots and the leather jacket I bought in Italy—a suede so soft it feels like velvet. I'm hoping Magnus will take me for a ride after the meeting. My hair brushed into a silvery waterfall, I know I'm looking good. Hell, I could do a shoot looking the way I do right now.

The group leader, Mrs. Svenson, greets me warmly, and the people in the group ask where I went, and I end up sharing that I have a "new job" that makes me travel a lot, but that I battled temptation overseas and won.

All the time I'm talking, and as the circle of experience, strength and hope moves on, I am looking for Magnus. He doesn't appear and my belly feels hollow and tight.

Finally, when we're standing up and holding hands for the

Serenity Prayer, I spot him entering through the side door. He has a woman with him.

My stomach plummets.

I turn to the girl standing next to me as the meeting ends and begin an animated conversation with her, watching Magnus out of the corner of my eye.

He's waiting for me, I can tell. He's all in black leather, looking dangerous, brooding and mysterious and oh so bad, but I know how good he makes me feel, how good he is inside. How good he is in every way.

It's no problem breaking up with Brandon if I can have Magnus.

Finally, the girl I'm talking to breaks away from me, confused by my overly friendly behavior, and Magnus catches my eye.

His hair is loose over his shoulders in coarse black waves. I see, more than I ever noticed before, the Native American ancestry in the blades of his cheekbones, the curl of that sweet hard mouth. The woman beside him is all in black too, tall and narrow-hipped, with an angular face and shimmering black hair. I hope she's a cousin or a relative of some kind. Anything but his woman.

He crooks his finger at me.

I flush at how embarrassing that is even as I leave the circle of chairs Mrs. Svenson is beginning to fold up, and approach him.

I can't let this woman see how totally under his spell I am. I try not to think of his voice in the dark, telling me how to touch myself.

"Hey, Magnus." Elaborately casual.

"Pearl." He inclines his head in acknowledgement and indicates the woman beside him. "This is Valley. Valley, Pearl."

"Hello." I shake her cool hand. Valley's face has a quality

better than beauty—a kind of charisma that makes you want to keep looking at it, though her mouth is too narrow, her eyes too wide-set.

"I've asked Valley to be your sponsor. You need someone to call when you're tempted to slip, someone to tutor you in the principles of the program."

I turn to him, my mouth opening to protest. "I don't need a sponsor. I have you."

"You do need a sponsor. I've been filling that function, no matter what I've called it, and I've done badly by you." Magnus almost bites off the words. I see red at the tops of his cheekbones.

"You've been great," I whisper. "The best." I feel like my heart is in my eyes, showing how I feel. How I want. How I *love,* though I haven't dared to call it that, even to myself.

He deliberately looks away. Tightens his jaw. Looking at the far wall, not at me, he says, "You need to be working on your sobriety with a woman. And Valley has been where you've been."

I cut my eyes over to Valley. Her mouth is a little quirked, and I see sympathy in her dark eyes.

"I'm going away for a while," Magnus says, his voice firm and low. "And I didn't want you not to have someone to call."

I want to throw myself bodily on him and hang on for all I'm worth. "Now?" My voice comes out a squeak. "Why?"

"Work. You need to focus on your modeling, anyway." He pushes away from the wall. "So this is goodbye. I know you'll do fine."

"No!" I exclaim. "You can't just shuck me off like...scraping gum off your shoe!" My voice rises. The few people still in the room look over at us. I don't give two shits that I'm getting loud, frankly. Magnus is not just dumping me off on this woman.

Valley pushes away from the wall with a mysterious half-smile, and saunters gracefully over to where she's left a helmet on the floor by the back doorway. *So she even rides a motorcycle!* But I'm too terrified of what Magnus is saying to worry about offending her.

"Pearl." He looks around, takes me by the arm, tugs me around the corner into the hall. He tries a doorknob and it opens into a storage room piled with extra chairs and smelling strongly of mothballs. He tugs me into the room, shuts the door. "You're making a scene."

"I don't care. You can't just—hand me off like a package." My throat's constricting, my eyes welling up. "You've helped me so much. What you did in Venice. . ." I can't complete the sentence; I'm too devastated.

"It wasn't good for us to go there. Physically. I should never have resorted to that," he says. "I can't get involved with you. It was a mistake."

"No!" I stomp my boot and it's unsatisfyingly muffled by the stacks of smelly chairs. "It wasn't! It helped me. I'm not the same! I cried for Dad the other day. I grieved, like I never have since he died. You kept me from using. You kept me from hurting myself!"

"But not the right way." Magnus finally looks at me with those deep brown eyes, so dark I can't see the pupils. He has the longest lashes. I want to lay my cheek against them and feel them touch me like butterfly wings. "I'm going away. I knew I was, and I never should have let you get attached to me. I'm sorry." He pushes away from the wall. "Give Valley a chance. She's a great sponsor and she can even take you out on her bike."

"No!" I cry again, and grab the front of his jacket with both hands, desperate, terrified. Every fear I've ever had is activated. Abandonment is trying to suck me into a nameless void of rejection and loss. I'm pretty sure I'm going to die of the pain, the feeling of my heart breaking.

"Pearl. Jesus, honey." He takes hold of my hands, tries to pry them off his jacket. "You're young, you're gorgeous. You're going to be a star supermodel. You don't know what you're feeling, what you're saying. I'm just the first guy who didn't take advantage of you—well, maybe I did. I couldn't help myself. But I do know I'm going to be gone for two years, and you won't be able to keep in touch. This, whatever it was, is over."

I won't let him pry my fingers off. I just latch onto the leather in another place.

"No. I know I meant something to you. I know I did. Please don't do this. Please." I realize that tears are rolling down my cheeks, catching on my lips, running into my mouth and choking me. I know I'm acting like a clingy psycho but I can't seem to help myself. "I'll let go if you tell me it meant something to you. If I wasn't the only one to feel something. And if I decide to wait for you, that's my decision." I gulp down sobs, letting the tears fall where they may.

He stands still, for such an agonizing moment. Then, just when I feel my legs are giving out and I'll fall to my knees in front of him, those hard arms come around me and crush me close. My wet face is buried in his jacket, dampening the leather, and his arms stroke me and hold me, from the top of my head, down my back, tracing the length of my hair, tangling in the locks.

"Oh, Pearl. You're a drug to me," he breathes into my ear. "You have no idea what you've done. Yeah. It meant something, but I wish to God it never happened—for both our sakes."

A protracted, sweet moment. Our hearts are thundering in the same frantic rhythm, our breaths mingling in sync.

I matter to him. He matters to me. There's nothing better in the world than right now.

And then he pushes me away, so hard I stagger backward into a stack of chairs, and by the time I right myself and stand back up, he's gone and I'm left in the room alone.

I sink to the floor, weeping, and it feels like that other time in the park with Brandon, like a dam breaking, like all the grief and shame and regret I ever had are flowing out. And there's a lot of it and it goes on awhile.

Suddenly the door cracks open, and I look up through the fall of my hair blearily, hopefully, but it's only Mrs. Svenson. "Pearl! Oh my goodness. We're locking up the building and someone said they heard crying in here!"

Her ruddy, comfortable face crumples with concern, inciting me to fresh crying. She lifts me up, hollering for help into the main room, and who comes to her aid but Valley, her fox face carefully neutral as she hoists me up on one side and the therapist the other, and they force-march me out of the building.

In the bracing light of the afternoon sun on the sidewalk outside the church, I try to pull myself together, dabbing my face and blowing my nose with a handful of paper napkins Mrs. Svenson hands me.

"Do you want a ride home with me on the bike? Or should we call your family?" Valley asks.

I gaze at her. Some other day I'd think she was really cool. I'd want to know her better. Today I'm too gutted to care about anything except that she's the only connection I have to Magnus Thorne. He gave her to me, so she must be the right thing to do next.

"Please take me home," I say. "On your bike."

And that's how I come to be riding a low rider down Mass Avenue, the sharp wind drying the tears off my face, trying to scrape together what's left of my heart.

CHAPTER TWENTY

Valley drives us around for a while, and while not as thrilling as when I'm with Magnus, it's still a totally immersive experience. By the time she brings me home on the back of her bike, I'm calm if wrung out. She parks the motorcycle in front of the brownstone.

"I'd like to come in, if I can. Meet your family. Introduce myself as your sponsor," she says.

"Okay." I am too flattened for anything but agreement. Valley is cool and charming with Rafe and Ruby and I can tell they like her as she explains that she's a computer programming major at Boston College and in recovery herself, and happy to take me to meetings when she can. They invite her to dinner in a couple of days, and she agrees.

Finally, I say, "I'm so tired. Jet lag from Italy. Can I call you later?" and she gives me her phone number and I can finally go upstairs and pour myself into bed, where I fall asleep instantly.

I wake up disoriented, in the dark. It's probably midday in Italy or something, but it's pitch black here, and I look at the glowing digital clock on the bedside table.

I slept for twelve hours.

I roll onto my back and stare at the ceiling. It's painted the very faintest pink, though it's shadowy darkness outside at four a.m. Still, I've watched the dawn come up outside the windows before, and the ceiling, with its delicate coffering and old-fashioned glass light fixture, blooms slowly into reflecting the faintest salmon glow, like the sky over Saint Thomas lighting with dawn.

That's why I love this room, which is much too pink everywhere else.

Something terrible happened yesterday. That's why I feel like I've been twisted and squeezed through an old fashioned washing machine. My throat is scratchy and sore, and my nose is stuffy. I'm sick, I realize, and I'm sick at heart, too, because I finally remember that Magnus broke up with me and has gone somewhere. I can't even contact him for two years.

Two years is an eternity. Two years ago, I was an innocent sixteen-year-old who'd hardly been kissed. Now? I don't even want to try to define what I am. And I have no idea who I will be, where I will be, or even what I will be doing, in two more years.

Where could he have gone? Some sort of military duty? He just doesn't seem the military type, with that long hair, all those earrings in one ear, all that leather. A spy? He seems too... rule breaking, rebellious, rough-edged. But maybe he's like James Bond. Going undercover in a foreign country, living among the natives.

I indulge in a brief fantasy of Magnus in the robes of a desert sheikh, with nothing on underneath. Or perhaps in South America, wearing nothing but tribal markings and a loincloth. Maybe he's in the jungles of Colombia, carrying a machine gun and wearing fatigues. He could pull off any of those looks easily and blend with the population.

But it doesn't matter what I imagine he's doing. He hasn't told me, and I can't keep in touch. Do I really want to try to wait two years for a man who told me that we weren't right for each other?

The answer's yes. An unequivocal yes. I've never felt about anyone like I have for Magnus. Call me crazy, because I hardly know the guy. He made sure I hardly knew him. But there's something about him I'll never, ever forget, even if I never see him again.

But do I have the willpower? I've never shown much willpower before. I've been someone who bounced from temptation to temptation. Someone who hasn't taken my sobriety seriously, or even been willing to admit I really had a problem.

But I get it now. And I've been given marching orders from Melissa. Break up with Brandon, and *no men*.

Focus on work.

That should be easy with Magnus gone, and maybe it will be enough to keep me on the straight and narrow for two years.

Two. Years.

I'm crying again.

The breakup with Brandon is two-stage. First, a phone call telling him there's someone else and I can't see him anymore, sniffling and sneezing through the really terrible cold I've picked up on my travels. I do this with convincing acting ability and even some tears, because there IS someone else... Just not someone I can be with, either.

As I suspected he would, Brandon shows up at the house

the next day. With flowers. I meet him in my robe and slippers, with a pocketful of tissues. I look as horrific as I ever have.

"Oh Brandon, no." I wave away his attempt to hug me. "I'm germy. Listen, I've fallen for someone. Like I told you. And I need to focus on work."

His golden-hazel eyes are fixed on my face, intent, but not angry. "Who?"

His eyes remind me unnervingly of Melissa, and that she's going to fire me and cut me off from any work in the industry if he doesn't believe what I say. And as challenging as it is, I already love modeling.

"You don't know him. It got started before I met you." Well, it did—I spotted Hot Motorcycle Guy in the twelve-step meeting the first time I went, and that preceded the mugging at the park that brought Brandon to my rescue, and into my life.

"We can take a break. I could tell you were iffy about going out with me in Italy." Brandon ignores my comments and takes my hand. We sit on the bottom step of the sweeping staircase.

"I mean it. Really. I can't see you anymore." My nose and eyes start running. "I have to go." I yank my hand away and run up the stairs and back to bed.

I hear the murmur of voices as Mrs. Knightly lets him back out. I don't know if that's the last I'm going to see of him, but it's a start.

Here goes the rest of my man-free life.

I cry myself to sleep again.

CHAPTER TWENTY-ONE

Ruby wakes me up much later with a tray loaded with soup and tea. She sits on the end of the bed, and doesn't leave after I sit up and start slurping.

She loops her arms around her knees. Her little pregnancy belly is still small enough that she can get away with that, and she leans her chin on her knees as she watches me eat.

"What's going on, Pearl? Spill. It's time for us to get caught up."

Ruby and I used to be close. Well, as close as you could be with a four-year age gap. And even though I knew it was what she had to do, truth was I never really forgave her for leaving me on Saint Thomas, going away to college, and getting married after her freshman year.

Things might have turned out a whole lot different for me if Ruby hadn't left.

Even so, I know it's not fair to blame her. Ruby always had a dream for herself—to live somewhere far away and different from sleepy Saint Thomas, and to be a lawyer. And she made it happen, and along the way, snagged one of the most amazing men on the planet.

I wish I could hate her for it, but she's shared everything she has, up to and including her home. I'm not a planner like she is. I take things as they come. I seem to have been lucky to fall into modeling and be good at it, and I like it. It's a good thing because I can't see myself getting all passionate about school and doing a career that takes years and years to build.

"Italy was good," I say, sipping my tea, deciding how much to tell.

"More is going on than Italy." Ruby's green eyes drill at me. She uses them to get her clients to tell all their illegal secrets, and I can feel them working.

"I have man problems."

"This is news?"

We both erupt in snorts of laughter. She crawls over and takes the tray off my lap, snuggles beside me, stroking my hair off my forehead. "You're crying more than I've ever seen you cry. Even when Dad died."

I can't tell her what really happened when Dad died. Ruby adored Dad and was his favorite daughter. She'd never forgive me if she knew, and I feel my belly tighten at the mere idea of her finding out. But I can tell part of the truth. Connor told me once, "If you lie, mix it with truth and keep the story simple. Tell your version and don't budge from it. The part that's truth helps you believe it, and if you believe it, others will."

Connor, with his wide streak of darkness, was right.

"Now that I'm sober and taking my program more seriously I'm able to really grieve for Dad," I say. "I didn't let myself feel it, before. And having man problems seems to have brought it all up. I've really fallen for Magnus, and he's gone somewhere for two years. I can't even keep in touch. And I have to break up with Brandon. Melissa's orders."

I tell her the details, and the thought of not seeing Magnus makes me cry again. "*Two years.* It might as well be an eternity."

"Aw, Pearl. You just aren't used to delayed gratification." Ruby keeps stroking me, and it reminds me of Mom. I miss her, and I regret what a bitch I was to her when we parted ways in Saint Thomas after I refused to go with her to Eureka. I haven't even talked with her on the phone in three months.

I'm a bad daughter. Bad in a whole lot of ways. "I need to call Mom and apologize. I've been awful to her and she never deserved it."

Ruby's stroking hand pauses on my brow. "Now I know you're sick."

We both giggle a little.

"Do you like Brandon? Is it worth getting fired to keep seeing him?"

"I do really like him. But not enough to get fired for it."

"What about Magnus?"

A pause. I sigh. "I wish I felt about Brandon the way I do about Magnus. Then there wouldn't be a question."

Ruby sighs too. "So you're going on a man vacation. I did that too, and it was an important time in my life." She tells me the story of the situation she briefly described before, about how she ended up in a relationship with three guys at the same time. How she had to put them all on hold and sort it out.

"It was worth it in the end. I made the right choice."

"Rafe was definitely the right choice for you," I say. "But two years? Even if I thought I was capable of that, it still might not work out. Magnus could reject me like he already has."

"But you'll be more mature. More ready for a real relationship. Solid in your sobriety. Established in your career, whether that turns out to be modeling or something else. A two-year man vacation is just what the doctor ordered. After all, I was a virgin until Rafe and I got married so I didn't get into too much trouble with it all, though it was awful at the time. You, on the other hand..."

I grab a handful of her hair and give a yank. "How much harder to give up sex, knowing what I'm missing!" I groan. "But unless I want to give up working with the Melissa Agency, I don't have much of a choice."

"You always have a choice," Ruby says. "Being trapped is an illusion."

"You're better than Dr. Rosenfeld. Ever considered hanging out a shingle as a counselor?"

"That's what they call us lawyers," Ruby grins. "Counselor."

"So, any idea how to get over Magnus?"

"Work. Lots of work. Going to the gym. Staying busy. And masturbation."

"Ew! You didn't just say that." I feel my cheeks flame. I'm already learning a bit more about that than I ever imagined.

"I did, and I stand by it. Tomorrow, back to work and your meetings. I also set up an appointment with Dr. Rosenfeld. You can hash all this out with her."

When the cold eventually runs its course, I get on with my man vacation.

I check in with Melissa each day. Go on shoots, attend sobriety meetings. Fend off Brandon until he seems to give up. Go to workouts to keep my new, leaner figure nicely honed and toned. Spend time with Valley exploring my triggers to use drugs, which we identify as rejection, abandonment, and feeling like I failed.

I recap all that to Dr. Rosenfeld, and eventually graduate from going to her.

I never tell anyone but Magnus about what happened to Dad. There are just some things too terrible to ever be told again.

I finally get my first paycheck after three months. Even after Melissa takes her cut, it's enormous. Rafe and Ruby want me to put it in investments, or to save for college "after your career" which is a nice way of saying when I'm too old and ugly for modeling.

I decide to buy my own motorcycle instead.

Valley takes me to the Harley dealer, where I get to try riding the bike on a stanchion and get a brief lesson in gearing and driving. It only takes five minutes for me to determine that this is definitely how I want to get around. Well, maybe not in the dead of winter, which it is right now.

I pay cash for the bike, but I don't know how to ride yet and the snow is swirling down. Valley talks me into renting a storage unit to park the snazzy blue Superlow in until spring, and in the meantime she'll take me out when she has time, and teach me to ride.

I hug the delicious secret to myself as I work on my high school correspondence courses, go to shoots and meetings. I know Rafe and Ruby will shit a brick when they find out; better to keep it secret until I know how to ride and am ready and able to use the bike for my transportation.

Spring rolls around, and by then I've begun international travel again. Amsterdam. The Bahamas. Even, memorably, Paris, where I'm part of a new runway show that's lingerie only.

We're all dressed as fairies, with different kinds of wings. I wear a tiny hot pink demi-bra and thong panties, and it's so outrageous and so little coverage there's nothing to do but work it hard.

I've been practicing my runway prance, a sort of combination of cha-cha hip swing with an arrogant stomp, and I go into that faraway mental place where I'm not me, I'm the idea of me: all Rapunzel hair, hourglass curves and long legs, striding that runway like the otherworldly creature they've made me.

I meet real supermodels there: Kate, Naomi, Linda, Christy and Claudia are all there, and I can't believe that I, the hick from Saint Thomas, am in such company. It's terrifying and heady and intimidating, and I deal with it by pretending I'm just the idea of me, and it doesn't matter.

Because, in some weird way, it *doesn't* matter. This bizarre career happened as a twist of fate, and it can be over just as easily. In a way it has nothing to do with me. I'm not responsible for the genes that made me tall and what others have decided is beautiful.

The part that does matter is the discipline I'm learning. Keeping regular sleeping hours. Taking care of my skin and hair. Working out. Staying clean and sober. No parties, no men, and only a few friends: Megan, Kayla, Valley, and my sister Ruby.

After the big show in Paris, they give us gauzy robes to wear and we mingle with all the bigwigs who came to the show in an afterparty. Rafe and Ruby have taken the private jet to Paris to support me. Looking amazing in tux and evening gown, they attend and both give me congratulations.

My hair is woven with tiny, battery-operated silver lights that pulse randomly, and I'm covered with so much body glitter every movement sparkles, but at least I got the wings off so I could cover up with the robe.

"We brought you a present," Ruby says. "It's a birthday present from us and Mom. Happy nineteen, Pearl." My birthday happened today, but we were too busy with the show to even sing happy birthday.

Standing next to the champagne fountain I open the small gold box.

I open the box, feeling terrible that I still haven't so much as called Mom. The more time goes by, the harder it is to break down the distance between us. Inside the box is a glowing baroque pearl the size of the pad of my thumb, on a lengthy snake chain.

"Oh, how beautiful." I put it on, touching it as it dangles between my breasts, feeling sadness in the midst of gratitude. My life is so strange, now, and yet I wouldn't have it any other way—except that Magnus would be in it. "Thank you."

"It's time for a whole family visit to Eureka," Ruby says. She and Rafe have brought my tiny nephew, baby Peter, with them in the jet. "Mom and Jade need to meet Peter. We got time off for you, a whole week, and we're all going to California after this."

"You wouldn't believe how hard it was to get you that time off." Rafe flexes his jaw, blue eyes hard. "Melissa thinks she owns you."

"She kind of does," I murmur. "But a visit sounds good. I need to see Mom."

And then Naomi shimmies up to me, a graceful Amazon in ridiculous gold platforms. "I hear there's a birthday girl in the house!" She drags me off onto the dance floor.

CHAPTER TWENTY-TWO

The plane might be a jet, but it still takes extensive time to get from France to Eureka, California. We pass the time playing cards while Peter is sleeping (which is often) and taking naps ourselves. Baby Peter is adorable, a soft bundle with dark hair and blue eyes, and he sleeps a lot, which Ruby assures me is what month-old babies do. She's taken to motherhood like a pro, but then there isn't anything I've come across that Ruby can't do well.

I realize, waking up from my second nap, that it's already almost been six months since Magnus disappeared, and the time's actually going pretty fast. Ruby's in the living room area of the jet with its padded seating area nursing baby Peter, so I pull my brother-in law aside.

"Rafe, I want to find someone. I can pay."

He lowers his brows. They're very dark, and his eyes very blue, so it's somehow a scary effect. "What for?"

I blow out a breath. "Remember Magnus? The motorcycle guy?"

"Who could forget that little chapter in the misadventures of Pearl Michaels?"

"Hey. He was a good guy, and now... he's disappeared. I'm worried about him." I don't want to tell Rafe that Magnus dumped me like yesterday's garbage. "He introduced me to Valley and got her hooked up as my sponsor, and then just— dropped out of circulation. I want to make sure he's okay."

Rafe stares at me. I can tell he's not buying it.

I sigh again.

"Okay. Magnus left for some reason. He said he was going to be gone for two years and that I couldn't keep in touch. I want to find out where he went."

"Shouldn't you take the hint?" Rafe says, no longer scary. Gentle, now. "He's not into you."

I shake my head. "No. Yes. It's complicated. He's into me, he just thinks he's too old for me, and then he had this mysterious thing to do for two years. Didn't want me to wait for him."

Another penetrating stare from Rafe. "When a guy says goodbye, it's usually over, Pearl. I know you're not used to having that experience, but I'm starting to like Magnus now that you told me he said he's too old for you. I agree."

"You're eight years older than Ruby, and look how well that turned out. Just because I'm young doesn't mean I'm stupid." I'm hissing now, because Rafe's a hypocrite and he knows it. "Never mind. Forget I asked you for help. I'll find him myself."

"You can do that. But it won't make two years go by any faster," Rafe says. He sits back, rubs his hands together, looks at them a moment, glances at me. "So you're serious about this guy?"

"Yes. I. . ." It's hard to put into words the effect Magnus has on me. How he's got under my skin. I'm not sure, because it's never happened before, but only one word I know describes how I feel. "I think I might love him."

Saying it feels surprisingly good.

"What do you know about him?"

"I know he lives outside of Boston. In a cabin on a big piece of land with a barn. His mother lives in another cabin on the land."

"What does he do for a living?"

"I don't know."

"Have you called him?"

"Of course. The number's disconnected."

I can tell Rafe's getting interested in spite of himself. "What else do you know about him?"

"He's clean and sober. He drives a motorcycle. He carries a gun."

Rafe glances quickly at me. "What kind?"

"I don't know. It was black metal." I trace the boxy shape. "When I asked him why he carried it, he said it was for protection. He didn't want to talk about it."

"Interesting." Rafe slaps his thighs, gets up. "Sometimes we need to get information for the business, so I know a private investigator. I'll check with him when we get back to Boston. But I warn you, Pearl. Go sticking your nose where it isn't wanted, and you might not like what you find."

He walks to the front of the plane, and leaves me to stew on that.

Mom looks older. That's the first thing I notice when I see her, walking behind Jade, who's running to meet us on the tarmac of the small landing strip in Eureka. Mom's auburn hair is in a braid, as usual, but it's got more silver in it than before and the weight she lost after Dad died has stayed off. She was always a sturdy woman, but she looks stooped now, as if bent over by worries, and though she's smiling widely and reaching out her arms to take the baby from Ruby, I feel the weight of her cares. And I know one of them has been me.

Jade, on the other hand, has grown taller in the ten months since we packed up the house on Saint Thomas and moved in different directions. She's filled out, grown into a long-legged, lithe beauty. Ruby tells me she's an avid ballet dancer, and I see grace in the way she moves.

I hug Jade. Holding her feels good. Looking into her dark green eyes smiling at me through her thick glasses, I feel really bad for shucking them off like I did. More to feel bad about— and I never did that well.

"When're you getting some contacts, Jade?" I ask. "You should let those pretty eyes shine."

Jade doesn't answer, and turns away. Either she doesn't want contacts, or there's some reason she can't have them. Ruby squints at me and mouths, "Be nice."

Finally, Mom hands the baby reluctantly back to Ruby and turns to me. Her hazel eyes well up, and so do mine.

"Mom." I fall into her arms and squeeze tight. Being in her arms, I feel the best I've felt since Magnus left. She loves me. I feel it to my bones. I want her to feel my love too.

"You're all over the place in the magazines," she whispers in my ear. "My beautiful Pearl."

"I'm sorry I've been so awful, Mom. I know I was terrible to you when Dad died." As I say it, I suddenly know why. *I wanted Mom to protect me from the Carvers.* To somehow know what had happened to me that night, and rescue me. In some weird way, I even blamed her for Dad's death, because if she'd kept me away from them he'd never have seen what he did, a sight so shocking it killed him.

It all makes no sense, and I know it, and yet I know it also to be true. That's why I was so horrible to her, so defiant and angry. If I'd told her about that night, that I knew I was raped but not how it happened, or who exactly had done it, instead of believing the boys' version—things might be very different for all of us.

The thought makes me tighten my arms around her, pressing my face into her neck. It's not her fault I didn't tell her. "I love you, Mom."

Rafe and Jade are unloading our bags with the pilot's help while Ruby joggles baby Peter, giving Mom and me our moment.

We pick up a rental car. Jade piles in with us, and she and I sit on either side of Peter's car seat, gazing down at him.

"I can't believe I'm an aunt," Jade says. I study her face. Now that I am so tuned into faces, how they look, what they show, I notice Jade's beauty. She has a longer face, olive skin, a smattering of freckles across her nose, and sweet, full red lips. I wonder how she'd photograph with auburn hair like Mom's loose around her face, no glasses, and a little mascara bringing out her amazing eyes.

"So how's Eureka?" I ask.

"It's okay." She's still withdrawn from me, after I said that stupid thing about the glasses. I bet Mom can't afford them.

"Listen, I'm sorry for what I said about the glasses. Let me buy you some contacts. I owe you a birthday present," I say.

Jade finally looks at me. She frowns. "You think everything is about looks. Some of us care about other things."

I snort. "You're fifteen. It's high school. You need every advantage you can get."

"Not everyone's a frickin' supermodel," Jade says, and now I see tears in her eyes. "You know how hard it is to be Pearl Michaels' sister?"

"Hey," Ruby moderates from the front seat. It feels just like when we were girls together on Saint Thomas, bickering.

"Hey yourself," I tell Ruby, and turn back to Jade. "I was saying that because you're really pretty, Jade, and you could be prettier. In fact, I could get you a test shoot if you want to try modeling. I'm not trying to yank your chain, either."

Jade scoots to the far side of the car and stares out the window. I notice she's buttoning and unbuttoning her cardigan sweater.

"Leave her alone, Pearl. She's just fine the way she is," Rafe rumbles from the front.

"I didn't mean that she wasn't. I just wanted to help." No one's listening, and I look out at the nondescript buildings of Eureka as we enter the town.

I haven't really been fair to Eureka. The area is beautiful, with redwoods growing abundantly and the ocean nearby. The ocean's a deep slate blue, so different from Saint Thomas, or even the greener color of the Atlantic near Boston.

The town of Eureka itself has a grubby utility about it, grown up as it did to serve the lumber trade on the coast, but it also has charming restored areas. My grandpa retired from the lumber mill where he was a foreman, and he and Nana live in a Victorian on the edge of town. I've been coming here annually since childhood to visit Mom's relatives.

Rafe and Ruby got rooms for the three of us at a nearby Holiday Inn, so we drop off our baggage and then drive to the house.

Jade disappears into her room the minute we return, and I wonder if she's still obsessively washing everything like she did after Dad died. Even as involved with the Carvers as I'd been at the time, I noticed. But she's avoiding me, so I decide to leave her alone.

It's just about the dinner hour, so eventually Jade reappears, helping with the food, and we all sit down at the big mahogany table and catch up with Nana and Grandpa and Mom's doings.

Nana looks like an older version of Mom, with her thick white braid and good bones. Grandpa is stooped, and hard of hearing, and makes heavy-handed conversation with Rafe as Mom tells us about her new business. "I took my experience with our vacation rental management business to managing rentals for the college students in Arcata," she says. Arcata is the small town one over, where Humboldt State University is located. "The students over there are always moving and needing places. It's going well."

"Good for you, Mom." Ruby glances over at Peter's carrier, but he's angelically asleep as usual.

"So, Pearl, tell us about your job." Mom cuts into her meatloaf. "I understand there's a lot of traveling? What's modeling like?"

"It's really hard work, actually." I tell them about the long days, the boredom that can happen, the struggle to be able to turn on emotion when I'm tired or down. "I also can't date. The Melissa Agency is really strict."

"What?" A huge grin breaks across Mom's face. "I can't believe they can do that."

"Yep. I can't do anything that will compromise my looks or reputation. So I've been on a very short leash between work and Rafe and Ruby," I tell her. "But I'm most proud that I have been clean and sober for almost a year."

A silence falls, and I realize Nana and Grandpa may not have known everything. I look into my grandfather's uncompromising eyes. "I had some problems in Saint Thomas. That's why I didn't come with Mom. I needed to go a different way."

"Sounds like you found it," Nana finally says. "Kate said you had behavior problems."

"I did." I nod my head. "But that's all in the past."

And I honestly think it is.

The visit goes well. We spend a lot of time doing puzzles and playing with baby Peter. Jade and I get past the scratchiness though she never accepts my offer of contacts or a photo shoot, and I notice she still does a lot of tidying and hand washing.

Too soon the week is up, and we're hugging and saying goodbye and getting on the jet. "We're going to see you every couple of months, now," Ruby declares. "We'll send the jet for you, right, Rafe?"

"Of course," he says, and kisses her a little longer than he should in front of family. "Whatever my honey wants."

I still envy what they have, but it's good to know it exists.

When we get back to Boston, I get cold feet about the investigation into Magnus Thorne.

"Don't tell me about finding him," I tell Rafe. "Except if he's in prison. If he's in prison, I want to know."

Rafe's dark-blue eyes crinkle at the corners. "Glad you thought that could be one of the reasons for his disappearance. All right. I'll only tell you if he's in prison."

And I get back to the whirlwind that's my life as a supermodel.

International travel. Magazine shoots. Workouts. Seaweed wraps. Fending off gross older men who think they can buy me becomes a regular thing as I get a higher and higher profile, and I'm shocked by some of the things they think will win my affection. On another shoot in Italy, I hold up a gold charm bracelet for Odile to see. Every charm is in the shape of a male anatomy part. "Makes me hot to look at this," I say. "Ooh. I'm so inspired by these charms."

Odile laughs. We're getting along great now, and Melissa

has actually hired her to be my personal manager, so she accompanies me on shoots and takes care of everything to make things smooth and easy.

A few months later I track down Rafe in his study. "Is he in prison?" I ask, hands on my hips.

Rafe looks up from his computer. People are using those more and more for business, and he has his own at home. "Not in prison," he says. "Want to know anything more?"

"No. Just--it's been eighteen months. Is he going to be back in six months?"

"Yes."

"That's all I need to know." I turn and leave, going to my familiar pink bedroom. I could afford my own place now, but I'm home so seldom, and I love being with family when I am.

I flop on the bed, fold my hands over my stomach, and stare at the pale pink ceiling, thinking about Magnus.

It's been eighteen months with no contact, no news, nothing to treasure but the frayed business card he gave me with his name on it, printed with a disconnected phone number.

If I shut my eyes, I can hear his voice in my ear, talking to me. Knowing that I was trying to hurt myself. Telling me what to do instead.

I think of his cabin, and his mother, and the horse named Onyx.

Maybe I can find it.

It's a beautiful day, and I don't have work today or tomorrow. The perfect time for a motorcycle ride.

I jump up and get the leathers and helmet I bought secretly. Rafe and Ruby still let me use the old Beamer when I'm home, so in no time I'm driving to the storage unit in Cambridge where Valley helped me stash my bike.

It's been something of a disappointment, the whole thing,

because I am always working and so seldom get to ride. When Valley was done teaching me, I took the new bike to the Department of Motor Vehicles and took my license test.

Between weather challenges and my schedule, I hardly ever get to take it out, but today's gorgeous, and I have all day to tool around and try to find the mysterious cabin Magnus took me to so long ago.

I'm not ready to deal with the crap from Rafe and Ruby about safety so I still haven't told them about the bike, my first big purchase with my modeling money. I change into my stiff new leathers in the storage unit, hot as it is, and take a moment to open a map of Boston and surrounding areas on the floor.

I look at the arteries into and out of the city and shut my eyes, thinking back to that night. The feel of the wind in my face. The swirl of the passing lights. The feel of Magnus in my arms, the smell of his jacket, the roar of the road.

We went across a bridge and out of the city to the north. Using a pencil, I trace what I think is the route. It took us about forty minutes, and that puts me in a suburb outside of Boston.

It's finding the turnoff to that bumpy dirt road that's going to be challenging.

I put my helmet on. It's sleek and black but has a clear face guard. I don't like looking through a lot of tinting.

I kick down the stand, start the bike, and roll out of the unit, hitting the remote I got with the rental to close the door again.

I feel totally anonymous on the bike. Everything that makes Pearl Michaels, international model, recognizable is hidden--my hair is in a fat braid that touches my butt, tucked inside my jacket. My face is hidden and my body, usually on display in those scraps of lace and silk, buried under the sturdy leathers.

And I feel different, too. More powerful. The mistress of my destiny. I'm finding the man I want, not just sitting around waiting and hoping, having my mogul brother-in-law track him down like a felon.

As I roar through the tunnel on Massachusetts Avenue out of town, I'm glad I had Rafe rule out prison. It could have easily been that, a two-year stint for something, and would I have still wanted Magnus at the end of that?

The answer's yes.

Yes, I would have. Because as mysterious as Magnus has kept himself, I know the essential him. He's honorable. He takes his sobriety program seriously, and if something from his using past caught up with him, who am I to judge?

I killed my father.

I roll through the gears and feel that exhilaration that riding brings me surge through my body as I weave in and out of the traffic down the freeway, over the bridge, and out into the suburbs. It's a glorious day, the sun is shining, the trees are the intense green of recent rains, and I love being alive.

At the forty-minute mark I slow down. The main artery of the road out of Boston has narrowed to a two-lane highway, peppered with mailboxes and driveways heading into leafy forest areas.

I turn down the nearest one, drive down to an unassuming ranch house with a barn, turn and go back.

I do this for several hours before I decide I must have got on the wrong road out of town, but it's been a great afternoon and I can do it again tomorrow.

The summer winds on into fall. Days off, I search the countryside, but I've begun to give up. I don't know what I'll say, anyway, if I find the place, I think one afternoon as I ease the bike down yet another potholed dirt road. So I find it. He won't be there, and his mother wasn't the most welcoming soul I've ever encountered.

There are pine trees leaning in over the road, and broad chuckholes that would be puddles at another time of the year-- and suddenly I recognize it, and know where I am even before the weathered gray boards of the huge barn appear, and the two small cabins, run-down in the light of day, with the strip of unpaved road between them.

There are no cars parked anywhere but as I pull the bike up in front of the barn, I hear a neigh from inside.

Onyx.

I turn off the bike, put down the stand, and swing my leg over. Taking my helmet off, I hang it from a handlebar and look around.

The place looks deserted. No smoke coming from either cabin's chimney, no vehicles parked in view.

I go to the barn and push one side of huge swinging double doors open carefully. "Hello?"

My voice startles a flock of doves which fly out with a rush of wings that startles me. I wrinkle my nose at the musty smell of hay, straw, and horse manure that waft over me. Inside, light sifts down in arrows from chinks in the cedar shake roof, illuminating the dusty floor in spots.

Directly ahead of me, draped in a black canvas cover, is a motorcycle.

My heart speeds up. Magnus's bike, no doubt about it, bigger and heavier than my Superlow. As I walk to it, I trail my fingers across the cover. They are powdered with dust when I get to the hornlike protrusions of the handlebars.

Another neigh. I see Onyx's handsome head looking at me, his eyes lustrous in the low light.

"Hello, beautiful." I stroke and pet him, straightening his forelock, scratching under his muzzle. He thrusts his nose at me, whuffling loudly, and I know he smells the apple I stuck in my pocket as a snack.

What the heck. I get the apple out and he takes it delicately off my open palm, crunching it in half and shutting his eyes in bliss as he chews.

I hear barking suddenly, and the barn door opens. Onyx starts back and pulls his head into the stall. Magnus's dog Whiskey gallops up to me and thrusts his head into my crotch for a good sniff, his tail lashing my legs.

His mother Raven must be home. She enters, and stands silhouetted against the open barn door. "Who's that?"

Her voice is resonant and deep, a vibration in it that reminds me of Magnus. She's wearing jeans this time, and moccasins. She still looks too young to be his mother. I dust off my hands and approach her.

"Hi. I met you a while ago. I'm Magnus's friend, Pearl." I extend my hand to shake hers.

She doesn't take it, only looks at my eyes. "How did you come here?"

"I'm looking for Magnus. Where is he?" I decide the direct approach is best.

"If you really were a friend, you would know." I'm close enough to see that her large, dark eyes, so like his, are hard and wary.

"I know he's gone for a while. I just want to know when he'll be back."

"Like I said. If you really were a friend, he'd have told you. Now get out of my barn and off my land."

And I see that what I thought was a walking stick in her hand is a shotgun.

CHAPTER TWENTY-THREE

"Okay. Tell him I came by, will you?" I'm hurrying now, out of the barn, my heart thundering. I can feel a burning place between my shoulder blades where she wants to shoot me.

I can't get the bike started and out of there fast enough.

On the way back to the city, tears pour out from under the Plexiglas face guard. Whatever I expected, it wasn't that hostile. I can't go back there again.

Maybe it's time to give up.

I deal with guys hitting on me daily, men asking me out. Most of them are older and I can tell they're looking to say they date a model. I'm nothing but a body and face to them, arm candy that they want to bang. But there are a few younger ones I've met on the set and even a male model or two who've elicited a tingle.

And there's always Brandon, who sometimes shows up at shoots and stands in the background, watching me, his face unreadable. I know that if I gave him reason to hope, he'd be at my side in a heartbeat.

But then there's his mother to contend with, and she owns me.

What is it about these mothers? They just don't like me.

I'm finally feeling better by the time I get home, wrung out and cleansed. Riding the bike does that for me. And there's a shoot this afternoon and a meeting to go to. I have a life. Magnus isn't in it, and I'm really fine.

Six months or so later, I'm twenty, not that I'm counting or anything.

I'm in my favorite lunchtime meeting and it's about to begin. I'm talking to Mrs. Svenson, stirring hot chocolate in a Styrofoam cup, when I feel something change in the room.

I look up, toward the door. Just like it happens every day, Magnus walks in. He takes off his helmet, setting it on the floor against the wall, and strides to the circle of chairs with easy grace, never taking his eyes off me.

He sits on the chair across from me. Extends his legs in black leather pants with the heavy buckled boots into the circle. Crosses his arms on his wide chest. His brutal mouth wears a curl of knowing smile. His black hair is braided, past his shoulders now. There's a fresh scar on his forehead, a livid red line, and his eyes on me are dark and hot.

I don't know how I'm going to get through the hour. I feel myself going warm and cold, unable to get comfortable on my chair. I alternate between terror, anger, and a sexual hunger so fierce I want to leap across the circle and tear his clothes off right in front of everyone.

Somehow I manage to keep it together, mainly by playing the scene where Magnus pushed me away in the storage room over and over in my head. The sharing of the meeting swirls around me, meaningless background noise. I look at the floor and make myself breathe.

Just because he's back, doesn't mean he wants me.

I sneak a look at him.

Oh, he wants me. He hasn't taken those black-olive eyes off me since he came in the room.

But just because he wants me doesn't mean he's going to let himself have me.

And then, there's the tiny issue of whether or not I should show some dignity, some self-respect, and try to act like I've moved on. Like I'm not a pitiful teenager who fell under his spell and hunted down his house and sent a private detective after him like some stalker fan-girl.

I should act like the international supermodel, with tons of men after me, that I actually am.

I sneak another look at him, keeping my lashes down, and let my eyes wander up those dark scuffed boots, along his heavy, leather-clad legs, past the bulge beneath his belt buckle, up the thick chest and all the way to his smoldering eyes.

My body jerks like I've been zapped with a hot wire as we make eye contact.

I yank my gaze away and cross and uncross my legs, turning to the side to pay attention to Mrs. Svenson, who's wrapping up the meeting with exhortations to pay attention to triggers this week. And then we're standing, and holding hands and saying the Lord's Prayer, and I swear to all that's holy I feel his energy reach all the way through all the hands between him and me, and touch me with a warm caress.

But when I look up, and try to decide if I'm going to approach him or if he's coming to me, all I see is his powerful back walking away. He reaches down and scoops up his helmet, and slips out the door.

I'm alone again.

CHAPTER TWENTY-FOUR

I want to scream with rage, chase Magnus out the door and pound on that rejecting back with my fists. Instead I go into the bathroom and sit on the toilet and take some breaths, and try to think of what to do.

My choices remain the same: pursue and approach him, and risk getting rejected again, or move on and get over him. I feel the impossibility of either option.

I hear the door of the bathroom open. Footsteps. A gentle knock on my stall.

"Pearl?"

Valley's voice. I registered her presence in the meeting on some level, but not consciously until now because Magnus so completely absorbed my attention.

Valley has truly been a gift in my life, a gift that Magnus gave me. She's been an incredible sponsor, holding me accountable to do my twelve-steps, available by phone day or night. And she helped me buy my motorcycle and taught me to ride.

"I know you're in there." Her husky voice is gentle.

I stand up and flush, for form's sake, and step out of the stall.

She's directly in front of me, this incredible woman in black leather, her jet hair in a braid, silver feather earrings flashing in her ears. Her eyes are sad and kind.

"You need to get over him, Pearl."

I open and close my mouth. I go to the sink, put my hands under the water and wash with soap. Rinse. I let them fill with cool water and splash it on my hot face. Look at that face in the mirror.

That famous face. Even without makeup or retouching, my face is something people want to keep looking at—I know, because I live in it, and feel eyes on me all the time. *The idea of me.*

Such false advertising.

My full mouth that promises sin hasn't even kissed a guy for two years. My trademark hair that one article described as "climbable" is skinned back from my brow into a braid that no one but a hairdresser or myself has so much as brushed. My eyes, those eyes that my Melissa Agency bio says "can launch a thousand ships" look haunted, purple shadows under them like I've been punched.

"I'm trying to. If there's anything you can say that will make me hate him, tell me. Please."

Valley puts her hands on my shoulders, squeezes. She's refused to answer any questions about Magnus this whole time, except to say they're cousins and have been friends all their lives.

"I told you I promised him I wouldn't answer your questions. All I can tell you is that Magnus decided you two weren't going to be together, and he's a very stubborn man."

"He judged me," I say. "And he's underestimated me. I've

been single for two years, waiting for him to come back. It's not fair that he gets to decide what happens."

Our eyes meet in the mirror. Valley shrugs. "That may be true. What are you going to do about it?"

I feel a reckless, crazy courage rise up in me. "I'm screwed either way, so I'm going to try to get Magnus to change his mind."

She smiles, a slow wide arc that turns into a grin. "Go get him, Pearl. And if it doesn't work, I'll be here to help you pick up the pieces."

One thing I know is seduction; it's my daily stock in trade, and I'm about to go on the ride of my life to undertake it. I need a plan. A plan to blow Magnus away, and a plan to deal with his gun-toting mother if I run afoul of her.

I slip into our brownstone quietly. I can hear Mrs. Knightly vacuuming somewhere. Rafe and Ruby are at work, and baby Peter is at his daycare.

I shower, shave everything. Rub down with some lotion I bought in France that's infused with real rose oil—something like a thousand crushed petals per drop, to make that oil, and it smells amazing. I get out a favorite panty set which I kept after a runway show. It's a satin demi-bra printed with tiny flowers that push my round, high breasts higher. It's paired with panties in the same fabric cut to make my legs look even longer.

I did a whole line of photos with this underwear and made the brand a bestseller. Maybe I can make one man want me enough to get over his ridiculous scruples.

I get into my leathers. He's not going to expect that, not going to know I have my own bike, and I hope he likes it. I know the leathers make me look good. They fit smooth and tight as a black glove against my figure, and more importantly they make me feel good. Confident. Badass. A woman who rides a Harley, by God.

I pack a small backpack with supplies I might need, and I leave a note that I'm at a friend's and will be gone overnight. Rafe and Ruby trust me now, and I deserve it. I haven't had one slip in two and a half years of clean and sober living and nonstop working. I've wrestled my demons and won. I've even reconciled with my mother.

I can seduce one stubborn man.

And if I can't, I'll survive. And I won't use over it. No matter what, I'm never going back to that dark place.

I pick up my backpack and my helmet and stride out the door.

The ride to Magnus's house in the country calms my racing heart, cools my hot cheeks. Centers me. Motorcycle therapy—it works for me. I turn down the bumpy, long dirt drive with its overgrown pine trees leaning in as if trying to hide the narrow road.

I navigate the potholes, thinking of what to do if Magnus isn't home. I plan to hide my bike so his mother doesn't see it, and break into his house and wait for him.

Yes, I'm desperate as an addict who will do anything for a fix.

At least I know the dog likes me.

I hear a roaring sound that penetrates even through the helmet, and as I come around the last overgrown pine tree into the clearing between the cabins and the barn, I see Magnus directly ahead of me.

He's wearing safety goggles and work gloves and a lumberjack shirt in red plaid, and he's chainsawing a pine tree.

I brake the bike, and put my feet down, and wait for him to notice me. I get to stare at him in his heavy work clothes, ear muffs canceling the sound of my approach, and watch the way he slings that heavy saw like it's a battleax and the tree is his enemy.

It makes me melty in the knees to watch him work.

Whiskey the dog spots me and runs over, barking and wagging his thick tail, and Magnus looks up. Sees me. Cuts the motor on the chainsaw. Lowers it until the pointed end is resting on the ground. He's gone still and alert, but I can tell he's not sure who I am.

This is my moment.

I take off the helmet. I shake loose the pile of curls I bundled inside. My hair tumbles down around me. I'm fully aware of how my shining, creamy blond locks contrast against the supple black leather I'm wearing. I put down the kickstand and swing my leg off the bike. I hang the helmet from one of the handlebars, all without breaking eye contact with him.

I stride toward Magnus with that sway and stomp, my patented sexy runway walk, and as I get closer I see that his mouth is hanging open and his eyes are wide behind the safety goggles.

I get to him and stand in his space. He hasn't moved, hasn't closed his mouth. I reach up and take off the safety goggles. Tuck them in his shirt pocket. I hook an arm around his neck and pull his mouth down to mine.

CHAPTER TWENTY-FIVE

The hot wire that zapped me in the meeting is nothing to the feeling of his lips. I am electrified, every hair on my body springing to attention, and as my leather-clad pelvis presses against his, I can tell that's not the only thing springing to attention.

He lowers the chainsaw with a clatter and groans into my mouth. His arms circle me and press me so close that I can't breathe, and I couldn't care less.

Our kiss is deep, a probing of souls as well as mating of tongues. He tastes of coffee and sorrow to me. There's a desperation in the kiss, a longing for life. Something terrible has happened to him. Perhaps it had, before, but I never tasted it so clearly—and terrible things have happened to me too.

Our wounds meet and meld and merge and it's delicious and painful too, as one of his big hands in the leather work glove clasps my buttock and hauls me closer and higher against him, grinding me against his erection.

I couldn't love it more, the dark intensity, this tearing need roaring through both of us without a word exchanged.

We stumble backwards, somehow making it to his little porch, up onto it, all the way to the front door of his cabin. Magnus lifts his head, eyes hazy as he fumbles with the knob.

"You sure you want this? You don't know what you're getting into."

"Oh, God, yes." There is no hesitation in me whatsoever.

"It's on you, then." He hoists me up by my ass like I weigh nothing, applying his mouth to mine. My legs wrap around his hips as he slams the door open. We're kissing and consuming each other as he carries me inside.

He backs me up against the bed and I let go of his shoulders and fall backward onto it.

He strips off the work gloves. "I must be dreaming. You, here in my bed. Wearing leathers."

"You left. I had to get my own motorcycle therapy." I let my hands drift over my body. One of them circling my breast, feeling its full, taut peak through the leather as the other hand slides down to my hips. I can feel my core heating even more as I watch him undress.

He's tearing at the long-sleeved, heavy lumberjack shirt, finally getting it off. His torso is ridged with muscle across the chest and abs, lightly hairy in a shape that only emphasizes his physical magnificence as he leans down to undo the heavy work boots. I'm rendered speechless by the way the light coming through the window gleams along the deep groove of his spine, across the rippling muscles of his shoulders.

"I should shower," he mutters, fumbling with the laces of the boots. I worry he's trying to gather steam for second thoughts.

"I want you just how you are." I can't bear to wait any longer. I surge back up to grasp his belt. I undo the buckle and slide down the zipper as he gives up on the boots, straightening up to tangle his hands in my hair as I slide the jeans down off his lean hips.

His erection is fighting the fabric of his boxers. Finally slowing myself down, this time so I can savor, I lower the fabric to his knees.

His shaft is proportional to the rest of him, and just the thought of him in me makes me groan. I put my mouth on him, circling and swirling with my tongue. He throws his head back as I take him in deep, my hands clasping his hard buttocks, digging into the thick muscle as I surge forward, slide back, and do it again.

"Oh, God. Pearl," he says hoarsely. It undoes me, this cry from the man I've wanted so long. The sound of my name in his mouth makes me so hot I find myself pressed against his legs, making tiny mewing sounds in my throat.

He detaches me by pulling my hair back. "Slow down. I want to savor this."

I sit back on the bed and let him wrestle off his boots and jeans, and finally he's totally naked in front of me and I can feast my eyes on the tree trunks of his legs, the stacked vee shapes of his body—but not for long, because he puts a knee between my leather-clad legs and pushes me backwards, a wolfish grin on his face. "Your turn."

He captures my hands in one of his and lifts them above my head as he slides the zipper of my jacket down. I moan and toss beneath him, rubbing myself against his leg, shameless and wanton as he takes his time stripping off the leathers.

When he has me down to panties, he stands up to look at me. I can't see past anything but his erection, but I feel his gaze wandering over all of me like a caress.

"You're so beautiful, Pearl."

"Yeah, yeah." I've heard that too much before. I'm coming

unglued, rubbing myself in those pretty panties against him. I feel close to coming already, and we haven't even got down to business. "I need you. Please. Now."

He looks around. "I have a condom somewhere." Another too long delay as he finds one in a drawer, leaving me to wonder who he does bring home to make love to. But I don't have long to think about that before he's finally got the panties and bra off me. Lying beside me, he lifts himself on his elbow and strokes me from breast to hip and back again, his firm hand igniting a trail of fire with every touch.

I turn on my side, facing him, and stroke him too, savoring the different textures under my hands: the thick muscle, hard and yet covered in silky skin with the tensile roughness of hair adding textural interest. I lean in and flick my tongue over his nipple. I feel his erection leap against my leg and he tenses.

"I'm trying to make this last, Pearl, because I know it won't take long once I'm in you."

I look into his eyes. Really look into a brown so deep it's like bitter chocolate. His lashes are a thick fringe that make them even darker, and up close they are so beautiful.

"It doesn't matter if it's over fast. We can just do it again, and take our time the next time."

He moves quickly now, rolls the condom on and rises above me, and I open for him. He tries to go slow, easing into me, holding himself high above me on straight arms trembling with strain, but that's not how I want it.

I wrap my legs around his hips and pull him into me with all the strength four times a week on the Stairmaster has given me.

He makes a harsh sound in his throat as he sinks in fully, and I arch and cry out at the deep penetration, my tissues unused to anything like this for so long. He freezes, afraid he's hurt me, but I buck my hips, wordless and begging for more.

And he gives it to me, thrusting so hard I slide backward, and we grapple with each other in a wrenching depth of feeling and need that is wordless and endless and all consuming—and, just as he predicted, over too quickly in a rush of inarticulate cries and mind-bending ecstasy.

CHAPTER TWENTY-SIX

He lies beside me, and returning to awareness of the here and now, I smell the faint, sweet smell of cut pine clinging to his skin and hair, along with the musky scent of us. My hand, indolent and possessive, wanders over his chest while his strums my ribs gently.

To stop touching each other is to know this is over, this precious, forceful, incredible first time. I'm afraid. Afraid he will push me away now that his thirst is slaked. Now that I've taken him off guard, broken through his defenses, and had my way with him. Because I know I'm responsible for what has just happened, for bowling him over. I don't regret it but I'm afraid he'll suddenly get up and walk away, or just point a finger at the door and tell me to leave.

Connor, my boyfriend, did that at least half the times we were together. He'd screw me, because I'll never call what we did making love, and sometimes he'd just point his chin at the door afterward, his eyes hooded, and if I was too slow gathering my clothes, he'd even push me to get me moving faster.

I shut my eyes on those humiliating memories, letting

myself sink deeper into the mattress, which is surprisingly good quality, deep and supportive but firm. The sheets smell fresh and crisp. I try not to think of his mother making up the bed for his return. I'm afraid of her too.

I keep my eyes closed so I can enjoy the way Magnus's fingers stroke along my skin, wander up my sternum and finally circle my nipple, pulling it into a tight, sensitized, hard point.

My breath hitches, and I pay him back by doing the same to his nipple. He sucks a breath. His voice is a rumble in the deep chest beside me. "I really need to shower."

"Me too." So we get up together, our hands still on each other, and in the narrow stall, under an inadequate stream of warmish water, we explore each other more fully.

He is so wonderfully made, this man with the almost-black eyes. I fill my hands with shampoo and wash his hair. At first he bends his head forward so I can reach it, and I use my thumbs to rub the base of his skull while working the suds into the thick black length with my fingertips as he moans at the good feeling. Finally, he lets me turn him, and straightens up, and I rinse the suds out and slide my hands up and down the hard, brown length of his body, slipping and sliding over the contoured muscles and strange scars there. Some look like cuts, and one near his shoulder is a divot of lighter-colored flesh.

"This is a bullet hole," I say in shock, tracing it with a fingertip. "Who shot you?"

He doesn't answer, just captures my questing hand in his and turns me to face the shower wall.

And this time when he presses against me, I feel him want me again, and he bites the back of my neck and it sends a thrill rippling down my spine and my core melts in a heated flush of readiness for him. He doesn't enter me yet, though. Instead he turns washing me into foreplay, a delicious, torturous exploration with lips and tongue and teeth, and intermittently, soap.

"Open your legs," he says, and I do, and he works me from behind until I come against the wall of the shower surround, my cries of helpless pleasure drowned in the flow of water and swallowed by his mouth on mine.

Only then does he turn me and lift me, entering me and pumping into me as I slide up and down the wall, my hands on his shoulders, helpless and gasping, overwhelmed with feeling and sensation, tears mixing with the cooling flow of the shower.

He pulls out at the last minute and I feel his deep shudder of release against my side, the water washing it instantly away. I have a weird sense of loss as I breathe in the damp place between his neck and shoulder. I want to have him totally in me, bare and completely mine. All of it, everything. Maybe when I'm on birth control. . .

I can hardly stand after that. He moves my heavy, sated body out of the shower, wraps me in a capacious towel, and carries me back to bed. He gets in with me, and we pull the covers up and fall asleep.

I wake to the feeling of Whiskey's tongue on my face.

I push him away. "No, boy! Ew." I sit up, and the covers fall to my waist. Magnus is at the stove, and he turns to me, a spatula in hand. He grins.

"Your hair. Maybe we should have dried it or something."

"I have a shoot the day after tomorrow, so no worries. The hairdresser will have something to work on." I push the snarled, damp, frizzing mass of locks back behind my shoulder.

"Eggs? I got home yesterday and haven't had time to shop. Found some of these out in the coop this morning."

Got home from where? But I don't say it. I know he won't answer, and I don't want to pop this delicate bubble we're in.

177

"Smells great. Yes, thanks." I draw my knees up under my chin, the sheet modestly draped, and watch him at the stove as Whiskey leans against me from one side of the bed.

I enjoy the quick economy of his movements, the sun shining on his thick tumble of hair and bare torso. He's pulled on a pair of jeans and that's all, and I like just looking at him.

He brings me the plate of eggs. They have canned chilies mixed in, and salt and pepper, and as we sit eating in bed, I think I haven't tasted anything better in my life.

When we're done, he sets the plates on the floor and Whiskey licks them. He lies back, and tugs my hair so that I lie back too. I pillow my head in the notch between his collarbone and the bulge of his shoulder. Almost idly, his hand plays with my hair.

"You seduced me," he says meditatively. "I would dare a saint to resist how you got off that bike and shook that hair out over your leathers."

"I did seduce you. What happened is all on me. And thank you for the compliment, I think."

"We shouldn't be together."

"I've never understood why not. You underestimate me."

"I guess that much is true." His hand turns my chin toward him, and I look up into his face. His dark eyes hold just as many secrets as before. "Now what are we going to do?"

"Keep having amazing sex as often as possible?" I know I sound too hopeful.

Magnus chuckles, but it's sad. "I'm afraid not. Because, Pearl, nothing has changed."

CHAPTER TWENTY-SEVEN

Pearl

I ride my Harley through the earliest stain of new day. The air is chilly, and cuts across my leathers, finding every seam and the crannies around my neck and wrists, slicing across my tender, heated skin. I would normally have other clothes on underneath, but not this time. All I'm wearing is the tiny bra and panties set I put on yesterday, hoping to seduce Magnus Thorne.

I succeeded. The underwear is a little worse for wear, and now, heading home, there's nothing much between me and the early-morning cold but one layer of black leather.

There's little traffic so early on a Sunday morning, so I can flatten out between my handlebars and really put down some speed, weaving in and out of the few cars on the road, the roar of the Superlow's engine, the absorbing feel of the power between my legs, the beauty of the wide-open bridge over the Charles River into Boston almost enough to distract me from my second broken heart from the same man.

Magnus Thorne.

I wish his name was something ordinary. Ignorable. Like Matt, or Doug maybe. I can't imagine someone named Doug being able to eviscerate me.

The pain of our breakup feels fatal but distant, like I got my head chopped off but neither my head nor my body has quite gotten the message yet.

I crank on some more gas. Traffic has begun to clog going into the Massachusetts Avenue tunnel, but I don't slow down.

I need the challenge of trying to weave between the vehicles without slowing, to hold off that pain just a little longer.

I roar under the familiar billboard that marked my modeling debut two years ago. Two years that feels like a lifetime. Two years that have taken me from being a hick teenager from Saint Thomas to international fame as a supermodel. Two years in which I grew up a lot, and took some responsibility, and owned my addiction and faced my past.

Not that any of it made a bit of difference to Magnus. That fame. That growth. Or that past, either.

A car switches lanes without signaling ahead of me, and I brake.

Too hard.

The bike swerves, cranking to the side, and I'm in danger of laying it down right in front of a Mack truck. I see the driver's eyes wide and mouth open at what he can't prevent sliding right up into his grill—but as I'm going down, I hit the gas, just a little, and downshift to first, and the bike pulls out of the slide as the tires catch in acceleration.

But there's hardly anywhere to go between the vehicles, and I barrel into the tight space between two cars moving parallel. I clip my handlebars on one of the mirrors. That almost spins me out again but I manage to get ahead of both cars and into a lane, moving at a more reasonable speed.

My whole body, amped with adrenaline, bursts out in sweat at the near miss.

We're still in the Mass Avenue tunnel, and I throw back my head and howl—a wail of anguish and pain, of determination to survive and go on in spite of it. I scream again, and it bounces around in the tunnel and makes children strapped into car seats glance at me with startled eyes.

I don't care that people are looking. I never have. But now I'm done with my crazy fit of angst. And for just today, I resolve not to use any substances to numb my pain. *I can do this.*

I've just had my heart ripped out by the roots, but it's my own damn fault. I knew what I was getting into, seducing Magnus Thorne.

I drive more sanely into the Back Bay neighborhood where my sister Ruby and her hunky husband Rafe have a dignified old brownstone he inherited from his blueblood family.

I'm also done hiding my bike as of today. Until now I've kept it elsewhere in a locked storage unit. No, today's a day for revelations, and my sister and her husband can find out I've owned and driven a Harley for the last two years.

I turn into the narrow alley between buildings and find the garage I've never parked the bike in before. It's a small garage that only holds two cars. Rafe has a bigger storage facility where he keeps his car collection. Still, the Superlow's not a huge bike, and I know I can cram it in between the antique Jag Ruby drives and Rafe's Mercedes.

I park the bike, unlock the garage with my house key, hit the button and roll the bike in between their cars, all the way to the front where there's an open area.

I take off my helmet and shake out my famous hair.

It's a waist-length mess of snarls and frizz from the shower Magnus and I took.

Oh, that shower.

The memory of him moving in me, sliding me up and down the wall of the surround, my hands on his shoulders, my legs around his waist as he held me by the ass—it engulfs, arouses and devastates me.

That memory will have to sustain me.

The upshot was that my hair got a whole lot of action it wasn't used to, and no product, and no styling, and it's doing what long, naturally-curly hair does when it's subjected to such indignities.

I have a shoot tomorrow. The hairdresser can deal with it. I hang the helmet off the handlebars of the bike and walk in the back door.

Mrs. Knightly, the housekeeper, something of an auntie to me, jumps in surprise as I enter the house from a different direction than usual.

"Miss Pearl! What is that outfit you're wearing? Very dashing!"

"Thanks," I say, without elaboration. "Got any ice cream?"

"Yes, I do. Mr. Rafe brought some home recently. But I thought you were supposed to be counting calories?" she lets her voice trail off delicately, eyeing me over her half glasses.

"It's an emergency. If anyone calls, I'm not at home. I'll be up in the bath, with my ice cream." I brush past her to the big silver Sub-Zero fridge, so yuppie I could puke, and take out the whole pint of designer ice cream, a brand called Ben and Jerry's. "Cherry Garcia? I'll take it."

I head for the great swooping staircase that ascends from the black and white checkered marble entryway. I am intent on first aid for a broken heart: loads of ice cream calories eaten in a hot bath will have to take the place of drinking, drugs, or sex.

In the huge jet-ringed tub, bubbles up to my neck and Cherry Garcia melting on my tongue, I let myself think about Magnus breaking up with me.

I wasn't brave about it last night, or the first time he did it to me, two years ago. After our second round of lovemaking, in the sweet afterglow, he told me nothing had changed.

"I had good reasons two years ago not to sleep with you. You were a teenager, and just getting clean. Now those reasons aren't as important, but my work is. I can't talk about it, I can't share anything about it, and it requires that I'm randomly gone for extended periods."

He was playing with my hair as he said this, sifting it between his fingers. It fell from his hand like strands of tinsel, landing softly on my bare breasts. He picked up a handful again, let it sift through his fingers. He brought it to his nose, inhaled.

"I'm okay with that," I said. "I've stopped asking about your work. I know it's something that requires a gun and its secret, and you've been shot and you won't answer my questions. I get that, and I respect it." I'm determined not to give him any reason to push me away. "I have work that requires me to travel and be gone random times, too, but as you know it's very public."

"Which is another reason why I can't be with you, Pearl." He moves out from under my head, rising on an elbow to look down at me as I lie naked on the bed beside him. He strokes the hair he sifted over my breasts, plays with my nipple as if he can't keep from touching me.

As I can't keep from touching him. Even in the midst of this terrible conversation, I can't stop touching him. My hand slides up and down the knotted curve of his bicep. He's so different from me, dark to my light, rough to my smooth, hard to my soft —but the sum total of us is perfect.

He goes on. "I can't draw attention to myself. If a paparazzi snaps a photo of us together, if someone decides to write an article about your love life, it will be a problem. You're famous."

"Nobody cares about my love life. Besides, I can do something else." Even as I say this, I know it's a lie. I've got nothing but modeling.

He snorts. "Don't be ridiculous. You're succeeding in one of the toughest and most competitive careers in the world, and you need to work it as long and hard as you can. Make a ton of money on this body and face while you can."

He strokes me, and it feels so good, so tender, so gentle. *It feels like he loves me.* If I shut my eyes, I can pretend he does.

When I open them, I see banked fire in those eyes, dark as the smoky depths of a whiskey barrel. His lashes are so long they'd be feminine if it weren't for the dark slash of his brows, one of them bisected by a pirate-like scar.

He has another scar on his forehead, a new one, still a raised red line. I trace it gently with my finger. "I haven't even asked you about this. I won't ask you. I'll give you all the space you need. Only please, please don't do this to us. We both need it. This. What we have."

He shuts his eyes. I trace the scar again, and feather my fingers into the length of his coarse black ripple of hair. That's why I don't think he's military. If he was, they'd make him cut his hair. Instead of answering, he leans down to kiss me.

The kiss is a compass. It's like I've been wandering in a fog, holding a map, trying to find my way—and suddenly a light has come on, and I see home.

I feel tears fill my eyes as our bodies say what our words cannot, what our words destroy.

This third time his touch on me is gentle, and slow, and filled with tenderness. His mouth brands a row of kisses down my neck. Along my collarbones, finally arriving at my breasts.

He moves to lie over me with a deep sound of satisfaction, as if settling to a task he's always anticipated, and proceeds to make love to them.

Sucking. Licking. Biting, swirling, his hands and mouth everywhere.

All of my senses are filled by him: the scent of him. The overwhelming sensations of his hands and mouth. His weight holding me down. The gorgeous visual of his face as he draws my nipple into his mouth. The soft sounds we both make. The smell of us, musky and arousing.

I shut my eyes and give myself over to this moment.

But that's not the end, oh no, because when I've given up dignity and restraint for wanton cries and twitching helplessly, he works his way down my sternum, along the smooth firm dip of my waist, past my hips, to my center, hot and melting.

"So sweet. So good," he says, and feasts there for a while.

Good. Oh, it *is* good. I've never felt good before, but he makes me so.

I've never had this kind of attention giving me so much pleasure. It fragments me, over and over again, exploding, dissipating, re-gathering.

When he's finally inside me, we make it last and last, and the ending is hard and sweet. I dissolve into tears, which he sips as if they're precious nectar. I know it's the end, even though not another word was spoken after my heartfelt plea.

In the cooling bath in my sister's house, I take another bite of ice cream, get it down in a convulsive swallow, and then let myself cry, great wrenching sobs. I eventually set the Ben and Jerry's on the edge of the tub and sink beneath the water, just to silence the grief that's become too loud, too unbearable.

Under the water, curled in a fetal position, I'm feeling my feelings. Unmedicated. Unmanageable. Ugly.

Dr. Rosenfeld, my therapist, would be proud.

I spasm with the stabbing pain of my lungs and burst up out of the water.

"Geez, Pearl, I thought you drowned!" My sister Ruby is

standing over me, hands on her hips, green eyes worried. She takes in my swollen, reddened eyes, drops down beside the tub. "Mrs. Knightly said you were upset."

"Yeah." I reach for the Cherry Garcia, soft now. I slurp from the side of the carton.

"And what's that Harley in the garage?"

"Mine. Decided it was time you knew."

"Oh, Pearl, they're so dangerous!" Ruby puts her hands up to her cheeks like the kid in Home Alone. "And now what's wrong?"

"I broke up with Magnus Thorne. Again."

"Dammit, sis." Ruby props her chin on her hands on the edge of the tub. "What's with him? You waited the two years and everything! It's not like you don't have other options."

"I don't care about my options." The cool ice cream is soothing on my abraded throat. "But I do need to get over him. Move on. I think I need to go see Dr. Rosenfeld again and figure out why I pick men who can't love me."

"What about Brandon? He seems like a good guy. Genuinely smitten with you."

"I can't date him. Melissa's orders."

"Come on, Pearl. It's been two years and Brandon's still hanging around. Maybe it's time both of you stand up to his mother."

"I would if I felt about him like I do about Magnus." I fumble for a washcloth, blow my nose. "Maybe when I'm over Magnus. If I ever get over Magnus." And my throat spasms with sobs, and I hand Ruby the ice cream carton and slide all the way under the water again.

Magnus

She left in the earliest dawn today, getting up out of bed, slipping into her leathers, sneaking outside. I know she rolled her bike down the driveway, away from the cabin to start it, because I hear its throaty roar in the distance, and that's when I finally sit up, feeling like I've been sandbagged.

I pretended to be asleep beside her, but the truth was, I didn't sleep all night. I just lay holding her and listening to the soft sound of her breathing. Feeling her in my arms.

Wondering how the hell I'm going to survive giving her up.

Pearl Moon Michaels. Literally one of the most beautiful women in the world. In my arms. Loving me, even if she doesn't say the words.

What a travesty my life is.

I get out of bed in slow motion, knowing I'm feeling sorry for myself, that I can hardly move I'm so sledgehammered by pain of a kind I don't know how to deal with.

Physical pain I can take. Bring it on. Been there, done that, got the scars to prove it. But this pain? And no drugs, no drinking to take the edge off? It's asking a lot; it's really fucking asking a lot.

Dammit. This head trip isn't helping.

I get the coffee going with Whiskey watching me accusingly. "She had to go, Whiskey. She would never fit in here. Never fit in with my lifestyle." Whiskey blinks his eyes. Doesn't wag his tail. Puts his head down. Snuffles into his paws.

He liked her, too.

Pearl's amazing hair, perfect body, that stunning face—all famous, all known by the world. But it's not the obvious, show-stopping things about her that I treasure. No, it's the little things no one else knows.

The curve of her ear, so tender and pink, and that little hollow behind it where her scent hides. She jumps and giggles when I put my nose there to breathe her in. And just above her absolutely stunning ass, in one of the dimples just above it, is a tiny brown mole like an accent mark.

I love that mole.

I think I might have a tattoo of it done somewhere that I can look and remember.

I fire up the chainsaw as soon as I get my work clothes back on, trying not to think of the expression she had on her face as she watched me get those same clothes off yesterday afternoon.

She looked at me like I was the best thing ever she'd seen in her life, and I know that can't be true.

I tear into the half-cut tree from yesterday, and the total focus required drives her out of my mind for a few hours that I extend by working my way down the long rutted road. Loading the logs, I've cut into the truck, trimming the branches, then moving and stacking them to dry for firewood takes the rest of the day, during which I blast rock music through my headphones so I don't think of her.

I'm exhausted and numb and finally, almost done with the work. Branches still litter the dirt road, but things are looking better when Mom's battered white Ford turns in.

I'm thankful she was away at a council meeting yesterday or she'd have seen Pearl ride her shiny new bike up to me in those leathers. And she'd have been aware of what happened after.

Raven stops beside me and rolls down her window. She's in full tribal regalia, her own leathers and beads, and I'm doubly glad she didn't run into Pearl. I know Pearl's afraid of her, and she should be.

"You got a lot done." Her eyes are sharp on me. She reads me like tea leaves, always has, and she sees something in my face and pounces on it like the raven she is. "That woman doesn't belong here."

"She isn't here," I snarl. "Mind your own damn business."

She puts the truck in gear and drives past without further comment.

Mom doesn't like that Pearl's white. She's been on my case since I brought Pearl here so briefly two years ago. "So many nice girls from our tribe and you have to bring home a white woman." She's been relentless.

But that's not why I resisted Pearl two years ago, or why I sent her away, now. No. It's a much darker reason.

CHAPTER TWENTY-EIGHT

Pearl

I stop going to my noon meeting. I'm afraid to run into Magnus there. Instead I throw myself into work, and when I'm not at a shoot, I'm working out at the gym. Only when I'm really, savagely pounding the weights and running on the treadmill, am I exhausted enough to sleep.

In the three weeks since I made my play for Magnus and lost, I lose ten pounds.

This is good news. I've always been on the edge of too-curvy, getting scoldings from my personal manager, Odile, who will actually grab my waist and pinch if she thinks I'm getting too big. Now she smiles. "Finally you can do more runway work."

"I'm still too big for that." I don't really like runway work. It's hectic, and I don't enjoy the experience of being an exotic creature, prancing up and down like a show horse—because that's what I feel like, swishing my mane and tail as I sway and stomp back and forth.

Not really me. The idea of me. Which has always been

easier to tolerate in front of a camera than an entire roomful of critical people.

Odile must have told Melissa about my weight loss because my agent summons me for a meeting. She has my portfolio open on her desk when I enter the inner sanctum, and she's leafing through the various spreads. She looks up and smiles, her hazel eyes almost warm.

"Have a seat, Pearl." I park myself on one of the silk-covered chairs in front of her desk. "I'd like to review your progress with the agency so far." She looks me over assessingly.

I didn't wear makeup today, and my hair is down and loose. I dressed in a black turtleneck and jeans, my default outfit. I loop my interlaced fingers around one knee.

"I'm still happy with your management of my career."

"I'm glad to hear that." She takes retro-looking reading glasses out of a little crystal holder on her desk and puts them on. She leafs to a spread from a lingerie show, gestures for me to look at it.

It's the show where I debuted the bra and panties set I wore to seduce Magnus Thorne.

That set is now wadded into a ball, way in the back of my underwear drawer. I washed them, but I can't bear to wear them. *Or throw them away.*

"This." She taps a photo of me striding out in the underwear, rhinestone-covered heels sparkling on my feet. "This was the apex of your career so far. You were in a few shows with the Big Six, but you haven't broken in to the point that you've made it the Big Seven." She's talking about the Big Six supermodels, the "women of the nineteen nineties" so famous that they're only known by their first names: Christy, Linda, Naomi, Claudia, Kate, and Tatjana.

"I've been happy to do what I'm doing. I don't need to be Big Seven. I don't really like runway work."

"They don't do much runway work. Just a couple of shows a year—but those shows are important. And even if you're not ambitious for yourself, I'm ambitious for you." She taps her glossy nails together in that way she has. "Congratulations on your weight loss. It brings out your eyes even more, and your bones." She extends a fingertip to touch my collarbone ever so lightly. It's a possessive touch. I know she uses words like "copyrighted look," "product," and "asset," to describe me and the other models in her stable, and I know she thinks of us that way.

It doesn't bother me. I get it.

Melissa goes on. "I think we need a dramatic new look for you. A haircut. Something really cutting edge. Everyone associates you with Rapunzel hair. What if you didn't have it? What would you be known for then? Your features are special too."

"I don't know if I like that idea." I feel a quaver in my belly at the thought of losing my hair. It's been my trademark. And something to hide behind, if the truth be known, when I need to.

"I'm thinking about a whole rebrand. So far we've pushed you as the sweet, WASPy, milkmaid American girl. This new look would be edgier. You'd be saying, in effect, that you have this stunning hair and you're so beautiful you don't even need it. You can whack it all off and still be one of the most beautiful women in the world. I wonder if you're up for that. If you believe it yourself." Melissa cocks her head as she looks at me. I'm reminded of a blackbird eyeing something shiny.

"I don't have to believe it. The camera has to." I know that now, from my time in front of the camera so far. I can act, true, and I have a gift for projecting my emotions, but I don't always need to *feel* them for them to translate. The camera still seems to love my face, and sometimes my ambivalence translates to a hypnotic charm.

"You're my manager. If you think this is the way to go, let's do it," I say. Now that I don't have Magnus to look forward to, I find myself constantly pushing to feel something. Riding too fast. Staying out late dancing. So far I've kept it under control and nothing's happened, but the possibility of disaster somehow perks me up. And this haircut could be a disaster.

Melissa leans back and smiles. "You've always had guts, Pearl. I like that about you." She pushes a button on her desk. "Send in Chad and Francine."

A few minutes later Chad Wicke, whose test shots first "discovered" me, arrives with Francine, the stunning hairdresser I met on my first day at the Melissa Agency.

Melissa gestures to me. "Stand up, Pearl. Everyone, I want you to take a good look at her. She's been flirting with the edge of the Big Six for the last year, but things are going stale for her lately." I didn't know that. I keep my face carefully blank as she goes on. "I'd like your opinion on a radical styling and rebranding change. She's lost weight recently, and my idea is to give her a short, edgy haircut. Make a big event of it. Auction her hair for charity or something. Film the whole thing. Then, debut her as the blonde who's so beautiful she doesn't even need that hair."

Both Chad and Francine circle me. I gaze into the middle distance, unfocused, the place I go during shows. Chad pouts, pushing his lips into a little moue as he considers me. Today he's in lime-green stovepipe trousers and a horizontally-striped shirt that reminds me of a mime. Meanwhile, Francine lifts handfuls of hair and inspects me. Her skin is the rich color of creamy coffee, and she smells like gardenias.

"You sure about this, Melissa? I mean, this is good hair." She sounds regretful. It makes the quaver in my belly deepen.

"I'm sure. We need something drastic to kick her to the next level."

"Well, then, I'm thinking a really short cut. No halfway measures. She's got natural curl, so if I do an allover buzz on her, the curls will coil up all over her head like a little lamb." Francine is still sifting my hair thoughtfully as Chad leans in.

"That will really bring out her bone structure. I can redo her portfolio shots. This will be fun." He rubs his hands together in anticipation.

"I'm glad you all are enjoying this. Tell me where and when to show up," I say.

We set up a date and time and Melissa picks up the phone. "I'm calling Vogue and some other magazines for coverage. I'll have my assistant find the right venue to donate to." She meets my eyes and cocks a finger. "Enjoy your last few days of hiding behind that hair."

Melissa always sees too much.

Magnus

It's been three weeks since Pearl spent the night. I've kept busy around the place doing repairs, painting, cleaning up the barn. It's never looked so good, but my next deployment could come any day. Memories of Pearl ambush me and make the nights long. I've stopped going to the lunchtime recovery meeting where I met her, afraid to see her again. But every time I think of the meeting I should be going to, the first time I saw her there replays in my mind.

Pearl's long legs in black jeans were thrust into the circle, crossed at the ankle. A worn hoodie concealed and engulfed her. Under the hood, I could see a shadowed, stunning face, the lush mouth sad and angry.

She gave me a long once-over when I sat down, and then began to put on moves, batting huge blue eyes of a light crystalline color like a tropical ocean, fringed in ridiculous lashes. She twisted her legs together and wriggled on the seat in that way that told me she was aroused. Of course that got a response going, which I suppressed with the thought of how young she was. *Just a messed-up kid at her first recovery meeting, trying to pass the time by yanking my chain.*

When I didn't give her any encouragement, she unzipped the hoodie so I could get a load of the curves I was trying to ignore. Tossing back the hood, she let a waterfall of silver-blonde curls out of hiding. Her mouth was pouty as hell, and she licked her lips, staring me down. This girl knew what to do with her mouth.

I managed to leave her in the dust that day, but staking out the drug action in the park for one of my little off-the-books takedowns, I spotted her making a beeline to score, and I had to stop her.

I distracted her with a kiss that was playing with fire, and I got hooked on the feel of her behind me on the Harley, her sleek thighs tight on mine, her breasts pressed against my back as she begged for motorcycle therapy. Truth was, it would have taken a saint to resist Pearl when she wanted something, and I've never been a saint.

Mom tries to take advantage of me being home to get me involved with tribal crap. She drags me to meetings where I endure the rhetoric and bickering, and afterwards, the set-ups she's engineered with this cousin's daughter's best friend or that auntie's stepdaughter. On the third of these "just wanted you to meet someone" attempts, I'm nice to the girl because it's not her fault, but I confront Mom in the car.

"I'm not dating anyone, Mom. My job."

"You won't be doing that job forever." Raven doesn't know

what it is, but she knows better than to ask. "And I want you settled."

"Mom." I'm driving the truck this time, and I squint at her. "Getting me settled isn't up to you. Because I won't settle. When I'm ready, when it's the right time, I'm going to be with someone I want to be with. Period."

"We have to preserve. . ."

"Like you did?" I can't believe she's harping on this, when my father was an American Samoan of mixed heritage she met while they were both in the Marines. She got pregnant; he died in a military accident. She's had a hard road raising me on her own, but I'm hardly a pureblood anything.

"It's because I did what I did that I want something different for you."

"Well, give it up. It turns me off on anyone you're throwing at me the minute I get that vibe."

She subsides, staring moodily out the window. We often don't get along, and I wonder if I should move to Boston proper as I've considered numerous times. I'd be out of her reach and that would be good.

But it would be hard to find a place where Whiskey could have the care and space he needs, and I like the solitude of the country and access to my training course.

I'm so irritated with Raven I don't say goodbye, just park the truck and jog into the house. Whiskey's waiting, and he senses my mood and watches eagerly as I change into my workout wear. Donning my backpack and running shoes, I head out into the forest with Whiskey at my side.

It's a distance from the house to the training ground I built, and we settle into a good run. I need to burn off the negativity that seems to attach to me whenever I slow down, and this afternoon's meeting, with its argumentative dickering over the plans for the tribe's new casino, counts as slow.

The girl Mom sat next to me was small, with a nice body. Nothing like Pearl. Nobody's like Pearl, and it's really not fair to other women to compare them. Her name began with an S. Sherry? Sheena? I shake my head. I don't give a crap what her name was.

I remembered to pick up some weights at the last minute as I hit the trail, and I've been pumping two twenty-pound dumbbells this whole time. Reaching the training area, I've finally broken a sweat. I set down the weights and swing off the backpack. Whiskey noses around the bases of the trees, lifting a leg and finding good smells.

He'd hate living in the city.

And I'd be closer to Pearl. That's not a good thing.

I tie Whiskey to a tree so I don't accidentally hit him while working the course. I screw silencers on my weapons—no sense drawing attention to what I'm doing out here.

The training area is set up over a square half-mile area. Obstacles. Targets. Different hazards. I open my backpack. I get on the various holsters and holders I need for throwing knives, ammo, arrow quiver, the rifle and sidearm. I even use a blowpipe sometimes. Nothing better for quiet disabling of a close target.

I drink some water. Do some stretches.

As I hoist the distance rifle to my shoulder, I feel that mindless calm descend, that place of detachment where I go. It's a peaceful place mentally, and I need that ever since she came and disrupted everything. In that place I'm alert, processing all the sensory input from around me, but not engaged with it.

Everything around me is either a target or an obstacle now.

I set the watch timer on my wrist and move off at a run, hitting my first challenge. Using a short length of rope, I scale the sheer trunk of a lodgepole pine whose branches I've stripped. Forty feet up I reach the tiny platform I built. I find my first rifle target. It takes me two shots to hit it. I don't do any better with arrows or sidearm, and I'm irritated by that.

I shinny down the tree. Sprint to the next obstacle, an old wall of barn siding I dragged out and erected. It takes me longer than usual to get over. I crawl under the logs on the other side that I've tunneled out. I take shots at the targets with sidearm, rifle, bow and throwing knives—from ground level, knee level, shoulder level, overhead.

Aim is off. It's been too long.

At the end of one round through the course, I do more stretches. Drink more water. I'm sweating, but just getting warmed up. I'll do better next time.

I run through it again.

And again.

And again.

It's getting dark when Whiskey and I finally trot back out of the woods. I feel better, because I got better. Still not up to top times, but close. The call could come any day. I have to be ready.

No, there's no room in my life for the complications a woman would bring. Especially this particular woman.

But I can't go into the narrow enclosure of my shower without thinking of her with her legs around my waist, up against the wall. Can't go to bed without remembering her there, that silver-cream hair everywhere. Can't look out my door without glancing down the road as if she's going to appear on her bike like something out of a motorcycle magazine fantasy.

I should never have brought her here.

CHAPTER TWENTY-NINE

Pearl

I'm sitting on a raised haircutting chair in front of a plain black drape. There's a spot on us, because Chad has decided to do a series of shots that will feature my haircut, and Francine's beautiful hands cutting it. The whole thing is also being filmed by a man hidden in the shadows. I can see the ruthless eye of that camera, tracking my every gesture and sniffle.

"You ready?" Francine asks. Her smile is kind, her eyes warm. I'm grateful for that.

"Let's do it." My voice is perfectly calm. I really am ready. I feel different, harder somehow. I was confused before, hurting from the revelations I'd had about myself, Dad's death, and my rape, but some part of me was still naive, hoping for love. Hoping to be rescued and healed somehow. By Magnus, if the truth be known.

Now I know that this is all there is. This life on the screen and the page, representing beauty to sell products. What does it matter what I look like doing that? It's all what others want and decide anyway. At least my hair is going to Locks of Love. Some poor cancer patient will get it and maybe feel better.

Even so, the shearing sound of the first deep snip Francine makes into the cape-like covering of hair gives me a shiver.

The hair falls like silver rain in the spotlight, and I hear the whir and click of the shutters recording the whole thing, and I stare into the dark middle distance and indulge in a memory of my time with Magnus.

Those first, overwhelming moments as I walked up to him. The way our mouths met, and he dropped the chainsaw he was holding. How he looked, stripping out of that lumberjack shirt. How he rose over me, his charcoal eyes on mine as he entered me so deeply we both gasped with the power of it.

It meant something to him, too. It had to. I hope he's suffering even a tenth as much as I am, the bastard.

I feel my eyes welling with the deep emotion I'm suppressing.

"You okay?" Francine's got all the hair cut off at my chin line.

"Sure. No problem." I blink the moisture away, knowing the cameras have caught my feeling and will be misinterpreting it as grief at losing my hair, when I really couldn't care less about that.

Francine's true to her word, and after cutting the major length and gathering it for the charity into a two-foot plume tied with a rubber band, she shears the rest of my head down to an even couple of inches. Just as she predicted, soft, silvery curls tighten up into ringlets against my head, freed from the pull of gravity.

Finally, she shakes out the drape, and I stand up.

I've dressed all in black to provide contrast with the spot and the white backdrop. I move to a prearranged area a few feet over without speaking, and strike a series of poses Chad and I worked out ahead of time.

The cameras click some more. I feel lighter without the hair, exposed, and the face I show the world is the new, no longer naïve me.

Stripped down. Shorn of girlish hopes. Bared to the essence of skin, bone, and flesh.

"Amazing," Chad finally says. I hear the triumph in his voice that tells me he got the shot. The movie camera moves off me, and Francine claps her hands. The lights come up, and Melissa's in the back, clapping too.

"Guess that went well," I say.

Francine hands me a handled mirror. "Check yourself out."

The makeup artist had done me up in black eyeliner, heavy mascara, a light foundation and scarlet lipstick, knowing a lot of the still photos would be in black and white. My face looks unfamiliar with the short halo of curls around it, but as I turn my face back and forth, I see that my eyes are enormous, my cheekbones sleek and hollow, my mouth a pillowy red promise.

"It's fine."

Melissa is smiling with satisfaction. "You were amazing. The whole thing was a performance, and you owned it. This is going to rocket you to the next level, Pearl."

Heading home on my bike, my helmet looser without all the hair, I wish I had someone to talk to. I forcefully turn my thoughts away from Magnus.

I call my sponsor, Valley, when I get home. It's past time I caught her up on everything. And when I do, she tells me to let him go. "He can't handle a girlfriend. Not with his job."

"I know. I'm trying, Valley."

Having this confirmed by a woman who's both my friend and Magnus's cousin feels like a nail driving into my heart. I'm breathless and broken with the pain of it, and that night I take three sleeping pills so I can't wake up and remember.

Magnus

The call comes early in the morning. Packing my gear bag, I wonder why it's always some ungodly hour when they call, but it is.

I phone Mom. "I'm on assignment. Can you take care of Whiskey?"

"Of course. How long?"

"A week or so."

"Stay safe." It's all she ever says. I hang up, and a few minutes later the big black truck arrives. I throw my bag in the back and get in.

Derrick is behind the wheel. He's in blue camo fatigues, which means it's somewhere near the water. That's how I know what kind of assignment it's going to be: Derrick's outfit. He serves as my eyes, ears, and support in the field.

"Hey. Why is it always so early when you guys call?"

"We're no respecter of time zones. You know that."

"What's the job?"

"The usual. Got a task file for you." He hands a folder over and pulls the truck around.

As we head to the private airstrip on the outskirts of Boston, I familiarize myself with the target. He's a Turkish businessman, five ten and a hundred and seventy pounds, balding, favors bling, white suits, and too-skimpy speedos for sunbathing. His skin is leathery and his grin, bleached.

The preliminary recon site is for his boat, a yacht where he's currently entertaining guests off the Turkish coast.

One of the pages details the target's ties to terrorists and how he uses his oil connections to fund training camps. I think management includes that to help me stay motivated, so I feel like I'm justified in doing what I do. The truth is, I no longer bother reading that section. I just need to know what the job is. The less I know, the better I sleep.

We get to the airstrip. The Learjet is already idling and in moments, we're in the air.

"You'll get a bonus on this one," Derrick says, handing me the blue fatigues that the strategy team decided were the thing to wear. "Anytime the hit's over water, you get that extra."

"Whatever." I don't bother going to the bathroom to change, just strip down and get into the fatigues.

"'You seem distracted. Got your head in the game?" Part of Derrick's job is to monitor me. I know he writes a report to management on my performance, does a risk assessment before and after every job. Our company, Efficiency Solutions, specializes in private-contract black-ops. I got my start as a military sniper and when my tour was up, I had so many kills Efficiency offered me the same job with less hours and quadruple pay. I've been working for them ever since.

"I'm fine." I don't need Derrick hassling me. The last job was a two-year stretch, and I know he's been worried about how I was handling it. I was embedded in the jungles of South America, working with the Sandinistas, training them, and taking out strategic targets there. "It's good to be getting back to work. There are only so many trees I can cut down on the property before Mom starts getting suspicious."

Derrick barks a laugh.

We settle into our seats for the ride. I spend the time reviewing the job specs, which are put together by a stateside analytic team. They've proposed a stealth approach by night. Derrick's going to get me as close to the yacht as he can, then

I'm going to go in in dive gear, get on the boat, find the target, and get off with no one the wiser.

I can think of a million ways this can go wrong, and the analytic team has thought of them, too. I've been provided with a dozen scenarios and specialty tools for it to go easier.

I shut the folder and recline my seat to get some shut-eye. But instead of reviewing the possible snags in my job, I find Pearl in my head. Walking up to me in those leathers, with that stomp. Hooking her arm around my neck and pulling me down for a kiss that felt like a detonation.

I end up having to get up and go to the gym area near the tail of the plane to go through a workout before I can finally relax for the few hours left to me before action.

CHAPTER THIRTY

Pearl

The PR stunt with my hair goes off perfectly. *Vogue* does a whole story on my transformation, featuring the stills from the haircut that Chad did and a touching follow-up about the cancer victims who get my hair with a picture of them wearing the two wigs made from my famous tresses. *Sixty Minutes* uses the film documentation shoot to do a short feature on famous people donating their hair for charity, and *People Magazine* interviews me on my bold move. Suddenly "Pearl" is one of those single names known worldwide.

The calls flood into the Melissa Agency, and all I do is work, work, work. Today I'm doing a runway show in Milan with the Big Six, now the Big Seven. Five of us are here for the show, and we have massive TV and worldwide coverage.

Milan has never been my favorite Italian city. Give me Venice, Rome, or Siena any day, over Milan with its heat and crowded streets. But, it's the fashion center of the country, and what does it really matter anyway, where I go, what I do, what I wear?

Odile pinches my waist before the show in that way she has. "Don't get too skinny. You need your tits and butt. That's what people are looking for from you." In her French accent, "tits and butt" sounds like "teets and boot" but I get the idea.

"Never thought I'd hear you say that."

"Never thought I'd have to." She pinches my cheek this time, an affectionate gesture. I can't believe we actually like each other after our bumpy start when we met on my first international shoot in Venice.

She's brought me a mug of thick Italian hot chocolate. "Drink the whole thing."

I'm sitting on the hairdresser's chair, and the woman's messing with my short cap of curls. "Not much to do with this," she says to Odile, but she's speaking Italian so I'm not entirely sure that's what she said.

"That's fine," Odile replies. "Finally you get a break with this one, right?" The hairdresser has worked on me before, and it's always taken hours with my ton of hair.

Neither of them know I've been studying Italian, one of my "get over Magnus" side projects. I listen to those Rosetta Stone tapes on my Walkman during my workouts, muttering phrases under my breath. I treasure my little secret, and it's already come in handy to understand what's going on around me.

Pretty soon, after a little arranging, patting, spraying and gluing a couple of curls accented with glitter onto my cheeks, I walk toward Makeup, wrapped in the silver robe the design house provides us in between wardrobe changes.

Out in the hall, I spot Brandon Forbes.

He's standing at the end of the hall, hands in his pockets. I'd forgotten how tall he is, and he's filled out in the two years since we had our little thing, brief as it was. He looks mature, every inch the young tycoon, and I find myself grinning, trotting down the hall to give him a hug. I'm happy to see him, I realize, and the tingle I feel as he puts his arms around me is so good after the chill I've felt in my bones since that morning I left Magnus's cabin.

"Melissa sent me over on business," he says, putting his mouth close to my ear but not touching, and careful not to disturb my hair. "I wanted to see the new look myself."

I pull back, look up into his golden-hazel eyes. "And?"

"I never thought I'd agree, because I loved your hair... But Melissa was right." He touches my cheek, and his eyes are warm with admiration. "You're so beautiful that you don't need it."

"Yeah, yeah. I have to run, but—can we get together after the show?"

He cocks his head. "I thought there was someone else."

"Not anymore." I swallow down my inner resistance to spending time with any man but Magnus. I have to get over him. *I have to.*

"In that case, I'll be in the front row—the guy drooling so bad they have to put a bucket out."

I laugh, and turn into Makeup with my spirits lifted.

The show goes well. I go to that place, a mysterious half-smile on my face, ignoring the murmuring over the disappearance of my famous hair and the appearance of my cheekbones. Sway and stomp, sway and stomp. Spin. Pause. Spin. Pause. Sway and stomp back. Wardrobe change, hot and hurried in the crowded changing room. Sway and stomp again, spin. Pause. Spin. Pause. Sway and stomp back. And again, and again, until finally all the outfits have been displayed, and then the row of us, five of the Big Seven for this show, get out on stage and, holding hands, bow.

My vision is burned by flashes; my ears ring from applause.

At last I'm creaming the glitter and goo off my face and

getting into my black turtleneck and jeans and heading out into the after-party chaos, looking for Brandon.

He finds me, takes my hand, and we duck around the cluster of photographers interviewing the designer and the gaggle of models and journalists around Melissa. Brandon pushes open the side door. Laughing like teenagers, we run down the cobblestoned alley to the brighter main street.

"What do you want to do?" he asks me.

"This reminds me of Venice," I tell him. "I really liked Venice."

"I did too." He bends his head and kisses me.

I let him. I shut my eyes and try to like it.

I'm aware, so aware, that he's already in love with me. For him, this is the incredible moment that he's been waiting for. I feel it in the tension of his body, the heavy thudding of his heart against mine, the fervor of his mouth. It scares me, because I'm going to hurt him. I don't feel the same. I can't feel the same.

I detach, gently. "I'm sorry, Brandon."

"Why?" He frowns, and I see the pain dawning. I hate that I'm hurting him.

"This isn't going to go anywhere. I'm sorry." I wrench away and hurry back down the alley. I cry for both of us as I go back into the building. He deserves someone who can love him back, and I wish it could have been me.

Magnus

Derrick and I walk through the airport in Turkey after the op. We've mailed the gear bag ahead of time, to avoid declaring the weapons. Even though we have the Learjet, the airport makes us go through the Customs process. I'm wearing the fancy white suit and headdress Derrick gave me for this leg of the op, complete with a fake Rolex and my hair in a ponytail with gold clip, imitating some Middle Eastern sheikh. Derrick is doubling as my driver and general manservant, and I'm not above playing it up a bit.

"Get me something to read," I say, pausing at a newsstand. My eyes scan the American offerings, and I feel a jolt as I recognize Pearl's face on the cover of *Vogue*.

I point to the magazine. "That one. And the sports magazine, too."

Derrick rolls his eyes but goes in and buys it. He carries the paper bag under his arm as we get through the rigmarole in Customs, and eventually walk across the hot tarmac to the plane. Once inside, he slaps the bag into my chest.

"*Vogue*, huh?"

I don't say anything, because what can I say? I slept with the woman on the cover? Who would believe it, and even if he did, I'm sure Derrick and the company would shut us down as a security risk. That's why I shut it down myself, already.

I go to the back room, change into my usual shirt, jeans, and boots. We take off, sitting in the deep, buttery leather seats. Derrick busies himself with the usual post-op reports, and, settling back, I finally open the Vogue magazine.

"Didn't know you were a metrosexual," Derrick says.

"Broadening my horizons." I thumb to the spread on Pearl.

She got a haircut, and made an event out of it.

I feel a tight sensation in my chest as I look at the stunning photos of the whole process in arty black and white: the black woman's hands holding the silvery scissors, her hands contrasting like carved ebony against that moonbeam hair as it falls to the ground in great drifting chunks. Pearl's face is a remote, empty sculpture gazing somewhere and nowhere, her cheekbones stark, eyes enormous, and mouth sad and sexy at the same time.

One photo is shot straight on. Her hair is snipped off level with her ears, a shiny curling helmet. Her incredible eyes are brimming with tears. Deep emotion reaches out to me from the pages, grief and pain beyond beauty. Looking into those wide, shadowed eyes, I know she's thinking about *me* in that photo. The death of dreams on her face is because I killed them.

"Fuck!" I crumple the photo, ripping the pages out of the magazine, stuffing them in my pocket. I fumble with the buckle and shoot up out of my chair.

"What?" Derrick's thick blond brows draw together as he looks up from the portable computer console at this outburst.

"Nothing." I head to the gym at the back of the plane. I don't bother to change, just throw a bunch of weights on the bar and lie down on the bench, hefting at top speed with animalistic grunts. I've got too much weight on the bar, and I know it, but only working until I can't anymore is going to help this.

Because it hurts me to have hurt her, damn it.

Derrick holds a hand above and blocks me, and I can't push the heavily-weighted bar past him. "What the hell's going on with you, Mag?"

He's the only person in the world who gets to call me that. "Mind your own damn business," I snarl, and he pushes the bar down across my chest. I can't lift it, and it's compressing my lungs.

"You're my business," he says calmly, and pushes down harder on the bar.

I huff out a breath and push up, but seriously there's more than three hundred pounds on this bar plus the force of him pushing down. I can't get it off, and I can't breathe. I see stars and black dots.

Finally, Derrick hefts the weight bar off me and throws it into the cradle with a crash.

"It has to be a woman. Whenever a man's this fucked-up, it's always a woman," Derrick says as blessed air fills my lungs. "Who is she, Mag?"

"No one you need to know about. It's over."

"So that's why you're so miserable."

"I'm not miserable. I did the job. Everything's fine." And I did do the job. Not a hitch. Slid off the fishing boat that Derrick drove to the coordinates. Used a scuba transport to get to the anchored yacht. Climbed up the side in the dark, in my black wetsuit. Disabled the guard with a blow dart. Snuck inside, darted the chick sleeping in bed with the rich terrorist Turkish dude, and then took him out with a silencer and a pillow. Left the way I came.

No fuss, no muss.

I admit I was on autopilot the whole time. I never enjoy what I do, but the danger aspect of it is usually an adrenaline rush. This time, nothing. I felt like I was flogging myself through my obstacle course at home, but removed from the whole thing as if watching it under glass.

"Whatever you need to tell yourself, man. But I don't like it." Derrick stood up. "I'm going to find out about this woman, do a threat assessment. Or you can tell me, and I'll do a threat assessment."

"Screw you." I'm not telling him one thing about Pearl, and with any luck at all, he won't be able to find out anything.

I lift the weight bar out of the cradle and pump it some more. Derrick shakes his head, spins on his heel and leaves.

I pump until I can't anymore, and finally throw the bar back in the cradle. I lock it down with the in-flight safety straps and go to the rack mounted on the wall. Turn my back to the wall, rest my arms on the handles, and lift my legs straight out to waist height, and lower them.

I feel her fingers, cool and light, tracing the lines that run down my abs to my pelvis. "Visual poetry," she said at one point, and put her lips where her fingers had been.

I mutter a curse, turn my back and lift myself by my arms, crossing my dangling legs as I push my body weight up and down between the bars, my back flexing.

I hurt her. I hurt her so bad she let them cut all her hair off. And she's getting skinny, like all those other stick-thin models giving women complexes.

I hate the new look. The haircut everyone praises makes Pearl look like an orphan, vulnerable and too young—but too old at the same time.

I wonder if she's been tempted, if she's had a slip into using. I need to call Valley when we get back to check on how she's doing.

Until then, nothing will do but that I hurt too, just as much.

CHAPTER THIRTY-ONE

Pearl

Dubai is a freaky place. The air is so dry my hair goes flat instantly the minute I get off the plane, even in the sleek, luxurious airport. Out the window, heat shimmers over the desert in the distance. I'm staying in one of the luxury hotels built on artificial reefs out in the smooth aquamarine water of the Persian Gulf.

The sand has been tamed with oil money into luxe oases of palaces and homes, discreetly fortified behind white stone barriers and walls. I'm whisked by Odile and our stylists, along with the other models, to the crazy-high skyscraper where we're staying until the show.

The elevator is glass and on the outside of a building that really has no business being so tall. I'm fortunate not to be afraid of heights, but as we zoom into the stratosphere, several of the girls are clutching each other with their eyes on the door. I'm plastered against the glass, taking in the sight of the city: a green and glossy jewel set in the gold of the desert, the blue Gulf glittering against the land in stark contrast.

We're here for an international show of seven designers, and Odile is exuberant. "These Arabs have beaucoup money," she tells me as she slides a keycard into the door and lets me and Naomi into our palatial room. "They're bringing their wives and girlfriends to shop."

"As long as they don't plan on adding us to a harem or something, I'm down with it," Naomi says, taking off the platforms she loves to wear and flopping back on one of the satin-covered beds. "I need a nap."

"Great idea," I say, unwinding the laces of a pair of Louboutins from my ankles. They make my legs look great, but hurt my feet.

"You ladies do that. I'll send up the facialist in an hour or two. Tomorrow it's work, work, work all day, so today you need to exercise, rest, hydrate, and get your skin acclimated to the desert air."

"Odile, you have a way of making even a facial sound like work," I say. "I don't see when we're going to actually be exposed to any of that desert air." I walk over and look out the vast plate-glass window over the stark line of where the sea meets the desert at the edge of the city. We are on a palm-shaped, manmade extension into the Gulf, and I can see fantastical gardens, gleaming white yachts, and even an extreme-looking water park from this vantage point. Exciting as it looks, we've been on planes for twelve hours, and I feel my eyes getting heavy. "Anyway, I think I will lie down for a few minutes."

"Sweet dreams." Odile dims the light and as I stretch out on the other bed, she tucks the satin cover under my chin as if putting a toddler down for a nap. As I close my eyes I know I'm going to dream of Magnus again.

Damn that man...

Magnus

I've barely been home a couple of days when Derrick contacts me with the next job. "Pickup at oh-eight hundred," he says. "Plan for a week."

"Roger that." I call Mom about Whiskey. "Going out again."

"You were barely home. That dog mopes when you're gone," she complains.

I glance down at Whiskey, draped over my feet. He looks back up at me, his brown eyes sad. "Nature of the beast."

I hang up, not sure if I'm referring to "the beast" as my work, or Whiskey. Either way, I don't mind the hectic pace Derrick has me on. The busier I am, the less time I have to think about Pearl.

I clean my weapons carefully with rags infused with gun oil. I hope it's a distance mission this time. I can still see the pouf of feathers exploding from the pillow over the Turkish magnate's face, his girlfriend sleeping beside him, the red tuft of the dart protruding from her neck.

The flashbacks will fade after awhile, replaced by memories from this next job.

The post op debrief with Efficiency Solutions' psychologist, Dr. Barrett, was accompanied by the light bar used in Eye Movement Desensitization and Reprocessing. Best practice for post-traumatic stress, Efficiency Solutions rolls both an EMDR treatment and the op debrief into one session. Why wait for me to get PTSD from the job when they can do both at once?

I hate to admit it, but the sessions seem to help. I have fewer bad dreams the sooner they're held after a mission. Still. I've begun to have the feeling that my kills are impressed on me. It's as if the memories are stylus marks on wax, made through plastic. While the plastic can be ripped up and re-laid, the surface appearing unmarked, underneath the wax has been scored again and again and is a mogul field of gouges.

One day I won't be able to register any new impressions, and I wonder what will happen then.

CHAPTER THIRTY-TWO

Pearl

In the morning at the hotel, we rehearse the lineup and wardrobe changes. The show is going to be in a huge ballroom on a raised stage. The theme is springtime fantasy, and I find myself almost looking forward to the amazing hair and makeup the designers have planned. Tonight's going to be a big night.

After we're done with morning rehearsal, several of us, along with Odile, go shopping. I'm not a shopper usually, but it's a chance to see the opulent, completely enclosed mall attached to the hotel.

Striding along in a group with the other models, I feel more like a giraffe than ever. In our heels, we dwarf the Arab women, some covered in traditional garb, but many dressed in Western fashions. Everywhere we go, people stare.

I ignore it. *Just an idea of me, not really me.*

After the shopping, Naomi and I take a little rest in the darkened room with cucumber slices on our eyes—and then it's show time.

We meet the other models in the big, well-lit dressing area.

Pre-show music is playing to get everyone's energy up, and I feel the excitement bubbling. This is only my second big runway show since the haircut, and I am very aware of the feel of the air conditioning on my unprotected neck. The hairdresser has an idea to make me look like a dandelion, which sounds awful—but as usual, I have no say in the matter.

Still, by the time she's done coloring my short hair to a pale silver-blonde, has dried and styled and sprayed it so that every strand stands up in a nimbus around my head, I change my mind. With the heavy eye makeup and shell-pink lipstick they put on me, I embody otherworldly spring.

They strip me down, airbrush me with a white base, and then apply opalescent body glitter to every inch of my skin with an artist's brush. Standing in a tiny g-string and no bra, I'm surrounded by an ebb and flow of people. My almost-nudity doesn't bother me after so many times prepping in front of others.

The stylist hands me the first of the outfits and gets me carefully into it so as not to disturb the body glitter or my fragile hair creation, and when she's patted and adjusted and pinned to her satisfaction, she puts me in line to go onstage.

I'm third up from the lead. I can hear the swishing conversation of the crowd intertwined with the thumping techno music they're using to set the mood.

The music stops, the designers go out, are applauded, and say a few words. Models keep lining up behind me, three deep. My heart rate ratchets up as I mentally practice my runway walk, fiddling with one of the many tiny silver tassels swinging off of the outfit, a minidress they've paired with a pair of sky-high clear plastic platform heels.

And finally, the cue light goes off. The first woman walks out, and I hear the swell of the applause and exclamations, and when she's halfway down the runway the little red light signals the woman in front of me, and a minute later it pulses red for me. I step out, taking great stomping strides, giving a little extra oomph in the hip swing so the tassels catch the light with their movement.

I'm blinded by the lights in my eyes but I can see the silhouette of the woman in front of me, and I can feel my heart pounding as I move, and I walk to the heavy techno beat, keeping my gaze on the remote black of the middle distance, a little smile on my mouth that says I'm indulging in some naughty fantasy.

And when I reach the little dais at the end I spin and pause, spin and pause, and I hear the murmurs of awe, different reactions to my hair, an undercurrent of comment. Possessed by an impulse, I lift my arms overhead and twirl, not an easy move on these platforms, to a roar of applause and the bursting strobe of flashbulbs.

I step off the dais and head back for the next wardrobe change, feeling the adoration of the crowd lift and carry me.

Magnus

My mouth has gone completely dry and my heart stutters in my chest. The model on the runway steps up onto the dais and spins twice, silver tassels all over her skimpy dress swinging like a thousand fishing lures. Suddenly she shoots her arms up and swings them wide, tipping back her dandelion-head of pale blonde hair and spinning on crazy see-through heels like a little girl all alone in a field of flowers.

It's Pearl.

I recognize her body language, that physical joy she so easily projects, that sexy abandon with its hint of innocence gone wrong.

What the hell is Pearl doing here? I thought she only did magazine work. My brain just doesn't want to compute what I'm seeing.

I didn't recognize her at first because my eye has been looking through the scope at the target, a traditionally-dressed sheikh in flowing robes in a back row, a concubine on either side of him. We don't usually work targets in public venues like this, but this man is so elusive that this is one of his first appearances outside of his heavily-armed compound in years. Apparently he's backed one of the young Arab designers participating in the show, and wanted to show his support by appearing publicly.

I'm up in one of the ventilation shafts in the ceiling, the metal panel nudged aside to accommodate my weapon. Getting in here was a project, and getting back out won't be easy either. Crawling in a freezing metal ventilation tunnel wearing a tux and carrying a sniper rifle—not high on my list of favorite activities. At least I'm not out in the open of the hot sandy desert.

My earbud crackles with Derrick's voice. "Take the shot. Crowd is distracted."

I don't want to take the shot.

I know what will happen when I take the shot. When the concubines realize the sheikh has been hit, which will hopefully not be immediately, the hue and cry will set off a panic. Everyone will run. People could be trampled, including beauties wearing ridiculously sky-high heels.

But maybe if Pearl's backstage when it goes down, she'll be okay. I'll have to check on her regardless. I know that's a bad idea, but I have to. I can't leave without seeing her, somehow.

I refocus on the target.

The chair's empty. *He's gone.*

"Why didn't you take the shot? He's gone to the restroom." Derrick's voice is impatient.

"Doing my own threat assessment."

"That's what you have me for."

I don't reply. I've got my scope on the empty chair. I won't look at the models streaming along the stage anymore. I can't afford to.

Finally, the terrorist comes back. Sits down. Adjusts his robes. Reaches over to pat one of the women beside him. Both women are excited, talking and gesturing. I don't like watching that. It reminds me this is a man whose loss is going to bring grief and shock. Never mind what a monster he is, at least according to the file.

I look away to check on Pearl and make sure she's still backstage.

She isn't. She's in a different outfit, halfway down the stage. It's a drifty, gauzy thing, with iridescent panels that hang down like petals to brush her amazing legs. She's wearing yellow heels this time, and I realize she looks like a lily. That's probably the plan.

At the dais, she does the usual spin and pause, then a low, graceful curtsy, the skirt-petals lifted high to showcase her legs. The crowd goes wild. She's playing this up, and the kiss she blows to the room feels like it hits me alone, a warm reminder of all we shared.

"Dammit," I mutter, and refocus on the target.

"Get your head in the game!" Derrick hisses in my ear, and I take the shot.

CHAPTER THIRTY-THREE

Pearl

I hear screams break out behind me, and I whirl around, catching one of the crazy-high yellow heels on the floor and stumbling. I can see what's happening out there now that I'm out of the hot spotlights. An Arab man in white robes has collapsed, and people are hunching over him. There's a spreading red stain on his chest.

The lights come up, the music stops, and the entourage around the man is lifting him and carrying him away amid the screams of his female companions. People are standing up, milling around, looking uncertain.

Suddenly I realize that's not the only thing going on. Several men dressed in black are backstage with us, and they're grabbing the models. Cries break out as the women fight back and try to run away. The chaos happening around me translates to the audience around the stage, and full panic sets in as people knock over chairs, rushing for the exits, screams filling the air.

I dive into the darkness between the heavy black curtains

that separate the stage from the audience area. Whatever is going on is not good. I need to stay hidden and be able to *move*.

I squat down to hide between the dark draperies, unbuckling the tiny straps of the ridiculous shoes—and just as I've got them off, a hand grabs my arm, yanking me upright.

The man's face is masked, and he's all in black. He says something in Arabic as he hauls me up against him. He smells of garlic and body odor. I try to remember my self-defense skills, and elbow him and stomp his foot—but he's wearing boots. My feet are bare, and my struggles don't seem to do anything. He yells something and an accomplice appears. He has a black cloth hood in his hand, which he stuffs over my head, tightening it around my neck with a cord.

I scream then, really let rip with everything I've got as full-blown panic sets in—this is like the attack in Boston where I got mugged, only so much worse. I thrash wildly, flinging myself around, desperate to get away. One of the men smacks me in the head, hard enough to see stars, and now I'm dizzy, my ears ringing, unable to get enough air as they quickly secure my hands behind my back with a zip tie and, still yelling at me in Arabic, one of them hauls me out of my hiding place by the arms.

Rendered blind, desperately sucking for air inside the hood, I have no choice but to stumble after my captor.

I try to calm my breathing because I'm not getting enough oxygen. The fabric of the hood is not only blinding, it's stifling. I try to figure out where I am, but he's practically carrying me along, my bare feet stumbling and scraping as we go down stairs. The blackness all around me is filled with the chaos of screaming, the thunder of running feet.

I can't make it easy for this guy. Wherever I'm going can't be good. I go totally limp, buckle my knees, and collapse. He hits me in the head again, yelling at me, pulling on my arms, but now I'm dead weight. *I refuse to make this easy.* His accomplice grabs my other arm. They're dragging me now, but I'm making them work for it, sliding my feet and trying to slow them down.

I don't scream any more. It's a waste of breath I need.

Suddenly, close by, the sound of gunfire. One of my captors jerks and lets go of me. I throw myself forward so that the other one has to let go too. This wrenches my arm out of his hands, but I have no way to break my fall. My shoulder takes the brunt, wringing a groan out of me as my forehead cracks down on the ground right behind it.

Blam! Blam! Blam!

Gunfire, right over my head. I'm so dizzy and breathless inside the hood. And then, horribly, I feel someone fall on me. He's heavy, and smells of body odor, garlic, and the iron tang of blood. He's smothering me. I writhe, my arms crushed behind my back beneath him. I get a knee up, forcing a little room so that my laboring lungs can draw a breath inside the hood. I just have to breathe, and not panic.

Breathe.

Breathe.

But spots are closing in around me, and then darkness.

Magnus

It's all gone to shit, and I think I might have killed her.

There's nothing in the hall but the two fallen masked kidnappers, and one of them crashed down right on top of Pearl. I don't think I hit her when I was firing, but as I heave the body off her, she's face down, hands bound behind her back, not moving. There's a hood on her head, and she's barefoot. I only know it's her by the silly flower dress she's wearing.

Oh God.

227

I yank at the hood on her head but it's tied on tight. I pull my knife and slash the cord, ripping it off.

Pearl's totally pale, her eyes closed—but I remember she was painted white with that opalescent glitter stuff, so there's no way to tell anything. I hear running feet and more gunfire, so I can't take time to see if she's okay right here. I scoop her up, throwing her over my shoulder in a fireman's carry, and run down the hall toward the exit.

I'm supposed to rendezvous with Derrick in the op van outside the building—but if I take her there, our security is blown. *That's if she's even alive.*

I refuse to imagine that she's not alive.

I get to the emergency exit, push the bar, and maneuver her body out the door into the alley. It's hot and airless out here even after dark, and I remember I'm in Dubai and it's still desert, even at night. Looking around, the van's nowhere in sight. I remember I'm supposed to meet the van on the other side of the building.

"Black Two, this is Black One. In alley on north side of building."

"Roger that. Coming to your location." Derrick's voice crackles in my earbud. I've been keeping him updated—all except the little detail of rescuing Pearl.

I move over against the wall, behind the door in case anyone exits behind me. I can hear the hotel's alarm systems going off deep inside the shiny steel structure. Police are coming with their high-pitched, foreign-sounding sirens. This crisis will be over shortly, and it's imperative that I'm not caught up in it.

I squat carefully and lower Pearl to the ground, lying her down on her back. She's coming around, her eyelids fluttering— but that's when the steel exit door bangs open as someone else runs out. It's one of the kidnappers, and he's tugging another hooded model by the arm. He sees me and goes for his weapon, but I get him first.

He drops. The woman is standing there, screaming her head off inside her black hood. I jump up and haul her over next to Pearl, pushing her back against the wall.

"You're safe, now," I say. "Sit down, you'll be okay." I guide the woman, now sobbing, her hands still bound behind her back, into a seated position against the wall. I turn back to Pearl to check on her. Her eyes are open, fastened on my face, wide with shock.

"Oh my God," she whispers. "What are you doing here?"

"Shh." I draw her up against me for precious seconds, squeezing her hard. I know I stink of adrenaline and the terror of her coming to harm, but even with her hands bound, she leans into me, shivering uncontrollably. "You're safe now. Help is on the way."

I hear a screech—it's the op van turning into the alley.

"I have to cover you up. But you'll be okay now. Don't tell anyone you saw me. I'll explain later." I pull the hood out of my back pocket.

Pearl shakes her head wildly. "No! No!" she cries, but I can't let my team know she's seen me, and I put the hood over her head in spite of her struggles. The van screeches to a halt and the door bangs back.

"Get in!" Derrick yells.

I lean close to Pearl as I move her back against the wall, as gentle as I can be, but she's still yelling, "No!" and trying to thrash the hood off. I don't blame her a bit. I know she'll get it off in a minute. I just need to get away while she still has it on.

"Shhh," I say again, close to her ear. "Help's on the way. I'll see you on the other side."

"Get in!" Derrick yells again, from the driver's seat of the van. "What the hell are you waiting for? An engraved invitation?"

I stand up and do the hardest thing I've ever done—I leap into the van and slam the door. The vehicle peels away so fast I'm thrown backwards, but I grab the seat and haul myself into it.

"Why were you talking to that woman?" Derrick says.

"I just told her help was on the way." I throw on the safety belt and then begin my post-op check, going over my weapons and the items on my body for anything lost, standard procedure after a mission. The distance rifle I left in position after the shoot, per the op specs when the plan was for me to come out in a tux and blend.

That was before the kidnappers ambushed the show and I had to shoot three of them.

"Why did you get involved, dammit? You had a mission, and getting out clean is part of that."

"Those poor women were getting grabbed. What the hell, with that going on right during our op? Why didn't you know about it?"

"Pure screwed-up coincidence. We had no intel."

"Got any idea who was grabbing those girls? They were speaking Arabic."

"Probably either kidnappers grabbing them for ransom, or sex slavers."

"Seriously. Sex slavers?"

"You got a better idea?"

I didn't. I did know that Pearl was worth money as a kidnap victim. Her brother-in-law was loaded, and her sister Ruby would have made sure they paid. But what about the other women? And why in the middle of a show? "We should find out what's going on."

"Quite frankly, not our problem. What is our problem is

getting you out of here, without some model describing you after the sheikh was shot."

"They didn't see anything. But, I did take out three of the guys."

"That means you left trace. Slugs from your sidearm."

"Whatever." I shoot the clip out of the Glock .40 I carry. Only one round left. The Glock's a reliable gun, and so common it's like carrying a Bic lighter. Of course it's unregistered, serial number filed off, clean of any use, and my fingerprints are masked by a silicone coating better than gloves. I check my pockets and vest—all weapons and ammo accounted for.

The van weaves onto the highway as we head for the airport. I know I've got a lot of post-op debrief to get through even if we make it off the ground without being stopped—but all I can think about is Pearl, sitting bound and vulnerable in the alley without me.

CHAPTER THIRTY-FOUR

Pearl

It feels like forever, but I'm pretty sure it only takes a few minutes for me to get the hood with its broken drawstring off my head. By then Magnus is long gone. The model next to me is still sobbing, and the warm Dubai darkness is lit by a few yellow security lights throwing light into the alley.

Now that I can breathe, I'm aware of all of my aches and pains-- my wrenched shoulder, my hands, bound too tightly and so painful. I hear sirens getting closer and closer, and then a small, bright yellow police vehicle, light whirling atop its roof, screeches into the alley.

I don't have time to think about Magnus. What he was doing here, why he didn't take me with him, where he was going.

I need to get out of the bindings that are cutting off the circulation in my hands. I stagger to my feet, yelling for help.

It's hours later, and Odile slides the key into the door of my hotel room. She's solicitous, fussing over me, and behind us is the hulking shadow of the bodyguard the Melissa Agency has assigned to Naomi and me until we fly out tomorrow. The bodyguard pushes forward as she unlocks the door. He's big and brown with buzz-cut hair and one of those curly cords stuck into his ear.

"Need to check that the room's clear." He goes in ahead with his weapon, a sight that would have made me nervous just a day ago—but now, after what I've been through, it's just reassuring.

"Clear."

"Stay outside in the hall," Odile tells him. "We fly out in the morning."

He nods, and I go in and head straight for the bathroom.

I can't wait to get in the shower, get the caked-on makeup and blood spatter off me. Because I'm decorated with a fine spray of it along with a heavy smear that pooled on my back from the body. All that helped corroborate my story, which is the truth. A mysterious rescuer shot my kidnappers and took me outside. A few minutes later, he shot the man holding Bella, the model rescued with me. Escaped before I could get a look at him.

"Who was this man?" the translator must have asked me a hundred times. I said the same thing, over and over.

"I have no idea. He was strong enough to carry me outside, and he spoke to me in Arabic. I don't know what he said but I can tell he was trying to reassure me I'd be safe."

"How did you get the hood off?"

"I didn't. He took it off me, I think to see if I was alive because I passed out under the body. I was smothering."

"So how is it that you didn't see him, with the hood off?"

"He put it back on as soon as he saw I was coming around. I

never saw anything. After I heard his getaway car leave, I moved around until I could get the hood off."

I told the tale over and over. When I asked for a lawyer, they just stared at me with hard brown eyes. But finally a lawyer arrived anyway, hired by Melissa, and eventually they had to let me and the other models go.

Now I turn my face up under the wide, gentle, rain-like shower head and let the water cleanse me. I hear a rustle outside.

"It's Odile. I'm taking your clothing for the police. They asked for them as evidence."

"Whatever." I hope Magnus didn't leave anything behind, a hair clinging to my dress or a drop of his own blood—but in the chaos and the filth of the alley, how could anything trace back to him?

And why am I so intent on protecting him? What was he doing there, dressed in a black tux, shooting our attackers without batting an eye? He was as scary as one of the kidnappers, if better dressed.

But I trust him with my life.

I let myself remember all I can of the rescue, trying to puzzle out what his role could be. I'd woken up lying on my back on the cement in the alley, my arms still bound beneath me, and as I came to consciousness I was looking at Magnus, partly turned away from me but his body still protectively over mine, his eyes trained on someone in the alley. I saw the gun in his hand, the same one I'd found in the small of his back that time we'd kissed in the barn. He moved and fired, so fast it was a blur.

The report was deafening and the expended shell flew past me and tinkled on the ground. Lifting my head, I saw the kidnapper fall, heard the woman wearing a hood screaming. Only then did Magnus leap up, go to her, settle her beside me,

TOBY JANE

and finally turn back to check on me. I knew when he hauled me tight against him, our hearts pounding against each other in a kind of wordless desperation, that I meant something to him. Something more than he wanted me to mean. Whatever he was mixed up in was really dangerous.

I shut my eyes under the water and let myself savor the feeling of being held so close my breath was squeezed out of my lungs. I loved that memory—so much more than his hurried words telling me to be quiet, not to identify him. Then the moment that he put the hated hood back over my head. But I know that I wasn't supposed to have seen him. It was dangerous for me to have seen him.

I use soft creamy soap and a washcloth to scrub all the body paint off. Back out in the room, the lights are dimmed but Odile is making up the trundle bed. Naomi's already a humped shape, turned away from the light.

"I'm sleeping in here tonight," Odile says.

"Thanks. So do you know anything about our attackers?"

"I kept asking the police. They wouldn't tell me anything, but Mr. Singh, the lawyer Melissa hired, says they were taking you hostage. Those of you who could pay ransom they'd take that, and anyone that couldn't pay was going to be sold."

"Sold? Like a slave?"

"Yes." Her nod is an abrupt movement. My stomach lurches. Thank God Magnus came when he had. "Who was that man that rescued you and Bella? What was he doing here?"

"Like I told the police a hundred times, I have no idea." I dried the short fluff of my hair with a towel. "But thank God he got us away."

"Yeah. They took three other girls. We're working with Interpol on their ransoms. I'm not supposed to say anything to you, but I thought you should know."

"Thanks." I slide into my sleep tee, and even though I'm a-jangle with exhaustion, I know sleep is a long way away.

"Besides the private detail Melissa hired, Interpol has agents deployed all around the hotel," Odile said. "You're safe."

"I won't feel safe until I'm back in the ol' U S of A," I say, getting into bed. "Do you happen to have a sleeping pill?"

"I already gave one to Naomi. You can see they work," Odile smiles, and hands me a yellow capsule along with a carafe of water.

"So what did that sheikh getting shot have to do with the kidnappings?" I ask.

"What sheikh getting shot?"

I tell her what I saw just before the attack on the models.

"I don't know anything about that. Maybe you were in shock." She's tucking herself into the trundle bed beside me, clearly done talking.

"Maybe," I murmur. It's not worth debating. That pill really does work, because a few minutes later, darkness pulls me under.

The trip back to the States is anticlimactic once we reach the airport the next day, heavily guarded until we get onto the Emirates Air jet and take up the entire first class. I sleep most of the time, and arrive in New York feeling feisty—at least, that's the word that comes to mind to describe how I'm eager to get on my Harley and drive out to Magnus's place and demand he tell me what the hell's going on. What was he doing there, so conveniently? Our kidnapping attack is all over the international news I watch on the flight and on the internet, but I can't find one word about the sheikh whose blood I know I saw.

It's almost like the chaos and drama of our attack covered up the sheikh's death. Forty-eight hours have gone by since the three models that were nabbed were rescued, after their ransoms were paid.

Odile informs me that I have a meeting arranged with my psychologist, Dr. Rosenfeld. "Your sister set it up. Don't worry, Melissa's paying for any trauma counseling you need after this incident."

"I don't need counseling," I snort. "I need to pack a gun from now on. Good thing counseling is already arranged." She forwards a memo to my phone.

"We'll see." I'm planning to be talking to Magnus Thorne tomorrow, and hopefully getting some answers.

It's late the next morning before I'm able to get out of the house and Ruby's worried hovering, with the excuse that I have to go to Dr. Rosenfeld's. But before I leave, I pack my backpack with a couple of changes of clothes and don my sexiest lingerie, the black G-string and demi-bra set.

I plan on going to Magnus's place. I'm hoping to have tons of sex and get some answers. That'll help me sleep better than any amount of therapy or sleeping pills.

CHAPTER THIRTY-FIVE

Magnus

It's two days after the op and I drive my bike out of the private airstrip outside Boston toward home. I feel a sort of bone-deep weariness that's more than physical.

I've been debriefed about my actions during the op at length. First, by Derrick, then by management, who put me on furlough while they wait for the shit to die down and see if I've compromised the company with my "reckless sentimentalism."

Screw 'em all.

I've just added four more bodies to a count I prefer not to keep. Pearl or no Pearl, I'm feeling brittle. One more stress and I'm going to need to stop by that woman with the knitting bag that I staked out on the Common so long ago. Getting high will only be the beginning if I go off that cliff. I'm hanging onto clean and sober by my fingernails right now—and if I slip, it'll be the end of the line for me.

Even the wind, the freedom of the bike and the road as I leave all the bureaucracy shit behind, isn't enough to blow the funk out of my brain.

I'm a killer. I can call it being a patriot, a soldier. I can justify it and dress it up like I've been doing for years, but the truth remains. I go out and kill people for mission and for money. Hopefully the dogs I put down are people who deserve it, but I haven't made sure of that.

Looking into Pearl's eyes as she lay on the ground in the alley, seeing the trust there, and the questions too—I know I'm going to have to tell her something. I have no idea what.

More lies and dishonesty, probably. I'm just a blunt instrument for the company, not even a government employee since they don't want to be associated with the dirty work I do for them.

At least Derrick waited until we were in private on the Lear and safely leaving Gulf airspace to tell me he knew about Pearl.

"That model you rescued. I bet it was Pearl Michaels, that chick you've got a hard-on for in Vogue." Derrick wagged a finger at me, disguising anger with fake humor. Open space in the living area of the Learjet separated us by a foldable table and a stretch of carpet. I still had the belt on from takeoff, but I'm straining against it reflexively at Derrick's words. "Don't look at me, your oldest friend and partner, like you want to kill me. What did you think? That I couldn't buy a Vogue magazine, track the pages you ripped out, find out where she lives and that she goes to your favorite twelve-step meeting? You forget who I am." There's steel in Derrick's voice as he lays down his beef with me. "You compromised the mission for a piece of ass, Mag."

"She's not a piece of ass." My arms are twitching with desire to inflict bodily injury. "And she's not in my life. I already made sure of that."

"Maybe not, but you've still got an itch for her. Not that I wouldn't be tempted, too. She's an extra *fine* piece of ass."

I throw the belt off and launch myself at Derrick, but he's ready. Even as we roll around the open carpet thumping each other, I know he's baited me deliberately to find out what she means to me—and I've fallen for it. I've never been much of a poker player, but knowing Derrick has manipulated me into attacking him gives me the extra I need to get in a punch to his face.

"Dammit!" Derrick yells as blood gushes from his nose. "You've got it bad, asshole! You broke my nose!" The Lear's cleaning crew isn't going to like this. I get up and run for the paper towels.

"You shouldn't say shit about her." I tip my friend's head back and stanch the blood with a handful of paper towels. "But like I said, we're not together."

"Keeb tellig yourself thad," Derrick says from behind the paper towels.

"Leave it alone, will you?" I push him hard so that he tips over onto his back. He stays there, the paper towels to his face.

"We hab to dalk."

"Later. I'm taking a shower." I go to the tiny head, and under the stream of water, decide on my story.

And I stick to that story when Derrick questions me later, taking an official statement.

Yes. I know Pearl from our twelve-step meeting, where she knew nothing about me but my name. We weren't lovers, but I liked her and thought she was hot. Who wouldn't? I was aware of her career from the meeting, and I recognized her at the show and saw she was in danger. I rescued her, as I would any friend.

Yes, I was aware I put the op in jeopardy and killed three kidnappers doing it.

At least they didn't know Pearl had seen me. There would be hell to pay if they knew that. She might even be in danger from the company. I was never sure what security measures management might deem necessary. Derrick, for all his buddy-sidekick-partner relationship with me, is as cold as they come when he needs to be.

The furlough from work is coming at a perfect time, because I'm as close to burnout as I've ever been in my life.

Shadows are slanting deep beneath the pine trees as I turn the bike onto the dirt road to the cabins. Things look much better since I cut all the trees back. The road is also more pleasant since I'd filled the potholes with gravel. I turn around the last pine tree of the driveway to see something that makes my stomach knot with worse apprehension than facing an armed enemy.

Pearl is standing on my porch, going toe-to-toe with my mother.

Pearl

I arrive at Magnus's house and park my bike out of view, next to the cabin. There's a little smoke coming from Raven's cabin, but I don't see the truck or Whiskey. Magnus's cabin is locked, so I settle into one of two Adirondack chairs on the porch, cover myself with a hand-woven blanket, and take a little nap.

"What are you doing here?" The voice that wakes me is hard, with a husky edge that reminds me of Magnus.

Raven. From her tone, she must be standing right over me. I keep my eyes shut, gathering my resolve. If I let her bully me, I'll never be able to come here regularly. It'll be a problem for me and Magnus.

I need to show her I'm not intimidated.

I pop my eyes open wide and sit up quick and alert, hoping

to startle her. It works, because she was leaning over me close, studying me, a contemptuous twist to her mouth, and now she takes a good step back.

"What do you think I'm doing here?" I have steel and sass in my voice. "I'm here to see Magnus."

"You don't belong here."

"He'll be the judge of that." I stand up as gracefully as I can. With my heeled boots on, I'm just a little taller. She refuses to back off, so now we're way too close. I look down my nose into dark, flashing eyes, narrowed like she wants to put a hex on me. She's surely too young and beautiful to be Magnus's parent. "I'm sure Magnus will be thrilled to know his mother thinks she can choose his woman."

"White whore," she hisses. "Get back to the city, where you belong."

"Nasty old witch," I snarl. "You don't scare me."

The throaty growl of Magnus's bike penetrates our stare-down and we both turn as he pulls the bike up in front of his porch and cuts the engine. "Nice to see my two favorite ladies getting to know each other."

"This bitch was just leaving," Raven points toward the road.

"Your sweet mother has been welcoming me," I say. "She apparently still thinks you're a little boy who needs his mother's help choosing friends."

Magnus takes off his helmet, shakes his hair back. His dark eyes, when he looks up at us, are deeply weary, ringed in shadows. "Please, Mom," he says. "Don't do this."

A moment goes by as Raven absorbs the fact that she's been bested. *He's chosen me.*

"We'll talk later," she says to Magnus. Her denim skirt swishes as she walks with long angry strides toward her cabin. She reaches it and opens the door. Whiskey comes bounding out to greet Magnus, comically excited, an antidote to Raven's venom.

"I apologize for my mother." Magnus swings his leg off the Harley, patting Whiskey. "She's old-fashioned. Has ideas about me marrying a girl from our tribe."

"She'll be lucky if you find anyone at all." My voice is cold. "Man like you, with so many dangerous secrets."

"You got me there. We do need to talk. But I'm tired right now. I need something to eat and a shower. Can we do that first?"

This whole scene is totally not what I planned. Standing on his porch in my leathers with nothing but tiny underwear underneath, I'd been hoping to jump his bones. Seduce him, like I did last time. Then, I'd sweetly ask if we could keep having sex as often as possible, for as long as possible, and when we were both satiated, which I imagined would take a while, I would finally ask what the hell he was doing in Dubai.

"Shower. Eating. Of course." I stand aside as he comes up the steps.

He unlocks the door, absently touching Whiskey's head as the dog ecstatically rubs against his leg, whimpering with happiness. I envy that dog. I want to rub against Magnus just that much.

The inside of the cabin smells shut up and musty as I follow him inside. He drops his bag, flicks on some lights.

"I'm going in to shower—it would be great if you could find something for us to eat." Magnus shrugs out of his leather jacket and hangs it on a hook behind the door.

"No problem." I'm determined to salvage the situation somehow. He goes into the bathroom. In a minute, I hear the water running in the tiny shower.

Oh, that shower.

I toy with the idea of joining him in there, but the last thing

I need right now is more rejection. Whiskey parks in front of me, wags his tail, looking up at me, brown eyes hopeful.

"Hungry, boy? I bet that witch didn't feed you." I begin opening cabinet doors in the little galley-style kitchen and eventually happen upon a galvanized trash can filled with dry dog food under the sink. I put a couple of scoops in the dog's bowl and freshen his water.

As the retriever eats, I continue my exploration, pretending to myself I'm not listening to the rush of water and picturing Magnus naked under it, bending his head to fit under the shower head, water running down his long black hair, forming streams over his hard, sinewy muscles, trailing over the topography of his chest hair, his washboard belly, and down lower...

I find myself staring out the window above the sink at the trees beside the barn, one hand on the open cupboard, the other turning on the tap. I have no recollection of doing either thing.

I shake my head to clear it, turn off the water, and open the cupboard beside the sink. This is, apparently, what passes for a pantry in this stark bachelor pad. Cans of chili, a gallon jar of pinto beans, a rack of tuna cans, a tin of coffee and a jar of pimentos were all that occupy the space. I open the refrigerator and reconnoiter in there, finding a bag of corn tortillas, a hunk of slightly moldy cheddar, a head of wilted lettuce and a carton of half-and-half, spoiled.

I throw out the half and half and heat up the chili, frying the corn tortillas in a skillet, paring off the mold and grating the cheese, chopping the lettuce.

Magnus comes out with a towel around his hips, rubbing his hair with another towel. He glances at me over the little breakfast bar that separates the stove from the living area. My mouth falls open, the spatula held poised, as I gaze at his body. It's as amazing as I remember, huge and chiseled as a gladiator's as he walks through the room. His buttocks flex under the towel, which I greatly wish would fall off and let me get a good look at all the magnificence I plan to get my hands on as soon as possible.

He disappears into the bedroom and shuts the door.

I close my mouth and turn over the burning tortilla on the skillet in front of me.

Clearly he isn't in the mood.

Maybe after eating, he'll find a little more gas in the tank. I'll even do all the work. He can just lie back and let me have my way with him. I grin to myself, thinking of all the ways I want to do that.

I manage to pull together some pretty-edible tacos from the meager selection of food, and I'm setting our loaded plates on the breakfast bar when he comes out, clad in jeans and a black T-shirt.

"Smells good out here." He opens the fridge and locates a ginger beer. "Want one?" He holds up another.

"Sure." I crave a real beer, actually, but we're both off that. Permanently, alas.

He pops the tops, and sits down on one of the stools. I peel off a couple of paper towels and hop up beside him.

My arm brushes his, and I feel it ripple through my whole body and tighten my nipples, but when I glance at him out of the side of my eye, he gives no sign. He picks up a taco, folds it in half, and eats it in three bites.

He consumes the food in about five minutes without looking at me, nor any conversation. I'm still on the first of two measly tacos I've allowed myself when he finishes his ginger beer and moves the dishes to the sink. He goes in the bathroom and I hear him brushing his teeth.

My mouth has gone dry and my stomach is tight with disappointment and rejection. I sip my ginger beer carefully. Expressionlessly.

"I'm sorry, Pearl. I'm beat. Can we talk after I get a little shut-eye?" He's standing next to me. His eyes are bloodshot and half-closed already. Maybe he really is just tired.

I slide off the stool. "Should I just go?"

I make myself look at him. Let myself show the emotion that's gathering moisture, ready to spill from my eyes.

"Aw, girl." He hooks me in, clasping me close in those big hard arms. My face is pressed against his chest and I can hear the slow, heavy thuds of his heart. "I don't want you to go. But I haven't slept in twenty-four hours, and I can't function right now. Come. Rest with me." He slides a hand down to mine, gives it a tug, and leads me to the small, tidy bedroom.

I'm already familiar with the queen-sized bed that takes up most of the space and really is too small for someone of his size and anyone else larger than a midget, which I am not, but I follow him into the dim space. I watch as he shucks off his jeans and shirt, leaving just boxers.

I'm still wearing my leathers, which don't seem appropriate, and I don't want to strip in front of him when sex clearly isn't on the menu.

"I'll brush my teeth and change. I'll be right back."

"Okay." He throws back the Native American patterned blanket and sheets, and sprawls onto the bed facedown.

Back in the kitchen, I clear my half-eaten dinner into the trash, run water on the dishes, take my backpack out and change into the silk cami set I packed in case I spent the night, brush my teeth. There's no point brushing my hair. It riots over my head, curling and wild. Not that Magnus cares. He's given no sign that he even noticed I've lost several feet of hair.

Whiskey has settled into his basket beside the bed, and as I slide between the sheets, Magnus, still lying facedown and taking up most of the bed, emits a rumbling snore.

I've got it bad for him that his great sprawled form, snoring and taking all the room on the bed, just makes me feel warm and fuzzy and think how cute he is. I gently push him over so that I have enough room to squeeze in, and I pull the covers up over us.

Lying there, snuggled in his heat-shadow, I realize I want to be right here. All the time. Every day. I don't need to go all over the world. I don't need to be one of the Big Seven. I don't need anything but this man sleeping so deep beside me, this man who's clearly at the raggedy edge of his resources.

It's in me to love and care for him in whatever small way he'll let me, even if it's just making tacos out of chili.

I stroke his damp black hair, my hands sliding lightly over the mountain of his shoulder, the tip of my finger grazing the bullet hole in his back, the corrugated lines of scars whose origin I don't want to think about. I slide another inch closer, my breath slowing, my heart rate settling, my eyes growing heavy. I tumble after Magnus into a deep well of sleep.

Magnus

I'm too hot, and I throw the covers off in that halfway state before waking. My arm encounters something that doesn't belong.

My eyes fly open as I wake, fully alert. It's deeply dark and the curtains are drawn, but now I've remembered Pearl's here.

Pearl is here, in my bed.

I dimly remember how earlier I felt like I was on a speeding elevator down into some subterranean place, and now I've shot to the surface too quickly, because the blood has left my head and is pooling somewhere lower. I turn over toward the softness I touched.

I can hear her breathing. Soft, tiny breaths. I sit up a little, tweak the curtain over the bed open.

She's barely squeezed onto the bed, turned on her side away from me. Moonlight falls on her cropped hair and turns it to silver curls. She's wearing something silky and skimpy, and as I lean over to get a look at her, I can smell her. Delicious skin, and vanilla.

Pearl managed to fix something edible in the bare kitchen. She has put up with my mother, and with my horrible manners. Shit, she probably even remembered to feed Whiskey. What I shouldn't do is make love to her without having that talk we need to have.

Aw, hell.

She wants me. I know she does. I saw it in her eyes as she watched me cross the room in nothing but a towel. She's putting up with all this shit because she wants me.

God knows I want her.

Now that my body's been minimally restored with some food and rest, all I can feel right now is blood throbbing in the hardest erection I remember since junior high.

I can't touch her with that or it's going to be over in minutes. But I can do a little something else.

I slide my hand up that silky thing she's got on, and damn if she doesn't moan in her sleep and push that luscious ass right into my lap. I hang onto my self-control and ease away so only my hand is on her. I'm not going to take her from behind with no foreplay like some caveman. She's probably wanting some wooing, especially after coming all this way and dealing with Mom—that would freeze anyone's blood.

I slide my hand up under the top, and her skin is unbelievably soft, her breast round and full, the nipple tight and begging to be sucked. So I roll her gently onto her back beside me, and suckle her through the fabric.

First one perfect breast, then the other. I don't need anything but moonlight and memory to show their round, perfect fullness to me, the skin like ivory satin, the nub I'm sucking the pink of a baby's fist.

She's moaning and writhing under my exploring hand, and my mouth's working her breast. I want to draw her in so deep that I suck her right into myself. It feels so right to pleasure her with my hands, my mouth all over her. She's like a vanilla milk-shake, unbelievably delicious and sweet and flavorful. I want to drink her in, and I know I'll never get enough.

"Magnus. Oh, please. I want you in me," she says, and guides my hand to her. She's so hot I can feel it through the fabric, damp and slippery and God, she'd feel so good. My hard-on feels like a stick of dynamite between my legs, dangerous and heavy.

"I don't know if I have a condom. I didn't expect..."

She sits up in a flash, ripping off her outfit which I have to remember to get a good look at in the morning, and she stalks naked over to a small backpack I can see leaning against the wall and unzips a side pocket. She pulls out a packet, and a roll of condoms spring out like a Jack-in-the-Box. "I did expect."

I laugh, and she launches herself at me, all bouncing breasts and silky skin and eager hands.

"I'll do all the work if you're still tired." She pushes me down, ripping open the condom packet with her teeth and rolling it down over me with panache. "You don't seem tired." She rubs the member in question, and I stop her hand.

"Please," I say through clenched teeth, and she gets that I'm barely hanging onto control. Without another word, she climbs aboard and straddles me, taking me all the way into her with a deep, heartfelt moan.

When I'm where I'm supposed to be, meant to be, destined to be—sunk hip-deep in her slick heat—she starts moving.

SOMEWHERE IN THE CITY

I try to make it last.

I think of ugly things. My mother, yelling. The cockroaches in Venezuela, the mold that grew on the inside of the tents, and the man with the smallpox scars and the little paring knife who tortured me for information.

Nothing works to slow down this freight train. Nothing works, because Pearl Moon Michaels, goddess in the flesh, is rising and falling on me, hands on my chest, breasts bouncing, head thrown back, panting and making little kitten noises.

I can't take it any longer. I fill my hands with her glorious taut ass-cheeks, pulling them apart so her pleasure is intensified as she's pulled tight around me filling her. She cries out and I can tell she's about to go, so I sit up hard. Our chests collide. Holding her ass, her hands on my shoulders, I drive into her again and again, and come in an explosive burst that wrings a groan out of me that's echoed by her cry as we slam into each other to an intense, totally satisfying finish.

I crush her close and fall back down with her in my arms. I clasp her tight against me, and she hangs on like a drowning victim.

It was over too soon, but so damn good I'm pretty sure I burst a blood vessel in my eye.

Pearl

My ear is right on top of Magnus's thundering heart. His arms are tight around me, and we're still connected. I know I have to get up, we have to deal with the condom, but right now all I can do is cling to him. Thinking of how close we came to dying in Dubai makes a wave of emotion swell through me. *I don't want to go through life without him*, I know that now. I don't even care what he was doing there. I don't need to know.

I gulp back a sob but can't stop tears from filling my eyes, running over to drip onto his skin. I snuffle a little, and his hand comes up to stroke my head, soothing, massaging, ruffling my curls.

"I hate the haircut," he says conversationally.

I let the sob out on a choked laugh. "It was all Melissa's idea."

He keeps stroking my head. "Grow, little hairs, grow."

It's almost as good as him saying that he loves me, and the tears ooze out some more, and he rolls to the side, still holding me. "Are you crying?" Alarm colors his deep voice.

"Just a little because... that was good." I wave a hand in the direction of his midsection, chickening out on any further revelations.

"Brought a girl to tears in bed. I can die happy now," he jokes, but there's a line between his brows and he rolls away and stands up. "Be right back."

Whiskey raises his head to watch and so do I as moonlight gilds Magnus walking away toward the bathroom. Yes, his ass is as amazing as I remembered, and those shoulders... *God*.

I wipe the tears off on the edge of the sheet and borrow half of the pillow to prop my head on. Well, he may be married to his secret dangerous job, but at least I know I don't have any competition from other women—there were no condoms here, and not even a second pillow.

I wonder where to go from this moment, what to do next. I'm terrified he's going to tell me to leave so I don't say anything as he returns, his face hidden by darkness but the moon lighting up that body I can't get enough of. Just looking at him, I can feel myself heating up again.

He slides into bed with me and lies on his side, propped on

an elbow. I reach up to play with the thick black hair falling over his shoulder. "My hair will grow. And in the meantime, you have enough for both of us."

"Let me look at you." He tosses the sheet back off my body so that moonlight bathes us like milk.

He tugs me close, so that my head rests on his bicep and I'm lying along his side. His eyes on me, he slides his free hand from the firm curve of my hip into the dip of my waist, up the plane of my belly to my ribs, circling the round of my breast, flicking the nipple.

I wriggle even closer, one hand questing down his abs, but he gently captures my hand and lifts it up above my head, curling my fingers around the iron bedstead.

"I need a little time to recover. Both hands up here. Hang on, baby, because this time, it's all for you."

I put both hands up and hold onto the bedstead, anticipation quickening my breath and loosening my knees, setting up an almost painful throb between my legs as he teases my nipple, pinching and rolling it, and leans over to suckle me.

His hot mouth on one breast and confident hand on the other make me arch and shudder, and, still suckling, flicking my nipple with his tongue, his busy hand continues its journey back down my body in a deep, smooth, slow stroke, feeling the silk of me. Through his hand on my skin, I can feel me too as he traces and discovers my hills and valleys, edges and grooves.

Up, down, around and around, suckling first one breast and then the other, skimming my mound but never going there, he drives me mad as I pull on the bedstead. I arch and shiver as he plays a masterful tune on the fiddle of my body.

"Please," I beg hoarsely, and then that questing hand skims across my mound and he slides a finger in. It nearly rockets me off the bed with sensation. I'm so hungry for him, so needy, pushing up with my hips into his hand as he finds the source of my pleasure and strokes me firmly, first two fingers, then three.

I find a fierce focus as he hits just the right spot, and it winds me tighter and tighter. I'm pulling on the iron bedframe with all I've got, plastered against him but only really aware of a fierce hot brightness that's burning between my legs. My body is extended and bowed, every muscle tight and trembling as I pant and beg, "Yes, yes, don't stop that. I love that, yes..." It's an unbearable long, long moment just before, and he extends it, varying the rhythm of his stroking, sucking one sensitized nipple then the other. My every muscle is rigid as he controls me with just the tip of his finger. I've become nothing but a steel spring coiled with unbearable tension, begging for release.

Then it comes, oh it comes, a tremendous lifting as a tidal wave of pleasure rolls over me, cresting as he plunges his fingers into me, curling them to touch my G-spot and extending the moment. My hips levitate off the bed as my body arches up, supported by my feet and head. I break over his hand and convulse against his body. My spine snaps back and forth, my head tosses, and my eyes are rolled back as he supports me on the muscle of his arm. My hands cling tight to the iron bar above my head as he takes me past the point of ecstasy.

And finally I dissipate, spreading like honey along his chest, belly and thighs, deliciously limp, utterly melted.

I can't move. I'm incapable of thought.

Magnus kisses my forehead tenderly, then reaches up to pull the curtain closed and the sheet up over me. He tightens his arms around me, holding me so close that my cheek is against his heart and every inch of us touches, and then we sleep.

I'm awakened by Whiskey snuffling in my ear. I crack an eye, and he's wagging his tail. The door of the little bedroom is shut, though, and I hear the rumble of Magnus's voice out in the main part of the house, fading with the sound of the front door shutting.

He's on the phone with somebody.

Morning lights the humble room, and this is the perfect chance for me to get a shower. I get up, slip into my cami set, beams of sunlight swirling dust motes around me. I feel like I could run a marathon I'm so strong and energized, but there's still a curl of apprehension in my belly for whatever comes next.

I push the door open gently. I can hear Magnus's voice intermittently on the cordless phone on the front porch. It sounds like business; business he clearly doesn't want me over-hearing. Whiskey follows me as I tiptoe across the living room into the bathroom. He'd follow me in there too, but I shut the door on his interested gaze.

I am tempted to linger in the shower, hoping Magnus will join me—but I have a sense that won't happen. We need to talk, and under the flow of water, soaping briskly, I consider my options.

I can pretend nothing happened in Dubai and wait for him to bring it up, and hope we can keep going the way things are going.

I can ask my questions, and see what happens.

I can plead my case first, tell him that I want to be with him regardless, and see what he says.

I decide on the first option. Say nothing, and hope he doesn't send me home. I'm a coward. The truth is, I'm in love with him and I don't care if he can't ever tell me about his job. I just want to be in his life. Every day, as much as possible.

I get out, use the hand towel to dry my hair. That's one

good thing about short hair—no fuss. I forgot to bring my backpack in, so I put the cami set back on without underwear, and
open the door.

Magnus is in the kitchen, and I smell bacon sizzling. My
stomach gives an instant rumble, and he widens his eyes at the
sight of me.

"So that's the little outfit you had on last night. Show me."
He makes a circling gesture with his finger.

I grin, lift my arms like a ballet dancer. The fabric of the
twin set is ivory silk, printed with tiny rosebuds but it's sexy
because of the cut. I swing my hips, do my runway spin and
pause, spin and pause. "It's called a babydoll."

"Oh, baby. You're a doll," he says, and I laugh, relief curling
through me. He's not going to kick me out, at least not yet.

"Got any coffee?"

"That I have. I went to the store, too, so there's half and
half." He points to the full carafe, and I go into the space with
him, reaching up to the cabinet, taking down a mug. He is
humming as he turns over the bacon. I've never heard him hum
before.

I pour the coffee, feeling the space between us vibrate with
attraction like trying to hold two powerful magnets apart, but
I'm determined not to crowd him and scare him off. He flicks
off the stove and moves the bacon, still in the skillet, to a back
burner. He turns to me.

"I can smell you."

My nipples tighten at his rough, husky tone.

"I smell bacon." I smile, playing it cool, but he plucks the
coffee mug out of my hand and pulls me in for a kiss, still
humming way back in his throat.

Something's changed, but I'm too afraid to ask what. I'm
just happy it did, as he kisses me thoroughly, his hands all
over me.

"So, shall we do this before or after breakfast?" He whispers in my ear.

"I thought it was breakfast."

"That's my girl."

I'm his girl.

Oh God, that's really what he said.

He lifts all five foot nine of me like I weigh nothing. I wrap my legs around his waist and hook my ankles, my arms around his neck, as he carries me back to bed, holding me against him by the ass.

He shuts a bewildered-looking Whiskey out, and the dust motes dance in the golden morning sunshine as he sits on the bed and positions me standing between his knees.

"I like this outfit." He slides his big hands around on the loose, skimpy shorts that I'm wearing without panties. He lifts one spaghetti strap onto a finger. "Because there's not much to it."

He yanks the shorts down and pulls me to him by the waist, kissing and caressing my belly, hips, and lower down until I'm clasping him by the hair, whimpering, my knees wobbling.

He stands up, and he's magnificently ready for me. "Where are those condoms?"

I point at the pile on the floor by the backpack, and it's an endless moment as he gets one on and then bends me over the edge of the bed. I'm panting, so hot for him, so eager I push my butt back toward him, but he pauses, sliding his hands all over it, stroking my core. He wedges my legs further apart with his knee.

"This is a world-class butt, Pearl," he says, "and it's all mine."

"Yes, please," I manage to say. He grasps me by the hips, his thumbs digging into the little dimples above my ass, and slides into my welcoming heat.

I throw my head back with a gasp at the incredible, over-whelming sensation, the utter possession of it. We both pause a moment to savor and adjust. Then, slow, deep and heavy, he moves into me. I gasp at each stroke, feeling ripples of sensation building toward a climax unbelievably quickly. He leans over my back and bites my neck, sending a thrill zipping down my spine as his breath tickles my ear.

"I'm never letting you go, Pearl. You're mine." His voice is low and stern, as if making a vow.

"Yes, please." I'm overwhelmed with relief. He's not sending me away, at least not now, and he makes a noise halfway between a laugh and a groan, and things get crazy, a vortex of sensation and movement and sound and smell and taste and touch.

I'm shattering, coming apart and mindless, and so is he. It's all anyone could ever want or dream.

I sit on his lap at the breakfast bar and feed Magnus bites of bacon, secretly letting Whiskey get a few bites too.

"How do you feel about a road trip?" he asks. I'm back in my cami set, and he idly fondles the skin of my knee as he takes a nip of bacon from my hand.

"Yes, please," I say, and this time we both laugh. "Where are we going?"

"Not sure. But let's take the bikes, go away for a while."

"I love it." I bite my lip to keep from adding, "and I love you," but I think he sees it in my eyes because he captures my cheek, turns my face to his. Kisses me. Then stands, setting me back on my feet.

"Make whatever calls you need to make. We can buy what-ever we need on the road."

I feel the same swell of emotion that brought me to tears earlier rise up, and my eyes prickle. I turn away to hide it, going to my little backpack and getting out jeans and a tee shirt, dressing quickly. I can't help glancing at the jumbled bed, smiling.

I hear the rumble of Magnus's voice, and a similar one, lighter and feminine. He's talking to his mother.

Oh, God. I'll just keep busy in here for a while. I decide to strip the bed and wash the sheets since we're leaving.

I hear the voices raised, moving away. Good. I don't want to hear what she has to say about me, and truthfully I hate that I'm a bone to pick between them. It's not a good thing long term.

If there is a long term.

I'm hoping there is, after he so totally laid claim to me, both in word and deed. I smile at the thought as I wash up the dishes. I find the apartment-sized washer and load the sheets, turning it on.

Magnus returns. His brows are lowered over those charcoal eyes, but he smiles when he sees what I'm doing. "Gorgeous, great in the sack, and cleaning up my kitchen. Am I dreaming?"

"I'm buttering you up so I can have my way with you later," I tell him.

"That's a given." He gets out a duffel bag, battered and patched. "Did you make your calls?"

"I wanted to get this done first. And give you time to talk to your mother."

He turns to me. He walks over, takes my chin, and brands my mouth with a kiss. "She'll settle down. She's watching the cabin and Whiskey for us."

Us. He said "us." I'm doing a happy dance in my heart. "Okay. I'll use the phone then. I need to call the agency and my sister. How long are we going for?"

"A week. To start."

My eyes flare wide. "You promise? Really? A road trip on our Harleys, for a week?" My voice has risen to a squeak of excitement.

"That's right. Down with that?" I can tell he's worried the squeak wasn't happiness. He just doesn't know me well enough yet, but he will.

"I'm down with that. Oh my God. I'm so excited."

It's a glorious week, riding across the great U S of A on my bike behind my man. He's got an atlas in one of his saddlebags, and when we stop along the route, we plan the road ahead. At night we find motels, and make an embarrassing amount of noise.

I never ask about Dubai, and he doesn't tell me.

We reach Vegas, and Magnus heads us in to get a suite in the Bellagio. Checking in, I look around the opulent lobby, everything trimmed in gold. My leathers are scuffed and my hair is plastered to my head with sweat and dust as I hold my helmet under my arm.

"Don't you think this place is a little much?" I whisper to Magnus.

"Past time we spent some of your world famous modeling moolah," he grins, and I elbow him.

"Fine. This one's on me." I take out my wallet at the counter and hand over my card. The concierge's eyes light up. "Pearl Michaels! I didn't recognize you."

"I'm traveling incognito," I whisper.

She giggles, cutting her eyes over to Magnus, clearly seeing what I so appreciate. "Our guests' confidentiality is always our highest priority, of course."

We go up in the elevator to the top floor. The suite is huge at the top of the hotel, a sprawl of mirrors, satin, and cheesy awesome overblown grandeur.

"I can't wait to get into the shower," I say, peeling off my leathers. "I bet they can clean these for us."

"I'm sure. I'm going to pop out for a minute," Magnus says. "Scout some shows."

"Oh good. I want to do the Cirque du Soleil. Find that one for us, will you? I'll feel a whole lot better with this road grime off." I'm heading for the bathroom as he heads for the door.

I stare at the crazy, heart-shaped, red satin bed on a raised dais. It has a ceiling mirror above it. I can't wait to get Magnus up on there and see what I can see.

Magnus still isn't back when I get out of the shower, but I call downstairs for a cleaning service to work over our leathers, and get into bed to wait for him.

It's the perfect bed, firm but still soft. I spot a button on the bedside table and touch it. The bed very slowly begins moving, turning in a circle on the raised dais. I look up at myself in the mirror overhead and grin. Oh, this is going to be so good.

I'll just nap a minute until Magnus gets back. My eyes fall shut and I'm gone.

Magnus

It took me longer than I planned to find what I need, and I'm hoping Pearl isn't pissed when I get back. She's been amazing on the trip: never complaining, eager to see everything, fine with hours on the bike, occasionally terrible food, and a series of lousy beds that we make squeak every way there is.

I needn't have worried she'd be fussy. She's out cold in that crazy bed, which is slowly turning under the ceiling mirror, a Las Vegas cliché.

I grin at the sight of her, positioned right in the middle of the turning heart, her cap of damp blonde curls darkening the satin pillow. I strip out of the travel-worn clothing I had on under the leathers and hop in the shower for a quick soap. She deserves my best, though again, she doesn't seem to care whether I come to her clean or dirty, shaved or not.

She's never said the three little words I can feel vibrating between us, but I can sense them between all the sentences, a layer of intensity that adds depth to the incredible sex we've been having.

No, not sex. *Lovemaking.* Because even whether it's rough and quick, or slow and tender, with Pearl it's all making love.

I towel off my hair and body and stalk back into the bedroom, climbing up on that silly bed and lifting the red satin comforter to look at her.

She's naked under there, of course, stretched out like a centerfold, and as the cool air touches her, those pale pink nipples tighten. I put my mouth on one of them, and she sighs, and opens her eyes, then grins like a Cheshire cat.

"I like the view."

I cock my head to the side. I can see my big hulking body leaning over hers. The contrasts of our colors, her paleness beside my dark, are nice to look at.

"Mmm," I say. "How about this bed?"

"Beats the ferns on the side of the road," she says.

Yeah, the last time we made love was in a patch of dry, crackling ferns under a tree on the border of Utah and Nevada. "I liked the ambience of that spot."

"I liked how the buzzards came to check us out." Her smile is so beautiful.

"I love your smile," I say. "I love you."

Her smile fades. Her eyes get big. She's tried to hide it, but I know she's been afraid I'll say we're over. But after I had her that time after Dubai and I knew how she felt in my arms and how totally necessary she'd become, I made up my mind.

She's not leaving my side. Ever again.

I pull the comforter all the way up over us, making a dim little tent over our heads. "I've got something to ask you."

"What?" Her voice is a thread. Her eyes are enormous in the dim, her lips pale. It scares me, her expression, and my heart feels like a taiko drum. *Man up.* All she can say is no. My stomach knots at the possibility. I'm not sure I can survive it.

"Will you marry me?"

I have the one-carat Harry Winston rock I bought down at the hotel jewelry store stuck on the tip of my pinkie, the only finger it will even kind of go on. I extend it to her, and even in the dim light, it sparkles.

Pearl covers her mouth with her hand, and those famous, glorious, enormous eyes fill with tears that brim over and run down her cheeks. She throws the comforter off and sits up. "You're not joking?"

I can't believe that this amazing woman is afraid I'm going to reject her when I'm petrified she won't have me—with my horrible past, my battle-ax of a mother, and very shaky prospects for the future.

"Hell no, I'm not joking," I growl. "You're killing me here. I love you, damn it, and I want you to be mine in every way there is."

"Oh." She frowns. "Are you sure?"

"Holy crap, woman." I know I sound aggrieved but I can't take the suspense. "Please. Really. Marry me. I'm pitiful. I'm begging."

"Okay then. Yes. If you're really sure." She giggles through tears at the sight of the ring on my pinkie, and plucks it off. She slides the ring onto the finger of her left hand and admires it. It fits perfectly. "I can't believe this."

"I can't believe you said yes without asking me anything." I haul her into my arms and kiss her, claiming what's mine. She gives it right back, pressed down, shaken together and running over.

When we come up for air, she says, "I love you. I love you so much." It's the first time she's said it.

"I know."

She smacks my chest, sniffling and laughing. "I was trying to be cool. I didn't want to scare you away."

"Yeah. One of the world's seven most beautiful women loves me and is worried about scaring me away—me, an unemployed mercenary who lives with his mother." I shake my head.

"So that's what you are? A mercenary?"

"In a manner of speaking. But, like I said, I'm unemployed now."

"Excellent. Even better," she says. "I'll pay for everything from here on out."

And so she does, from the Bellagio to getting our leathers cleaned, from the Elvis chapel where we get hitched to all the motels along our slow route back to Boston as we honeymoon and see the country on our bikes, happier than either of our dark-hearted souls deserve.

Company confidentiality policy dictates that we have to be married for me to disclose the nature of my work. Three days into wedded bliss, I talk to her about it.

"I was in Dubai on a job," I tell her. We're seeing Zion National Park during the day and staying in a little adobe motel on the outskirts at night, chosen for the sturdiness of its bed and thickness of its walls.

"The sheikh." Her eyes get big with memories of the trauma.

"Yeah. He was some sort of terrorist funder. Anyway, I couldn't believe it when I saw you there, and then when those guys grabbed you..." I can feel my throat working at the remembered terror.

Pearl puts her fingertips, then her lips, on the beating pulse in my neck. "You saved me."

"And you saved me." I bend my head to kiss her, and feel the truth of it to my bones.

EPILOGUE

Pearl

I'm in the yard at our new house, throwing the ball for Whiskey. It's been six months since Magnus and I got married and took our epic road trip. By the time we returned to Magnus's cabin, Efficiency Solutions, who'd refused to accept his resignation, had come up with a proposal: Magnus could "retire" from active duty and be a personnel trainer for their troops. He accepted.

We didn't want to live close to his mother, so Rafe and Ruby helped find us a nice place with a big fenced yard not far from Magnus's cabin. We bought it with my modeling money, and he developed his training course out in the forest on his and his mother's land for working his "boot camp" training program.

Six months later I'm still pinching myself that I get to wake up most mornings next to this amazing man and have this incredible life. Sometimes we travel for work, and I don't ask about where he goes or what he does. When he comes with me, though, we love exploring the cities where I'm doing shows or shoots and I never feel anything but safe and supported with my warrior husband at my side.

I've come such a long way from the damaged drug addict I was, all flashy anger on the outside but hurting inside. And this beautiful spring morning, Magnus walks across the grass to join me. Whiskey comes running back, the ball in his mouth.

"Got him tired out yet?"

"He's a retriever. He's never tired."

Magnus throws the ball this time, and it goes much further, the dog a golden streak after it. "I'm going to be at the cabin all this week. Got my trainees survival camping out in the woods. Want to sneak in and rendezvous one of the nights?"

"Can I make it past your mother's eagle eye?"

"Raven knows better than to say anything. Besides, she's finally figured out you're her best bet for grandbabies." He pats my tummy affectionately.

"Ha. Just because Rafe and Ruby went that way doesn't mean I'm the parent type." But even as I say it, I know I'd love being a mother. The thought of a sweet little baby with Magnus' dark eyes and my curls just melts me.

He shrugs. "We've got all the time in the world." He pulls me into his arms, nuzzles my neck. "Your hair is touching your shoulders now. Those little hairs are growing."

"I know."

"Didn't Melissa want you to keep it short?"

"She doesn't own me. You do." I turn and kiss him like I mean it, because my heart is given one hundred percent to Magnus Thorne.

Turn the page for a sneak peek of *Somewhere in the California*, Book 3 of the Somewhere Series.

SNEAK PEEK

SOMEWHERE IN CALIFORNIA, SOMEWHERE SERIES
BOOK 3

I can't grow even another half inch or my life is over. At five foot six, I'm pushing the limits of traditional height for ballet dancers, and standing in front of the judges at their table, my file of history and credits open in front of them, I wish I'd twisted my heavy bun onto the back of my head instead of on top, where it makes me look taller.

I'm dressed in the traditional pale pink of ballet clothing: tights, a leotard, toe shoes, a filmy pale pink skirt, and my own signature touch, a black velvet ribbon tied around my waist.

My waist is tiny. It needs to be. And the black ribbon provides a focal point for the eye when I do my audition.

"Thank you for joining us, Miss Michaels," one of the judges says. She's got the slender build and upright posture of a retired pro dancer.

"Jade, please," I say.

"According to this, Jade, you got started dancing at fourteen. Are you aware that's late for a professional career?"

"Yes. I grew up in Saint Thomas, Virgin Islands. There was

nowhere for instruction where I lived. My family moved to California and that's when I started dancing."

"Ah. So tell us what you're going to be dancing."

"Just a short piece from the Nutcracker. With adaptations."

"You are aware this competition is for a television show. Not just classical ballet?" The male judge, a harshly-handsome man crowned with the crest of a green mohawk, jingles an armful of copper bracelets impatiently. I can feel the eye of the TV camera boring into my back, and I ignore the little blinking red light of the camera in front.

"Yes, sir. I said 'with adaptations,' didn't I?" I smile as big and charming as I can. People have told me I ought to smile more, that I'm almost as pretty as my sisters when I smile, but that's hard to believe.

Still, it seems to help, because the grumpy male judge inclines his head and flicks a finger for the music.

My favorite song, *Total Eclipse of the Heart*, comes on.

I drop to the ground, folding in tight on myself. I know that song's a little old now that it's 1992, but it speaks to me. Speaks to what I long for—a love so big it sweeps me away. In secret, in the studio where I've been dancing and giving lessons for the last five years, I've choreographed my own routine to it.

As the music builds, I slide my legs out from beneath my tightly-wrapped upper body into full splits, then, pointing my toes in the shoes laced tightly up my legs, using full leg strength I draw my extended legs together, lifting my short upper torso off the ground by main force. I hear a gasp from one of the female judges at this new maneuver, but the music's changing and now I fling my arms wide and spin, and go into a moon-walk, still up on pointe. From there I segue into the breakdance sequence I taught myself by watching MTV, doing some upper body pop-and-lock, some shuffling with rubber legs, an Egyptian maneuver or two with my rib cage as my 'heart' beating in exaggerated twitches beneath my hand, startling another gasp from someone.

But I can't hope, or think, because next comes the laid-back leap extension, and the pirouette, and the mime-in-the-box followed by the sassy hip shake of my best partnerless cha-cha.

I'm waiting for the buzzer to end my audition. I've watched this show in its first season, and auditioners never seem to make it through a full minute of dancing, so I didn't choreograph more than two minutes.

But the buzzer doesn't sound, so I dance on, flinging myself into whatever feels right in the moment until finally the music throbs and cries its *total eclipse of the heart*, and I sink into a deep curtsy, heaving for breath and dripping with sweat.

When I lift back up, the judges are standing.

And applauding.

The eye of the TV camera zooms in on my face, my mouth falling open and tears welling from my eyes, because my heart has just been totally eclipsed by the dance.

"Congratulations," the mean male judge says, grinning so wide I don't recognize him. "You've got a golden ticket. You're going to LA!"

Suddenly my legs won't hold me up anymore. I sink to the ground in a weepy puddle.

Someone comes to help me. He lifts me up underneath the arm, helping me out of the audition area, settling me onto a hard plastic chair.

"Here," he says. "Jade Star Michaels." He hands me some-thing soft, and I mop my streaming face and blow my nose. "That was amazing."

"Thanks," I say, muffled in the material. "What is this?" I feel real cloth, silky and expensive, under my hands.

"Handkerchief. You can give it back another day."

I look up into the face that belongs to such a kind voice. Oh,

SNEAK PEEK

he's handsome, with short dark blond hair, golden hazel eyes, a full but firm mouth, a square chin.

"How did you know my name?"

He holds up a clipboard. "I'm of the producers. My name's Brandon Forbes." He seems to be looking at me intently. "And I knew your sister."

"Which one?" I ask, honking my nose again. I spot his initials woven into the corner of the kerchief. "I have two." Neither of them, nor Mom, know I'm here in San Francisco at this audition.

"Pearl. She and I dated at one time. Did she ever mention me?"

"No, I'm sorry. We're not close," I said.

Brandon's mouth tightens with a twist that looks to me like old pain. "Well. It was a long time ago."

"Yeah. She's married now." I don't want to talk about my supermodel sister. I stand up. "Thanks for the help. That was...overwhelming. I didn't expect to have to dance the whole song."

"That's never happened before," Brandon says, his golden eyes bright. He seems to be really seeing me for the first time. "You were really something out there. How old are you?"

"Nineteen. And thanks." I want to hand the kerchief back to him, but it's gross. I'm going to have to wash it before I return it. "What happens now?"

"Here's your golden ticket." He hands me a small packet. It's topped by a gold foil ticket that reads, *"You're invited to the next level of competition in Los Angeles!"* Clipped on the back are vouchers for United Airlines, a couple of taxi rides, and a Holiday Inn. "Stick around. Watch the rest of the auditions. And be at Universal Studios in Los Angeles next Tuesday."

"I'll be there with bells on," I say, and shake one of my ankles, where I've tied a little silver bell.

"Nice." Brandon pats my head as if I'm three. "See you around."

I look up at him, and smile. "You will."

Pearl Moon Michaels isn't going to be the only famous name in our family.

Download and continue reading *Somewhere in California* now: tobyneal.net/SSCwb

ACKNOWLEDGMENTS

Dear Readers,

I think I love writing romance.

First of all, there's no plotting. As a mystery writer, you have to plot. There are clues, and subplots, and red herrings. It's a lot of organizing. And then, there's the research. Half the time I'm writing about something I've never heard of before, so there are experts to consult, and Google searches on things like bomb deactivation, arson, and the best blade to dismember a body with.

Not so these stories. I'm a "plotter" going "pantsing" and the freedom and fun are dizzying! I start with the female character. I see her clearly, and her wounds and hopes. I develop her on the page. And then, dear reader, her love appears, and he's just absolutely right for her. I'm bedazzled by him too. And then complicated stuff begins happening that I never planned or imagined.

It's kind of like being a magical bartender. I decide on a main liquor, and turn on the blender, and suddenly ingredients start hopping in, and the drink takes on a life of its own as the story emerges. Organic. Emotional. Mystical, almost.

This is how it was with Pearl. She had such a different story from Zoe, from Ruby, and it was totally fun and satisfying to be with her until the happy ending that her wounded heart needed.

Chapter One of *Somewhere in California*, littlest sister Jade's story, follows. Happy reading!

With much aloha,

Toby Jane

FREE BOOK

Read Rafe and Ruby's story FREE when you join my newsletter list and receive *Somewhere on St. Thomas, Somewhere Series Book* 1 as a welcome gift.

tobyneal.net/TNNews

TOBY'S BOOKSHELF

ROMANCES
Toby Jane

The Somewhere Series
Somewhere on St. Thomas
Somewhere in the City
Somewhere in California

The Somewhere Series
Secret Billionaire Romance
Somewhere in Wine Country
Somewhere in Montana
(*Date TBA*)
Somewhere in San Francisco
(*Date TBA*)

A Second Chance Hawaii Romance
Somewhere on Maui

Co-Authored Romance Thrillers
The Scorch Series
Scorch Road

Cinder Road

Smoke Road

Burnt Road

Flame Road

Smolder Road

PARADISE CRIME SERIES
Toby Neal

Paradise Crime Mysteries
Blood Orchids

Torch Ginger

Black Jasmine

Broken Ferns

Twisted Vine

Shattered Palms

Dark Lava

Fire Beach

Rip Tides

Bone Hook

Red Rain

Bitter Feast

Razor Rocks

Paradise Crime Mysteries Novella
Clipped Wings

Paradise Crime Mystery
Special Agent Marcella Scott

Stolen in Paradise

Paradies Crime Suspense Mysteries
Unsound

Paradise Crime Thrillers
Wired In
Wired Rogue
Wired Hard
Wired Dark
Wired Dawn
Wired Justice
Wired Secret
Wired Fear
Wired Courage
Wired Truth
Wired Ghost

YOUNG ADULT

Standalone
Island Fire

NONFICTION
TW Neal Pen Name

Memoir
Freckled

ABOUT THE AUTHOR

Toby Jane is the romance pen name for author Toby Neal, a mystery author who can't stop putting romance into all of her books! Toby Jane is the place where she gets to indulge her passion for happy endings, big families, and loving pets..

Toby also writes memoir/nonfiction under TW Neal.

Visit tobyjane.com for more ways to stay in touch!

or
Join my Facebook readers group, *Toby Jane's Romance Readers,* for special giveaways and perks.

Made in the USA
Columbia, SC
20 May 2021